Talking It Over

Talking It Over

A NOVEL BY

JULIAN BARNES

ALFRED A. KNOPF   NEW YORK
1991

THIS IS A BORZOI BOOK
PUBLISHED BY ALFRED A. KNOPF, INC.

ISBN 0-679-40525-9
LC 91-52725

Manufactured in the United States of America

FIRST AMERICAN EDITION

to Pat

He lies like an eye-witness.
RUSSIAN SAYING

Talking It Over

1: His, His or Her, Their

Stuart   My name is Stuart, and I remember everything.

Stuart's my Christian name. My full name is Stuart Hughes. My *full* name: that's all there is to it. No middle name. Hughes was the name of my parents, who were married for twenty-five years. They called me Stuart. I didn't particularly like the name at first – I got called things like Stew and Stew-Pot at school – but I've got used to it. I can handle it. I can handle my handle.

Sorry, I'm not very good at jokes. People have told me that before. Anyway, Stuart Hughes – I think that'll do for me. I don't want to be called St John St John de Vere Knatchbull. My parents were called Hughes. They died, and now I've got their name. And when I die, I'll still be called Stuart Hughes. There aren't too many certainties in this great big world of ours, but that's one of them.

Do you see the point I'm making? Sorry, absolutely no reason why you should. I've only just started. You scarcely know me. Let's start again. Hullo, I'm Stuart Hughes, nice to meet you. Shall we shake hands? Right, good. No, the point I'm trying to make is this: *everyone else around here has changed their name.* That's quite a thought. It's even a bit creepy.

Now, did you notice how I said *everyone* followed by *their*? 'Everyone has changed their name.' I did it deliberately, probably just to annoy Oliver. We had this tremendous row with Oliver. Well, an argument, anyway. Or at least a disagreement. He's a great pedant, Oliver. He's my oldest friend, so I'm allowed to call him a great pedant. Soon after Gill met him – that's my wife, Gillian – she said to me, 'You know, your friend talks like a dictionary.'

We were on a beach just up from Frinton at the time, and when Oliver heard Gill's remark he went into one of his spiels. He calls them riffs, but that's not my sort of word. I can't reproduce the way he talks – you'll have to listen to him for yourself – but he just sort of zooms off. That's what he did then. 'What kind of dictionary am I? Do I have a thumb index? Am I bilingual?' And so on. He went on like this for a while, and ended up asking who was going to buy him. 'What if nobody wants me? Disregarded. Dust on my top fore-edge. Oh no, I'm going to be remaindered, I can see it, I'm going to be remaindered.' And he started thumping the sand and wailing at the seagulls – real Play for Today stuff – and an elderly couple who were listening to a radio behind a wind-break looked quite alarmed. Gillian just laughed.

Anyway, Oliver's a pedant. I don't know what you think

about *everyone* followed by *their*. Probably not very much, no reason why you should. And I can't remember how it first came up, but we had this argument. Oliver and Gillian and me. We each had a different opinion. Let me try and set down the opposing points of view. Perhaps I'll do the minutes of the meeting, like at the bank.

OLIVER said that words like *everyone* and *someone* and *no-one* are singular pronouns and must therefore be followed by the singular possessive pronoun, namely *his*.

GILLIAN said you couldn't make a general remark and then exclude half the human race, because fifty per cent of the time that *someone* will turn out to be female. So for reasons of logic and fairness you ought to say *his or her*.

OLIVER said we were discussing grammar not sexual politics.

GILLIAN said how could we separate the two, because where did grammar come from if not from grammarians, and almost all grammarians – probably every single one of them for all she knew – were men, so what did we expect; but mainly she was talking common sense.

OLIVER rolled his eyes back, lit a cigarette and said that the very phrase *common sense* was a contradiction in terms, and if Man – at which point he pretended to be extremely embarrassed and correct himself to Man-or-Woman – if Man-or-Woman had relied upon common sense over the previous millennia we'd all still be living in mud huts and eating frightful food and listening to Del Shannon records.

STUART then came up with a solution. *His* being either inaccurate or insulting or quite possibly both, and *his or her* being diplomatic but awfully cumbersome, the obvious answer was to say *their*. Stuart put forward this compromise suggestion with full confidence, and was surprised by its rejection by the rest of the quorum.

OLIVER said that, for instance, the phrase *someone put their head round the door* sounded as if there were two bodies and one head, like in some frightful Russian scientific experiment. He referred to the displays of freaks which used to take place at funfairs, mentioning bearded ladies, deformed sheep's foetuses and many similar items until called to order by the Chair (= me).

GILLIAN said that in her opinion *their* was just as cumbersome and just as obviously diplomatic as *his or her*, but why was the meeting being so squeamish about making a point anyway? Since women had for centuries been instructed to use the masculine possessive pronoun when referring to the whole human race, why shouldn't there be some belated corrective action, even if it did stick in a few (masculine) throats?

STUART continued to maintain that *their* was best, being representative of the middle course.

The MEETING adjourned *sine die*.

I thought about this conversation for quite a while afterwards. Here we were, three reasonably intelligent people discussing the merits of *his* and *his or her* and *their*. Tiny little words, yet we couldn't agree. *And* we were friends. Yet we couldn't agree. Something about this worried me.

How did I get on to that? Oh yes, everyone else around here has changed their name. It's true, and it's quite a thought, isn't it? Gillian, for example, she changed her name when she married me. Her maiden name was Wyatt, but now she's called Hughes. I don't flatter myself that she was eager to take my name. I think it was more that she wanted to get rid of Wyatt. Because you see that was her father's name, and she didn't get on with her father. He walked out on her mother, who was stuck for years afterwards with the name of someone who'd left her. Not very nice for Mrs Wyatt, or Mme Wyatt as some people call her because she was French originally. I suspected that Gillian was getting rid of Wyatt as a way of breaking with her father (who didn't even come to the wedding, incidentally) and pointing out to her Mum what *she* ought to have done years before. Not that Mme Wyatt took the hint, if the hint was there.

Typically, Oliver said that after the marriage Gill ought to call herself Mrs Gillian Wyatt-or-Hughes, that is if she wanted to be logical and grammatical and commonsensical and diplomatic and cumbersome. He's like that, Oliver.

Oliver. It wasn't his name when I met him. We were at school together. At school he was called Nigel, or sometimes 'N.O.', or occasionally 'Russ', but Nigel Oliver Russell was never called Oliver. I don't think we even knew what the O stood for; perhaps he lied about it. Anyway, the point is this. I didn't go to university, Nigel did. Nigel went off for his first term, and when he came back he was Oliver. Oliver Russell. He'd dropped the N, even from the name printed on his cheque-book.

You see, I remember everything. He went in to his bank and got them to print new cheque-books, and instead of signing 'N.O. Russell', he now signed 'Oliver Russell'. I was surprised they let him do that. I thought he'd have to change his name by deed-poll or something. I asked him how he'd done it but he wouldn't tell me. He just said, 'I threatened to take my overdraft elsewhere.'

I'm not as clever as Oliver. At school I sometimes used to get better marks than him, but that was when he chose not to exert himself. I was better at maths and science and practical things – you only had to show him a lathe in the metal workshop for him to pretend he had a fainting fit – but when he wanted to beat me, he beat me. Well, not just me, everyone. And he knew his way around. When we had to play at being soldiers in the Cadet Force, Oliver was always Excused Boots. He can be really clever when he wants to be. And he's my oldest friend.

He was my best man. Not strictly speaking, because the wedding was in a register office, and you don't have a best man. In fact, we had a silly argument about that as well. Really silly; I'll tell you about it some other time.

It was a beautiful day. The sort of day everyone should have their wedding on. A soft June morning with a blue sky and a gentle breeze. Six of us: me, Gill, Oliver, Mme Wyatt, my sister (married, separated, changed her name – what did I tell you?) and an aged aunt of some sort dug up by Mme Wyatt at the last minute. I didn't catch her name but I bet it wasn't original.

The registrar was a dignified man who behaved with the correct degree of formality. The ring I'd bought was placed on a plum-coloured cushion made of velvet and winked at us until it was time to put it on Gill's finger. I said my vows a bit too loud and they seemed to echo round the light oak panelling of the room; Gill seemed to overcompensate and whispered hers so that the registrar and I could only just hear. We were very happy. The witnesses signed the register.

The registrar handed Gill her wedding lines and said, 'This is *yours*, Mrs Hughes, nothing to do with this young man here.' There was a big municipal clock outside the town-hall, and we took some photographs underneath it. The first photo on the roll said 12.13, and we had been married three minutes. The last one on the roll said 12.18, and we had been married eight minutes. Some of the pictures have silly camera angles because Oliver was fooling around. Then we all went to a restaurant and had grilled salmon. There was champagne. Then more champagne. Oliver made a speech. He said he wanted to toast a bridesmaid but there weren't any around so he was jolly well going to toast Gill instead. Everyone laughed and clapped and then Oliver used a whole heap of long words and each time he used one we all whooped. We were in a sort of back room, and at one point we gave a particularly loud whoop at a particularly long word and a waiter looked in to see if we were calling for anything and then went away. Oliver finished his speech and sat down and was slapped on the back. I turned to him and said, 'By the way, someone just put their head round the door.'

'What did they want?'

'No,' I repeated, '*someone* just put *their* head round the door.'

'Are you drunk?' he asked.

I think he must have forgotten. But I remember, you see. I remember everything.

G i l l i a n   Look, I just don't particularly think it's any-one's business. I really don't. I'm an ordinary, private person. I haven't got anything to say. Wherever you turn nowadays there are people who insist on spilling out their lives at you. Open any newspaper and they're shouting Come Into My Life. Turn on the television and every second programme has someone talking about his or her problems, his or her divorce, his or her illegitimacy, his or her illness, alcoholism, drug addiction, sexual violation, bankruptcy, cancer, amputation, psychotherapy. His vasectomy, her mastectomy, his or her appendicectomy. What are they all doing it for? Look At Me, Listen To Me. Why can't they simply get on with things? Why do they have to *talk* about it all?

Just because I don't have a confessional nature doesn't mean that I forget things. I remember my wedding ring sitting on a fat burgundy cushion, Oliver leafing through the telephone directory looking for people with silly names, how I felt. But these things aren't for public consumption. What I remember is my business.

O l i v e r   Hi, I'm Oliver, Oliver Russell. Cigarette? No, I didn't think you would. You don't mind if I do? Yes I *do* know it's bad for my health as a matter of fact, that's why I like it. God, we've only just met and you're coming on like some rampant nut-eater. What's it got to do with you anyway? In fifty years I'll be dead and you'll be a sprightly lizard slurping yoghurt through a straw, sipping peat-bog water and wearing health sandals. Well, I prefer this way.

Shall I tell you my theory? We're all going to get either cancer or heart disease. There are two human types, basically, people who bottle their emotions up and people who let it all come roaring out. Introverts and extraverts if you prefer. Introverts, as is well known, tend to internalise their emotions, their rage and their self-contempt, and this internalisation, it is equally well known, produces cancer. Extraverts, on the other hand, let joyous rip, rage at the world, divert their self-contempt on to others, and this over-exertion, by logical process, causes heart attacks. It's one or the other. Now I happen to be an extravert, so if I compensate by smoking this will keep me a perfectly balanced and healthy human being. That's *my* theory. On top of which, I'm addicted to nicotine, and that makes it easier to smoke.

I'm Oliver, and I remember all the *important* things. The point about memory is this. I've noticed that most people over the age of forty whinge like a chainsaw about their memory not being as good as it used to be, or not being as good as they wish it were. Frankly I'm not surprised: look at the amount of garbage they choose to store. Picture to yourself a monstrous skip crammed with trivia: singularly ununique childhood memories, 5 billion sports results, faces of people they don't like, plots of television soap operas, tips concerning how to clean red wine off a carpet, the name of their MP, that sort of thing. What monstrous vanity makes them conclude the memory wants to be clogged up with this sort of rubbish? Imagine the organ of recollection as a left-luggage clerk at some thrumming terminus who looks after your picayune possessions until you next need them. Now consider what you're asking him to take care of. And for so little money! And for so little thanks! It's no wonder the counter isn't manned half the time.

My way with memory is to entrust it only with things

it will take some pride in looking after. For instance, I never remember telephone numbers. I can *just* about remember my own, but I don't rack up the angst if I have to extract the address book and look up Oliver Russell in it. Some people – grim *arrivistes* in the kingdom of the mind – talk about training your memory, making it fit and agile like an athlete. Well, we all know what happens to athletes. Those hideously honed oarsmen all conk out in middle age, footballers develop hinge-creaking arthritis. Muscle tears set solid, discs weld together. Look at a reunion of old sportsmen and you will see an advertisement for geriatric nursing. If only they hadn't taxed their tendons so fiercely . . .

So I believe in coddling my memory, just slipping it the finer morsels of experience. That lunch after the wedding, for instance. We had a perfectly frisky non-vintage champagne chosen by Stuart (brand? search me? *mis en bouteille par Les Vins de l'Oubli*), and ate *saumon sauvage grillé avec son coulis de tomates maison*. I wouldn't have chosen it myself, but then I wasn't consulted anyway. No, it was perfectly all right, just a little unimaginative . . . Mme Wyatt, with whom I was *à côté*, seemed to enjoy it, or at least to relish the salmon. But she pushed rather at the pinkish translucent cubelets which surrounded the fish, then turned to me and asked,

'What exactly would you say this might be?'

'Tomato,' I was able to inform her. 'Skinned, cored, de-pipped, cubed.'

'How curious, Oliver, to identify what gives a fruit its character, and then to remove it.'

Don't you find that rather magnificent? I took her hand and kissed it.

On the other hand I'm afraid I couldn't tell you whether Stuart was wearing his medium-dark-grey suit or his dark-dark-grey suit for the ceremony.

Do you see what I mean?

I remember the sky that day: swirling clouds like marbled end-papers. A little too much wind, and everyone patting his hair back into place inside the door of the register office. A ten-minute wait round a low coffee table bearing three London telephone directories and three copies of the *Yellow Pages*. Ollie trying to amuse the company by looking up relevant professionals like Divorce Lawyers and Rubber Goods Purveyors. No spirit of fun ignited, however. Then we went in to face this perfectly oleaginous and crepuscular little registrar. A flour-bomb of dandruff on his shoulders. The show went off as well as these things do. The ring glittered on its damson *pouffe* like some intra-uterine device. Stuart bellowed his words as if answering a court-martial and failure to enunciate perfectly at top volume would earn him a few more years in the glasshouse. Poor Gillie could scarcely vocalise her responses. I think she was crying, but adjudged it vulgar to peer. Afterwards we went outside and took photographs. Stuart was looking particularly smug, I thought. He *is* my oldest friend, and it *was* his wedding, but he was looking mogadonic with self-satisfaction, so I purloined the camera and announced that what the wedding album needed were a few art shots. I pranced about and lay on the ground and turned the lens through 45 degrees and stepped in pore-scouringly close, but what I was really doing, what I was after, was a good shot of *Stuart's double chin*. And he's only thirty-two. Well, maybe *double chin* is a little unfair: let's say a mere jowlswipe of pork tenderloin. But it can be made to bulge and glitter with a maestro behind the iris.

Stuart . . . No, wait a minute. You've been talking to him, haven't you? You've been talking to Stuart. I sensed that little hesitation when I floated the subject of his double chin. You mean you didn't notice it? Yes, well, in the dark with the light behind him . . . And he was probably sticking his jaw out to compensate. In my view the jugular podge wouldn't show up so much if he had longer hair, but he never gives that coarse mousy matting of his any *Lebensraum*. And with his round face and friendly little circular eyes peering at you from behind those less-than-state-of-the-art spectacles. I mean, he looks *amicable* enough, but he somehow needs *work*, wouldn't you say?

What's that? He wasn't wearing glasses? Of course he was wearing glasses. I've known him since he was knee-high to a schoolmaster and . . . well, maybe he's secretly taken to lenses and was trying them out on you. All right. It's possible. Anything's possible. Maybe he seeks a more thrustful mien so that when he goes to his nasty little hutch in the City and glares at his neurotically blinking little screen and barks into his cellular telephone for another *tranche* of lead futures or whatever, he comes over as just a trifle more macho than we all know him to be. But he's been keeping the opticians in business — especially the ones that stock really old-fashioned frames — ever since we were at school together.

What are you smirking at now? We were at school . . . Ah. Got it. Stuart's been bleating on about how I changed my name, hasn't he? He's obsessed by things like that, you know. He's got this really boring name — Stuart Hughes, I ask you, there's a career in soft furnishings for you, no qualifications needed except the perfect name, sir, and you've got it — and he's quite complacent about answering to it for the rest of his days. But Oliver used to be called Nigel. *Mea culpa, mea maxima culpa.* Or rather, not. Or rather, Thanks, Mum. Anyway, you can't go through the whole of your life being called *Nigel*, can you? You can't even go through a whole book being called Nigel. Some names simply aren't appropriate after a while. Say you were called Robin, for instance. Well that's a perfectly good monicker up to the age of about nine, but pretty soon you'd have to do something about it, wouldn't you? Change your name by deed-poll to Samson, or Goliath, or something. And with some *appellations*, the contrary applies. Like Walter, for instance. You can't be Walter in a pram. You can't be *Walter* until you're about seventy-five in my view. So if they're going to christen you Walter they'd better put a couple of names in front of it, one for your spell in the pram plus another for the long haul up to becoming Walter. So they might call you Robin Bartholomew Walter, for example. Pretty duff, in my opinion, but doubtless it somewhere pleases.

So I swapped Nigel for Oliver, which was always my second name. Nigel Oliver Russell – there, I pronounce it without an encrimsoned cheek. I went up for my first term at York called Nigel and I came back as Oliver. What's so surprising? It's no stranger than joining the army and coming home on your first leave with a moustache. A mere rite of passage. But for some reason old Stuart can't get over it.

Gillian's a good name. It suits her. It'll last.

And Oliver suits me, don't you find? It rather goes with my dark, dark hair and kissable ivory teeth, my slim waist, my panache and my linen suit with the ineradicable stain of Pinot Noir. It goes with having an overdraft and knowing one's way around the Prado. It goes with *some people* wanting to kick my head in. Like that deep trog of a bank manager I went to see at the end of my first term at university. The sort of fellow who gets an erection when he hears the bank rate's gone up a tenth of a percent. Anyway, this trog, this . . . Walter had me into his panelled wankpit of an office, classified my request to change the name on my cheques from N.O. Russell to Oliver Russell as not central to the Bank's policy for the 1980s, and reminded me that unless funds were forthcoming to camouflage my black hole of an overdraft I wouldn't be getting a new cheque-book even if I called myself Santa Claus. Whereupon I fell about in my chair at this with an effective simulacrum of sycophancy, then matadored the old charm around in front of him for a few minutes, and before you could say *fundador* Walt was on his knees begging me for the *coup de grâce*. So I allowed him the honour of endorsing my change of name.

I seem to have mislaid all the friends who once called me Nigel. Except for Stuart, of course. You should get Stuart to narrate our schooldays together. I certainly never insulted my memory by asking it to store all that routine junk. Stuart, just for something to say, occasionally used to go 'Adams, Aitken, Apted, Bell, Bellamy . . .' (I invent the names, you understand.)

'What's that?' I'd say. 'Your new mantra?'

He would look baffled. Perhaps he thought a mantra was a make of car. The Oldsmobile Mantra. 'No,' he would reply. 'Don't you remember? That was 5A. Old Biff Vokins was our form-master.'

But I don't remember. I *won't* remember. Memory is an act of will, and so is forgetting. I think I have sufficiently erased most of my first eighteen years, puréed them into harmless baby food. What could be worse than to be dogged by all that stuff? The first bicycle, the first tears, that old teddy with a chewed-off ear. It's not just an aesthetic matter, it's practical as well. If you remember your past too well you start blaming your present for it. Look what they did to me, that's what caused me to be like this, it's not my fault. Permit me to correct you: it probably *is* your fault. And kindly spare me the details.

They say that as you get older, you remember your earliest years better. One of the many tank-traps that lie ahead: senility's revenge. Have I told you my Theory of Life, by the way? Life is like invading Russia. A blitz start, massed shakos, plumes dancing like a flustered henhouse; a period of svelte progress recorded in ebullient despatches as the enemy falls back; then the beginning of a long, morale-sapping trudge with rations getting shorter and the first snowflakes upon your face. The enemy burns Moscow and you yield to General January, whose fingernails are very icicles. Bitter retreat. Harrying Cossacks. Eventually you fall beneath a boy-gunner's grapeshot while crossing some Polish river not even marked on your general's map.

I don't ever want to get old. Spare me that. Have you the power? No, even you don't have the power, alas. So have another cigarette. Go on. Oh, all right, please yourself. Everyone to his own taste.

2: Lend Us a Quid

Stuart   In a way it's a surprise that the *Edwardian* has survived, but I'm rather pleased it has. It's a surprise too that the school has survived, but when they were killing off all the grammar schools in this country and turning them into comprehensives and middle schools and sixth-form colleges, and everyone was getting shoved in with everyone else, there somehow wasn't anyone to shove St Edward's in with, and they sort of left us alone. So the school continued, and the old boys' magazine continued as well. I didn't take much notice of it in the first few years after I left school, but now I've been gone, what, fifteen years or so, I find quite a lot of interest in what's happened. You see a familiar name and it sets off all sorts of memories. Old boys write in from various parts of the world and say what they're up to. Good God, you think, I'd never have thought Bailey would be in charge of the whole South East Asia operation, you say to yourself. I remember when he was asked what the principal crop of Thailand was and he answered transistor radios.

Oliver says he doesn't remember anything about school. He says – what's that phrase of his? – he says he can drop a stone into that particular well and never hear the splash. He always yawns a lot and says *Who?* in a bored voice when I pass on news from the *Edwardian*, but I suspect he's interested. Not that he ever offers recollections of his own. Perhaps when he's with other people he pretends he went to a posher school – Eton or something. I wouldn't put that past him. I've always thought you are what you are and you shouldn't pretend to be anyone else. But Oliver used to correct me and explain that you are whoever it is you're pretending to be.

We're rather different, Oliver and me, as you might have noticed. Sometimes people are surprised that we're friends. They don't exactly say so, but I can feel it. They think I'm lucky to have a friend like Oliver. Oliver impresses people. He talks well, he's travelled to distant lands, he speaks foreign languages, he's conversant with the arts – more than conversant – and he dresses in clothes which don't fit the contours of his body and are therefore declared to be fashionable by people in the know. All of which isn't like me. I'm not always very good at saying what I mean, except at work, that is; I've been to Europe and the States but never to Nineveh and Distant Ophir; I don't have much time – literally – for the arts, though I'm not *against* them in any way, you understand (sometimes there's a nice concert on the car radio; like most people I read a book or two on holiday); and I don't give much of a thought to my clothes beyond looking smart at work and feeling comfortable when I get home. But I think Oliver likes me for being the way I am. And it would be rather pointless if I started trying to ape him. Oh yes, there's another difference between us: I've got a reasonable amount of money, and Oliver has hardly any at all. At least, not what anyone who knows about money would call money.

'Lend us a quid.'

That was the first thing he ever said to me. We were sitting next to one another in class. We were fifteen. We'd been in the same form for two terms without really speaking, because we had separate friends and in any case at St Edward's you were seated according to your exam results at the end of the previous term, so it wasn't likely we'd be close. But I must have done well the term before, or perhaps he was slacking, or both, because there we were together and Nigel as he then called himself was asking for a pound.

'What do you want it for?'

'*Such* colossal impertinence. What on earth do you want to know for?'

'No prudent money manager would authorise a loan without first knowing its purpose,' I replied. This seemed to me a perfectly reasonable statement, but for some reason it set Nigel off laughing. Biff Vokins looked up from his desk – this was meant to be a private study period – and gave an enquiring glance. More than enquiring, actually. Which only set Nigel off more, and it was some time before he could attempt an explanation.

'I'm sorry, sir,' he said finally. 'I do apologise. It's just that Victor Hugo can be so terribly amusing sometimes.' Then he started howling with more laughter. I felt rather responsible.

After the lesson he told me that he wanted to buy a really good shirt he'd seen somewhere, and I enquired into the resale potential of the item with a view to recovering my outlay in case of bankruptcy, which amused him further; and then I gave him my terms. Five per cent simple interest on the principal per week, repayment within four weeks otherwise the interest rose to 10 per cent per week. He called me a usurer, which was the first time I'd heard the word, paid me back £1.20 after four weeks, paraded at weekends in his new shirt, and we were friends thereafter. Friends: we just decided and that was it. At that age you don't discuss whether or not you're going to be friends, you just are. It's an irreversible process. Some people were surprised, and I remember we played up to this a bit. Nigel would pretend to patronise me, and I would pretend I wasn't clever enough to notice; and he would be swankier than he really was, and I would be more boring; but we knew what we were doing and we were friends.

We stayed friends even though he went to university and I didn't, even though he went off to Nineveh and Distant Ophir and I didn't, even though I went into the Bank and had a steady job while he flitted from one bit of temporary work to another and eventually ended up teaching English as a foreign language in a side street off the Edgware Road. It's called the Shakespeare School of English and has a neon Union Jack outside which flashes on and off all the time. He says he only took the job because the neon sign always cheers him up; but the fact is he really needs the money.

And then Gillian came along and there were three of us.

Gill and I agreed we wouldn't tell anyone how we met. We

always said that someone at the office called Jenkins had taken me to the local wine bar after work and we'd run into some old girlfriend of his and Gillian who knew this girl vaguely was with her and we sort of got on immediately and made another date.

'Jenkins?' Oliver said when I told him this story rather hesitatingly, though I expect my nerves were to do with talking about Gillian. 'Is he from Arbitrage?' Oliver likes to pretend he knows what I do, and chucks out the odd word from time to time to sound authoritative. I tend to ignore it nowadays.

'No,' I said. 'He was new. Well, he's old now. He didn't last long. Not up to the job.' This was true. I'd chosen Jenkins because he'd recently got the sack and no-one was likely to run into him.

'Well, at least he dealt you a *tranche de bonheur* while he was there.'

'A wotsit?' I asked, playing Dumb Stu. He smiled his smile, playing Sophisticated Ollie.

The fact is, I've never been very good at meeting people. Some people are naturally good at it and others aren't. I don't come from one of these huge families where there are loads of cousins and all sorts of people keep 'dropping in'. No-one 'dropped in' on our family the whole of the time I lived at home. My parents died when I was twenty, my sister moved up to Lancashire and became a nurse and got married, and that was the family gone.

So there I was, living in a small flat by myself in Stoke Newington, going to work, sometimes staying late, getting lonely. I don't have what is referred to as an outgoing personality. When I meet people I like, instead of saying more and showing I like them and asking questions, I sort of clam up, as if I don't expect them to like me, or as if I'm not interesting enough for them. And then – fair enough – they don't find me interesting enough for them. And the next time it happens I remember this, but instead of making me determined to do better, I freeze again. Half the world seems to have confidence and half the world doesn't, and I don't know how you make the jump from one half to the other. In order to have confidence you have to be confident already: it's a vicious circle.

The advertisement was headed YOUNG PROFESSIONAL? 25–35? WORKING TOO HARD FOR YOUR SOCIAL LIFE TO GET OFF THE GROUND? It was quite well done, the ad. It didn't read like some pick-up place where everyone went off together for topless holidays; nor did it make it seem as if it was your fault for not having a social life. It was just one of those things that happened to even the nicest people, and the sensible thing to do about it was pay £25 and turn up at a London hotel for a glass of sherry and an implicit promise of no humiliation if things didn't work out.

I thought they might give us badges to wear with our names on, like at conferences; but I suppose they thought this would imply we weren't even capable of uttering our own names. There was a sort of host who dished out the sherry and took each new arrival round the groups; though as there were quite a lot of us he couldn't remember all our names so we were forced to say them. Or perhaps he deliberately didn't remember some of our names.

I was talking to a man with a stammer who was training to be an estate agent when Gillian was brought across by the organiser. Something about the fact that this chap stammered gave me more confidence. That's a cruel thing to say, but it's been done to me often enough in the past: you find yourself saying ordinary things and the person next to you is suddenly being witty. Oh yes, that's happened to me often enough. It's a sort of primitive law of survival – find someone worse off than yourself and beside them you will blossom.

Well, maybe 'blossom' is an exaggeration, but I told Gillian one or two of Oliver's jokes, and we talked about being apprehensive over coming to the group, and then it emerged that she was half-French, and I had something to say about that, and the estate agent tried to bring in Germany but we weren't having any of it, and before I knew where I was I had half-turned my shoulder to exclude the other chap and was saying, 'Look, I know you've only more or less just arrived, but you wouldn't like a spot of supper, would you? I mean, perhaps another evening if you're not free.' I was amazed at myself, I can tell you.

'Do you think we're allowed to go this soon?'

'Why ever not?'

'Aren't we meant to meet everybody first?'

'It's not compulsory.'

'All right, then.'

She smiled at me, and looked down. She was shy, and I liked that. We went out for supper in an Italian restaurant. Three weeks later Oliver came back from somewhere exotic, and there were the three of us. All that summer. The three of us. It was like that French film where they all go bicycling together.

Gillian   I wasn't shy. I was nervous, but I wasn't shy. There's a difference. Stuart was the shy one. That was perfectly obvious from the start. Standing there with his schooner of sherry, perspiring a little at the temples, clearly not in his element, and trying painfully hard to overcome it. Of course, nobody *was* in his or her element. At the time, I thought, this is a bit like shopping for people, and we aren't trained for that, not in our society.

So Stuart began by telling a couple of jokes, which fell rather flat because he was so jumpy and I don't think the jokes were much good in the first place. Then France was mentioned, and he said something ordinary, like you can always tell you're there from the smell of the place, how you could tell even if you were blindfold. The point was, though, that he was *trying*, with himself as much as with me, and that's touching, you know. It's genuinely touching.

I wonder what happened to the man with the stammer who wanted to talk about Germany. I hope he's found somebody.

I wonder what happened to Jenkins.

Oliver   Don't tell me. Let me guess. Let me zero my telepathy in on the benign, rumpled and somewhat steatopygous figure of my friend Stu. Steatopygous? Means his bum sticks out: the Hottentot *derrière*.

Jules et Jim? Am I right? I think I can tell. He used to mention it at one time, but only to me, never to Gillian. *Jules et Jim.* Oskar Werner, the short, blond and – dare one say it – quite possibly steatopygous one, Jeanne Moreau, and then the tall, dark, elegant, good-looking one who doubtless had kissable teeth (what was his name?). Well, no problem with the casting, the only problem is remembering the plot. They all go bicycling together and run across bridges and *lark about*, yes? I thought so. But how pudgily typical of Stuart to choose *Jules et Jim* – likeable enough, but not exactly *central* to post-war cinema – as his cultural reference point. Stuart, I'd better warn you in advance, is the sort of person who knows Mozart's K467 as the Elvira Madigan concerto. His preferred idea of classical music is the sound of a string band imitating birds, or clocks, or a little chuffer train going up a hill. Isn't it so sweetly unstylish?

Maybe he'd taken a course in French film as a way of learning how to pick up girls. That was never his *forte*, you understand. I sometimes used to help him out with double dates, but they always ended with both girls squabbling over yours truly and Stuart sulking in the corner and displaying all the charisma of a limpet. Dear me, those were saturnine occasions, and I'm afraid our Stuart did tend to point the finger afterwards.

'You ought to help me more,' he once complained pathetically.

'*Help* you? *Help* you? I find the girls, I introduce you, I get the evening on an upward parabola, and you just sit there glowering away like Hagen in *Götterdämmerung*, if you'll excuse the cultural allusion.'

'I sometimes think you only invite me so that I can pay the bill.'

'If I were coining it down in the bull market,' I reminded him, 'and you were my oldest friend and out of work and you came up with two corking girls like that, I'd be honoured to pay the bill.'

'I'm sorry,' he said. 'I just don't think you should have told them that I don't have any confidence with women.'

'Oh *that's* what's bugging you.' Now I began to understand. 'The master plan was to put everyone at his ease.'

'I don't think you want me to get a girlfriend,' Stuart sulkily concluded.

Which is why I was pretty surprised when he excavated Gillian. Who'd have believed it? What's more, who'd have believed he'd *picked her up in a wine bar*? Imagine the scene if you please: Gillian on a bar-stool with satin skirt slashed to the hip, Stuart nonchalantly hefting his tie-knot while working out the current bodybuilder health of the yen on his wristwatch computer, a barman who knows without asking that Mr Hughes-Sir desires the 1918 late-landed Sercial in the special glass which concentrates the nose, Stuart sliding onto the next stool and casually emitting the subtle musk of his sexuality, Gillian begging a light, Stuart slipping the tortoise-shell Dunhill from the pocket of his unstructured Armani suit . . .

Come on, I mean, *come on*. Let's get some reality in here. I've heard the account in hushed and pulsing detail and frankly it was no more and no less squalid than you might expect. Some winklebrain from the bank who managed to get himself sacked the following week (and you really do have to be a winklebrain to get ejected from there) stepped out one evening with Stu for a post-*Arbeit* beverage at Squires Wine Bar. I made Stuart repeat the name to me several times: Squires Wine Bar.

'Are we to understand,' I cross-examined, 'that this is

an establishment owned by someone who deems himself a Squire; or, on the other hand, that this is a location sought out by Squires such as yourself when they desire to quaff?'

Stuart thought about this for a while. 'I don't follow you.'

'Then look at it this way. Where does the apostrophe go?'

'The apostrophe?'

'Is it *e* apostrophe *s* or *s* apostrophe? It does make a measurable difference.'

'I don't know. I don't think it has one.'

'It must have one, even if subliminally.' We stared at one another for a few seconds. I don't think Stuart at all grasped the point I was making. He looked as if he thought I was deliberately sabotaging his modern dress *Paul et Virginie*. 'Sorry. Do go on.'

So there they were, Vinkelkopf and Stu, lording it at Squire's or Squires' Wine Bar as the case may be, when who should step in but some *vieille flamme* of Herr Vinkel's, and this Fräulein had in tow none other than what turned out to be our own dear Gillian. Now the course of events for the trysting quartet from here on in would normally be predictable, except that one of the quatuor was Stuart, and Stuart on a double date is defiantly cognate with a breadstick still in its wrapper. How did he burst out of his crepuscular *oubliette* of unnoticeability on this occasion? I put this poser to him, though in a more tactful way, you understand. And I cherish his reply.

'We sort of got talking. And we sort of got on.'

Ah, that's my Stuart. Do I hear Tristan? Don Juan? Casanova? Do I hear the unspeakably naughty Marquis? No, I hear my mate and mucker Stuart Hughes. 'We sort of got talking. And we sort of got on.'

Oh dear, you're giving me that look again. You don't have to say it. I know. You think I'm a patronising pudendum, don't you? It's not really like that. Perhaps you're not picking up the tone. I only go on like this because Stuart's my friend. My oldest friend. I love him, that Stuart. And we go way back – way, way back, back to the time when you could still buy mono records, when kiwi fruit were yet to be devised, when the khaki-clad representative of the Automobile Association would salute the passing motorist, when a packet of Gold Flake cost a groat and a half and you still had change for a flagon of mead. We're like *that*, Stuart and me. Old Buddies. And don't you underestimate my friend, by the way. He comes on a bit slow, sometimes, and the old turbine up top doesn't always chug away like a Lamborghini, but he gets there, he gets there. And sometimes sooner than I do.

'Could I borrow a pound from you?' We were sitting on adjacent banquettes at whatever that school of ours was called (Stuart will know – ask Stuart). I thought it only civil to break the ice with this boy of hitherto laggardly intelligence who had somehow scrambled his way to a temporary plateau of scholastic proximity. But guess what? Instead of obsequiously handing over the dosh as any self-respecting minion temporarily permitted to breathe the upper air would have done, he started reciting terms and conditions. Interest, percentages, dividends, market forces, price/earnings ratio and what-have-you. He practically had me signed up for the European Monetary System when all I wanted was to touch him for a gold moidore. Then he asked why I wanted the money! As if it was any of his business! As if I knew! I just let out a giggle of disbelief which made the old gecko who ran the class flutter his ruff at me in disapproval; I calmed him with a quip and continued the negotiations with my round and financially tenacious new chum. Some months later I paid him back, ignoring his ridiculous caveats and quibbles about interest rates because they were frankly unintelligible, and we've been mates and muckers ever since.

He had a girlfriend. Before Gillian, I mean. Back in the days when a groat and a half, etc. And do you know what? I'm sure he won't mind my telling you this – *he wouldn't sleep with her*. Get that. No rumpy pumpy. He declined to make free with her narrow loins. When such Stakhanovite chastity over a period of months finally coaxed some forlorn gesture of affection from the girl, he told her *he wanted to get to know her better*. I said that this was what she'd been proposing, *dummkopf*, but Stuart wasn't having any of it. No, that's right, he wasn't having any of it.

Of course, he might have been lying, I suppose, but that would have been an imaginative step for him to take. And besides, I have other evidence. Boffins have definitively spotted the tie-up between sex, interest in/lack of interest in, and food, interest in/lack of interest in. (You doubt me? Then let me cosh you with this detail: one of the most important human pheromones, or sex-pongs, is called isobutyraldehyde, which in the mighty pulsing chain of carbon lies immediately next to – the odour of bean sprouts! Chew on that, amigo.) Now, Stuart, as you will discover if you have not done so already, believes that the principal *raison d'être* of food is to conceal from public view the hideous pattern on the plate beneath. Whereas few – not to boast – few are speedier on the draw with the old chopsticks than young Ollie.

Ergo, I've never had much trouble in the related department of human behaviour either. Family Hold Back has not
been my motto. Perhaps my reputation as a *coureur* emascu-
lates Stuart. And working at the Shakespeare School of English
doesn't exactly hinder me in that direction. After-hours individual tuition in a one-to-one personal interface situation. Stuart
must have rung my boudoir and learned how the telephone is
answered in about fifteen languages so far. But he's all right
now. He's got Gillian, hasn't he?

To tell the truth, I didn't have a steady girlfriend at the time
he swanned into the Café des Squires and exited with Gillian. I
was a bit blue, and being blue always makes me satirical, so I
expect the odd unfair jest might have escaped my lips. But I was
happy for him. How could I not have been happy for him? And
he was so puppyish that first time they came round together to
my place. So tail-waggingly, bone-snafflingly puppyish that I
nearly tickled him under the ears.

I'd tried not to make my apartment look too intimidating.
I loosely tossed a swirl of Moroccan curtain over the sofa,
slid Act 3 of *Orfeo* onto the revolving mat, lit an Al Akhbar
joss-stick, and left it at that. Rather a *bienvenue chez Ollie*
effect, I thought. Oh, I could have gone further, I suppose
– put up a bullfight poster to make Stuart feel at home –
but one mustn't entirely submerge one's personality, I find,
otherwise one's guests don't know whom they're meeting. I
lit a Gauloise as the bell went and prepared to meet my doom.
Or Stuart's doom, as the case might be.

At least she didn't ask why I kept my curtains closed
in the daytime. My explanations of this foible have become
increasingly baroque of late: I find myself announcing every-

thing from a rare eye disease to undying homage to the early Auden. But perhaps Stuart had warned her.

'How do you do,' she said. 'Stuart's been telling me about you.'

I did a touch of Makarova in *Romeo and Juliet* at that, just to put everyone at his ease. 'Oh God,' I replied, launching myself at the Moroccan fabric, 'he hasn't blown the gaff on my war wound, has he? Really, Stuart, I know it's not everyone who's descended from King Zog of Albania, but there's no need to blab the whole story.'

Stuart touched her on the arm — not a gesture I had ever seen come naturally to him before — and muttered, 'I told you not to believe anything he said.' She nodded, and in a strange way I suddenly felt outnumbered. It was strange because there were only two of them, and normally it takes a lot more than that to make me feel outnumbered.

Let me try and reconstruct what she looked like that day. I failed to deposit an accurate simulacrum of her visage and demeanour with the left-luggage clerk of memory; but I *think* she was in a shirt of a hue between sage and lovage, atop grey stone-washed 501s, green socks and a ridiculously unaesthetic pair of trainers. *Marron* hair pulled back and clipped over her ears, falling freely behind; lack of make-up bestowing a pallor which dramatised her generous brown eyes; petite mouth and jaunty nose, set rather low on the tapered oval of her face, thus emphasising the curved hauteur of her forehead. Ears with practically no lobes, I couldn't help noticing, a genetic trait of increasing popularity which no doubt Darwin could explain.

Yes, I think that's how she struck me.

Now, I'm not one of those conversationalists who maintain that the personal should only be approached after arduous circumnavigation. I do not take a lapwing diversion from the nest via such topical matters of the day as the political turmoil in Eastern Europe, the freshest African *coup*, the survival chances of the whale, and that surly ripple of low pressure currently pendant from Greenland's coathook. No sooner had I equipped Gillian and her Squire with a cup of Formosa Oolong than I asked her how old she was, what she did, and whether her parents were still alive.

She took it all in good humour, though Stuart seemed as twitchy as a rabbit's septum. She was twenty-eight, I discovered; her parents (mother French, father English) had separated some years previously when Pater had done a runner with a bimbo; and she toiled as a handmaiden of the arts, rendering fresh the faded pigments of yesteryear. What? Oh, she restores pictures.

Before they left I could not forbear to draw Gillian closer and impart to her the glittering counsel that wearing 501s with trainers was frankly *un désastre* and that I was amazed she had walked the streets to my apartment in broad daylight and escaped pillory.

'Tell me,' she replied. 'You don't . . .'

'What?' I urged her.

'You don't . . . You're not wearing make-up, are you?'

3: That Summer
I Was Brilliant

S t u a r t   Please don't take against Oliver like that. He
goes on a bit but he's basically very good-hearted and kind.
Lots of people don't like him, and some actively loathe him,
but try to see the better side. He hasn't got a girlfriend, he's
practically penniless, he's stuck in a job he hates. A lot of that
sarcasm is just bravado, and if I can put up with his teasing,
can't you? Try and give him the benefit of the doubt. For my
sake. I'm happy. Please don't upset me.

When we were sixteen, we went youth-hostelling together.
We hitch-hiked up to Scotland. I tried to get a lift from every
vehicle that passed, but Oliver only stuck out his thumb at
cars he really wanted to ride in, and sometimes even scowled
at drivers whose cars he disapproved of. So we weren't very
successful at hitch-hiking. But we got there. It rained most of

the time, and when we were kicked out of the youth hostel for the day we walked around and sat in bus shelters. We both had anoraks but Oliver would never pull up his hood because he said it made him look like a monk and he didn't want to endorse Christianity. So he got wetter than I did.

Once we spent all day – somewhere near Pitlochry, I think – in a telephone box playing battleships. It's that game where you make a grid on a sheet of graph paper and each player has one battleship (four squares), two cruisers (three squares), three destroyers (two squares) and so on, then you have to knock out the opponent's fleet. We played game after game. One of us had to sit on the floor of the phone box while the other stood up and rested on the shelf where you open out the directories. I spent the morning sitting on the floor and the afternoon standing up at the shelf. For lunch we had damp oat-cakes we'd bought at the village shop. We played battleships all day, and nobody wanted to use the phone. I can't remember who won. In the late afternoon the weather cleared and we walked back to the youth hostel. I pulled my hood down and my hair was dry; Oliver's was still soaking wet. The sun came out and Oliver linked his arm through mine. We passed a lady in her front garden. Oliver bowed to her and said, 'Behold, madam, the dry monk and the damp sinner.' She looked puzzled, and we walked on keeping step with one another, arm-in-arm.

I took Gillian to see Oliver a few weeks after we met. I had to explain him a bit first, because from meeting me you wouldn't necessarily be able to tell what my best friend was like, and Oliver can get up people's nostrils. I said he had various slightly eccentric habits and tastes, but that if you ignored them you quickly got through to the real Oliver. I said he'd probably have the curtains drawn and the place would smell of joss-sticks, but if she behaved as if nothing was out of the ordinary, all would be fine. Well, she did behave as if nothing was out of the ordinary, and I began to suspect that Oliver was a little displeased. When all's said and done, Oliver does like to cause a bit of a stir. He does enjoy some come-back.

'He wasn't as odd as you'd made him out to be, your friend,' Gillian said as we left.

'Good.'

I didn't explain that Oliver had been uncharacteristically well-behaved.

'I like him. He's funny. He's rather good-looking. Does he wear make-up?'

'Not to my knowledge.'

'Must have been the lighting,' she said.

Later, over a tandoori dinner, I was on my second lager, and something, I don't know what, got into me. I felt I could ask questions, I felt she wouldn't mind.

'Do *you* wear make-up?' We'd been discussing something else, and I said it out of the blue, but in my mind it was as if we'd just been talking about Oliver, and the way she answered, as if she thought we'd just been talking about Oliver too and there wasn't any break in that conversation even though we'd been through lots of different subjects in the meantime, made me feel very cheerful.

'No. Can't you tell?'

'I'm not very good at telling.'

There was a half-eaten chicken tikka in front of her and a half-drunk glass of white wine. Between us stood a fat red candle, whose flame was beginning to drown in a pond of wax, and a purple African violet made of plastic. By the light of that candle I looked at Gillian's face, properly, for the first time. She . . . well, you've seen her for yourself, haven't you? Did you spot that tiny patch of freckles on her left cheek? You did? Anyway, that evening her hair was swept up over her ears at the sides and fastened back with two tortoise-shell clips, her eyes seemed dark as dark, and I just couldn't get over her. I looked and I looked as the candle fought with the wax and cast a flickering light on her face, and I just couldn't get over her.

'I don't either,' I finally said.

'Don't what?' This time she hadn't picked up the thread automatically.

'Wear make-up.'

'Good. Do you mind if I wear trainers with 501s?'

'You can wear whatever you want to as far as I'm concerned.'

'That's a rash statement.'

'I'm feeling rash.'

Later, I drove her back to the flat she shared and stood leaning against some rusted railings while she looked for her keys. Then she let me kiss her. I kissed her gently, then I looked at her, then I kissed her gently again.

'If you don't wear make-up,' she whispered, 'it can't rub off.'

I hugged her. I put my arms around her and hugged her, but I didn't kiss her again because I thought I might cry. Then I hugged her again and pushed her through the door because I thought that if it lasted any longer I *would* cry. I stood on the doorstep alone, pressing my lids together, breathing in, breathing out.

We traded families. My father died of a heart attack some years ago. My mother appeared to be coping well – in fact, she seemed almost exhilarated. Then she got cancer, everywhere.

Gillian's mother was French – is French, I mean to say. Her father was a schoolmaster who went to Lyon for a year as part of his training course and came back with Mme Wyatt in tow. Gillian was thirteen when her father ran off with one of his pupils who'd left school a year earlier. He was forty-two, she was seventeen. There were rumours they'd been having an affair while he was actually teaching her, when she would have been fifteen; there were rumours the girl was pregnant. There would have been a terrific scandal if there'd been anyone present to have a scandal around. But they just took off, vanished. It must have been awful for Mme Wyatt. Like having a husband die and leave you for another woman at the same time.

'How did it affect you?'

Gillian looked at me as if that was rather a stupid question.

'It hurt. We survived.'

'But thirteen's . . . I don't know, a bad time to be left.'

'Two's a bad time,' she said. 'Five's a bad time. Ten's a bad time. Fifteen's a bad time.'

'I just meant, from articles I've read . . .'

'Forty wouldn't be too bad,' she said in a sort of bright, almost hard voice I hadn't heard before. 'If he hadn't bunked off till I was forty I think it might have been better. Perhaps they ought to make that the rule.'

I thought, I don't ever want anything like that to happen to you ever again. We were silent, holding hands. Only one parent out of four between us. Two dead, one missing.

'I wish life was like banking,' I said. 'I don't mean it's straightforward. Some of it's incredibly complicated. But you can understand it in the end, if you try hard enough. Or there's someone, somewhere, who understands it, even if only afterwards, after it's too late. The trouble with life, it seems to me, is that it can turn out to be too late and you still haven't understood it.' I noticed she was looking at me carefully. 'Sorry to be gloomy.'

'You're allowed to be gloomy. As long as you're cheerful most of the time.'

'OK.'

We *were* cheerful that summer. Having Oliver with us helped, I'm sure it did. The Shakespeare School of English had switched off its neon light for a couple of months, and Oliver was at a loose end. He pretended he wasn't but I could tell. We went around together. We drank in pubs, played fruit machines, went dancing, saw films, did silly things on the spur of the moment if we felt like it. Gillian and I were falling in love and you'd think we'd have wanted to be by ourselves all the time, gazing into one another's eyes and holding hands and going to bed together. Well of course we did all that too, but we also went around with Oliver. It wasn't how you might think – we didn't want a witness, we didn't want to show off that we were in love; he was just easy to be with.

We went to the seaside. We went to a beach north of Frinton and ate ice-cream and rock and hired deck-chairs and Oliver got us to write our names in big letters in the sand and photograph one another standing next to them. Then we watched the names being washed out as the sea came in and felt sad. We all groaned a bit and snivelled like kids, and we were putting it on, but we were only putting it on because underneath we *did* feel sad seeing our names rubbed out. Then Gillian said that thing about Oliver talking like a dictionary, and he did his scene on the beach and we all laughed.

Oliver was different, too. Normally when he and I were with girls he would be all competitive, even if he wasn't meaning to be. But now I suppose he had nothing to win, nothing to lose, and it made everything easier. Something in all three of us knew that this was a one-off, that this was a first and last summer, because there wouldn't be another time when Gillian and I were falling in love as opposed to just being in love or whatever. It was unique, that summer; we all sensed it.

Gillian   I started training in social work after I left university. I didn't last very long. But I remember something a counsellor said on one of the courses. She said, 'You must remember that every situation is unique and every situation is also ordinary.'

The trouble with talking about yourself the way Stuart is doing is that it makes people jump to conclusions. For instance, when people find out that my father ran off with a schoolgirl they invariably look at me in a particular way, which means one of two things, if not both of them. The first is: if your father ran off with someone only a couple of years older than you, what this probably means is that he *really* wanted to run off with *you*. And the second is: it's a well-known fact that girls whose fathers run off frequently try to compensate by having affairs with older men. Is that what you're into?

To which I would answer, first, that the witness is not before the court and has not been cross-examined on the matter, and secondly that just because something's a 'well-known fact' this doesn't make it a well-known fact about *me*. Every situation is ordinary and every situation is also unique. You can put it that way round if you prefer.

I don't know why they're doing this, Stuart and Oliver. It must be another of their games. Like Stuart pretending he hasn't heard of Picasso and Oliver pretending he doesn't understand any machinery invented after the spinning-jenny. But it's not a game I want to play, this one, thank you very much. Games are for childhood, and sometimes I think I lost my childhood young.

All I'd say is that I don't quite agree with Stuart's description of that summer with Oliver. Yes, we spent quite a lot of time alone together, started going to bed and all that, and yes we were sensible enough to know that even when you're falling in love you shouldn't live entirely in one another's pockets. But this didn't necessarily mean, from my point of view, that we had to go around with Oliver. Of course I liked him – you can't not like Oliver once you get to know him – but he did tend to monopolise things. Almost telling us what to do. I'm not really complaining. I'm just making a small correction.

That's the trouble with talking it over like this. It never seems quite right to the person being talked about.

I met Stuart. I fell in love. I married. What's the story?

Oliver   I was brilliant that summer. Why do we keep referring to it as 'that summer' – it was only *last* summer, after all. I guess because it was like one perfectly held note, one exact and translucent colour. That's how it seems in memory; and we each apprehended it subcutaneously at the time, *il me semble*. On top of which, I was brilliant.

Things were just a touch grim at the Shakespeare School before it occluded its portals for the vacation. A certain crepuscularity of spirit had sauntered in, courtesy of a misunderstanding which I hadn't bothered to trouble the prancing Squire and his Milady with; not fair, in their state of mind, I thought. But I had discovered one of the problems, one of the deep-seated wrinkles about my foreign students: they don't speak English very well. That was the cause of it. I mean, there she was nodding away and smiling at me, and Ollie, poor old dimwit braindead Ollie, actually jumped to the conclusion that these outward behavioural tics were reliable indicators of reciprocated attraction. Which not too surprisingly in my view led to a misunderstanding which, while ultimately regrettable, was surely purged of culpability on the part of the hapless instructor. And the idea that I resisted her desire to vamoose from my apartment, that I was unmoved when she burst into tears – how could I, an aficionado of opera, fail to respond to lachrymosity? – is a ridiculous exaggeration. The Principal, a frightful piece of lava from a volcano long extinct, actually insisted that I relinquish domestic tuition, simperingly permitted the murky phrase *sexual harassment* to hover in the air between us, and indicated that in the course of the aestival recess he might be reconsidering the terms and conditions of my employment. I replied that as far as I was concerned

his terms and conditions of employment were best used as a
rectal implant preferably without benefit of anaesthetic, which
roused him to suggest that perhaps the whole matter would
best be served by being turned over to the florid authority of
Her Majesty's Judiciary, via PC Plod, or at the very least to
some banal tribunal vested with the right to dilly-dally over
contretemps between master and servant. I replied that of
course such decisions were entirely his prerogative, then I
fell into a musing mood and sought to recall something Rosa
had asked me the previous week about English social customs.
Was it normal, she had enquired, for elderly gentlemen making
termly investigations into your scholastic progress to indicate
where you were to sit for interview by laying their hand on the
sofa cushion, and then, when you sat down, failing to remove
their hand? I acquainted the Principal with the burden of my
reply to Rosa: I had explained that it was less a question of
manners than of physiology, and that extreme decrepitude and
senescence did often lead to withering of the bicep and tricep
muscles, which in turn led to a breakdown in the chain of
command from cerebral GHQ to courting finger. Only later,
I told the now somewhat quivering Principal, only later, when
Rosa had gone, did it come to mind that one or two of the
other girls had made of me the same enquiry over the past
twelve months. I could not quite remember their identities,
but were those currently *in statu pupillare* to be assembled in
a *décontractée* atmosphere – rather like, say, a police line-up
– I felt sure that the whole matter could be discussed as an
appendix to their weekly class 'Britain in the 1980s'. The Principal had by this time become almost as fluorescent as the neon
sign outside his academy, and we eyeballed one another in a

spirit entirely lacking in camaraderie. I thought I might have lost my job, but I wasn't sure. My bishop pinned his queen; his bishop pinned my queen. Was it to be stand-off or mutual destruction?

All of which needs to be taken into account when assessing my brilliance that summer. As I say, I didn't trouble Stu and Gillie about my career hiccup: a trouble shared is not, in my experience, a trouble halved, but rather a trouble broadcast on the mighty tannoy of gossip. Ahoy there, anyone wish to evacuate from a great height upon the doleful Ollie?

Looking back, it might actually have helped that I was a bit blue. The fact that they reserved me a front row seat in the Big Top of their felicity did assist in throttling back the glooms. And what more practical way of repaying them than to ensure that their own little seedling of *bonheur* had time to sprout and shoot, to root and burgeon? By my dancing presence I kept the pests away. I was their aphid spray, their cat-dust, their slug-pellet.

Playing Cupid, I should have you know, isn't just a matter of flying around Arcadia and feeling your tiny winkle throb when the lovers finally kiss. It's to do with timetables and street maps, cinema times and menus, money and organisation. You have to be both jaunty cheerleader and lithe psychiatrist. You require the binary skill of being absent when present, and present when absent. Don't ever tell me that Love's dimpled pander doesn't earn his pesetas.

I'll let you in on a little theory of mine. You know that Gillian's father decamped with a nereid when his daughter was as yet but ten, or twelve, or fifteen or something – at what is falsely termed 'an impressionable age', as if all ages were not so characterisable. Now, I have heard tell in the sultry dens of Freudianism that the psychological scar inflicted by this act of parental desertion frequently induces the daughter, when she is of an age to start questing for a swain, to seek a substitute for the departed archetype. In other words, they fuck older men. This has, in point of fact, always struck me as behaviour verging on the pathological. For a start, have you ever looked at old men, the sort of old men who seduce young women? The roguish high-bummed stride, the fuck-me tan, the effulgent cuff-links, the reek of dry-cleaning. They snap their fingers as if the world is their wine-waiter. They demand, they expect . . . It's disgusting. I'm sorry, I've got a thing about it. The thought of liver-spotted hands clamped on tense juve breasts – well, hie me to the vomitorium *pronto*! And the other point which lies beyond the reef of my comprehension: if you have been deserted by Daddy, then why react by going to bed with Daddy-substitutes, by donating *la fleur de l'âge* to a line-up of old gropers? Aha, the textbooks reply, you're missing the point: what the girl is doing is seeking a replacement for the security that was roughly torn from her; she is looking for a father who *won't* desert her. Fair enough, but *my* point is this: if you're bitten by a pye-dog and the wound becomes infected, is it sensible behaviour to carry on hanging out with pye-dogs? I would say, on balance, not. Buy a cat, own a budgie, but don't hang out with pye-dogs. So what does the girl do? She hangs out with pye-dogs. This is, I have to admit, one murky compartment of the female psyche which has yet to benefit from the oven-scourer of Reason. And besides which, I find it disgusting.

How, you might ask, does this theory of mine apply

to the case in point? Granted, my steatopygous chum is not of an age with the aforementioned silver-haired Lothario who rode off into the sunset with a nifty piece of under-age crumpet strapped to his roofrack, i.e., Gill's dad. But one is forced, upon contemplating Stuart, to conclude that if he is not currently *d'un certain âge*, he nevertheless might as well be. Let us consider the facts of the matter. He is the owner of two medium-dark-grey suits and two dark-dark-grey suits. He is employed doing whatever it is he does by a bank whose caring *dirigeants* wear pin-striped underpants and will look after him until he retires. He contributes to the pension fund and has taken out life insurance. He has a half-share in a 25-year mortgage plus top-up loan. He is modest in his appetites and (sparing your blushes) somewhat attenuated in his sexuality. All that's stopping him being welcomed into the great freemasonry of the over-fifties is that he happens to be thirty-two. And this is what Gillian senses, this is what she knows she wants. Bohemian pyrotechnics are not what marriage to Stu promises. Gillian has landed herself nothing other than the youngest older man she could find.

But would it have been fair to point all this out as they nuzzled one another on some Anglian *plage* and assumed I wasn't noticing? That's not what friends are for. And besides, I was pleased for Stuart, whose *derrière*, voluminous and pensile as it was, had not spent much of its existence in the *beurre*. He clutched onto Gillian's hand with alarming gratitude, as if previously girls had always insisted on his wearing oven-gloves. He seemed to lose a little of his clumsiness when he was beside her. He even danced better. I mean, Stu would never attain anything more than a kind of addled bopping, but that summer he brought a certain careless vivacity to the matter of heel-and-toe. For myself, on those occasions that Gillian embellished my dance-card, I reined myself in, generously not seeking to provoke dismaying comparison. Was I even, at times, uncharacteristically gauche as I jig-a-jigged the parquet? Perhaps. Everyone must decide for himself.

So there we were, that summer. Woes were not on the agenda. At Frinton we played a one-armed bandit for two whole clattering hours and never attained three fruits in a row – but did we mope? I do, however, recall one moment of piercing sadness. We were on a beach, and someone – probably me in my cheerleader mode – suggested we engrave our names in big letters upon the sand, then one of us would mount the promenade and photograph inscription plus inscriber. A cliché in Beowulf's time, I know, but you can't keep coming up with new games. When it came to my turn to be recorded, Gillian went up to the promenade with Stuart. Probably he required help with the auto-focus. It was the end of the afternoon, an east wind was chivvying its self-important way across the North Sea, the sun was losing its heat, and most people had gone home. I stood alone on the beach next to the elaborate italics of *Oliver* (the others had done capitals, of course), and I looked up towards the camera, and Stuart shouted 'Cheese!' and Gillian shouted 'Gorgonzola!' and Stu shouted 'Camembert!' and Gillian shouted 'Dolcelatte!' and suddenly I had this crying fit. I stood there gazing up and blubbing. Then the sun got into my tears and I couldn't see anything, just a blinding coloured rinse. I felt I might cry for ever, whereupon Stu shouted 'Wensleydale!' and I just howled some more, like a jackal, like a pathetic pye-dog. Then I sat in the sand and kicked at the *r* of *Oliver* until they came and rescued me.

Shortly afterwards I was jolly again, and they were jolly too. When people fall in love they develop this sudden resilience, have you noticed? It's not just that nothing can harm them (*that* old suave illusion), but that nothing can harm anyone they care about either. *Frère* Ollie? Crying fit on the beach? Broke down while being photographed by his friends? No, that's nothing, call off the men in the white coats, send back the padded van, we've got our own first-aid kit. It's called love. Comes in all sorts of packaging. It's a bandage, it's a sticking-plaster, it's lint, it's gauze, it's cream. Look, it even comes as an anaesthetising spray. Let's try some on Ollie. See, he's fallen down and broken his crown. Spray spray, whoozh, whoozh, there, that's better, Ollie, up you get.

And I did. I got up and was jolly again. Jolly Ollie, we've mended him, that's what love can do. Have another squirt, Ollie? One last pick-me-up?

They took me home that night in Gillian's rebarbatively quotidian motor-car. Definitely not a Lagonda. I got out and they got out too. I kissed Gillie briefly on the cheek, and ruffled the pelt of Stuart, who was beaming concern at me. So I Nureyeved the front steps and flowed through the door in a single motion of Yale and Chubb. Then I lay upon my understanding bed and burst into tears.

4: Now

Stuart   It's now. It's today. We got married last month. I love Gillian. I'm happy, yes I'm happy. It finally worked out for me. It's *now* now.

Gillian   I got married. Part of me didn't think I ever would, part of me disapproved, part of me was a little scared, to tell the truth. But I fell in love, and Stuart is a good person, a kind person, and he loves me. I'm married now.

Oliver   Oh shit. Oh shit shit shit shit SHIT. I'm in love with Gillie, I've only just realised it. I am in love with Gillie. I'm amazed, I'm overawed, I'm poo-scared, I'm mega-fuckstruck.

I'm also scared out of my cerebellum. What's going to happen now?

5: Everything Starts Here

S t u a r t   Everything starts here. That's what I keep repeating to myself. Everything starts here.

I was only average at school. I was never encouraged to think that I should aim for university. I did a correspondence course in economics and commercial law, then got accepted by the Bank as a general trainee. I work in the foreign exchange department. I'd better not mention the Bank's name, just in case they don't like it. But you'll have heard of them. They've made it fairly clear to me that I'll never be a high-flier, but every company needs some people who aren't high-fliers, and that's all right by me. My parents were the type of parents who always seemed faintly disappointed by whatever it was you did, as if you were constantly letting them down in small ways. I think that's why my sister moved away, up north. On the other hand, I could see my parents' point of view. I *was* a bit disappointing. I was a bit disappointing to myself. I tried to explain earlier about not being able to relax with people I liked, not being able to get them to see what virtues I had. Now I come to think of it, most of my life was like that. I couldn't get other people to see the point of me. But then Gillian came along, and everything starts here.

I expect Oliver's given you the impression that I was a virgin when I got married. No doubt he used some rather choice language about this hypothesis of his. Well, I'd like you to know it isn't true. I don't tell Oliver everything. I bet you wouldn't tell Oliver everything either. When he's cheerful his tongue runs away with him, and when he's depressed he can be unkind. So it's common sense not to let him into every area of your life. We very occasionally went on double dates but they were without exception complete disasters. For a start, Oliver would always provide the girls and I would always provide the money, though naturally I had to slip him his half of it beforehand so the girls wouldn't know who was really paying. Once he even made me hand over *all* the money beforehand, so that it would look as if he was paying for everyone himself. Then we would go to a restaurant and Oliver would get dictatorial.

'No, you can't have *that* as a main course. There's mushrooms and cream in your starter.' Or fennel and Pernod. Or whatever and whatever. Do you ever feel the world is getting *too* interested in food? I mean, it does come out at the other end very soon afterwards. You can't store it, not for long. It's not like money.

'But I *like* mushrooms and cream.'

'Then have this main course and the aubergine starter.'

'Don't like aubergine.'

'Hear that, Stu? She cringeth at the glossy aubergine. Well, let's try converting you tonight.'

And so on. Then the business about wine with the waiter. Sometimes I used to go for a pee at this point. Oliver would start by addressing the table: 'Shall we perhaps essay a Hunter River Chardonnay *ce soir?*'

And having got our agreement in theory he would begin grilling the poor waiter. 'Would you advise the Show Reserve? Would you say it had enough bottle age? I like my Chardonnays fat and buttery, but not *too* fat and buttery, you understand. And how oaky is this one? I do find the colonials tend to be rather over-zealous in their use of oak, don't you?'

Mostly the waiter would go along with this, sensing that Oliver was one of those customers who did not, for all their enquiries, actually want any advice, and it was just a question of slowly reeling him in like a fish. Eventually the order would be placed, but this was not the end of my anxieties. Oliver had to be seen to approve of the wine he had himself chosen. At one time this involved a lot of slurping and gargling and half-closed eyes and many seconds of mystical contemplation. Then he read an article somewhere which said that the point of tasting a wine before it was poured was not to see if you liked it, but to make sure that it wasn't corked. If you didn't like the taste, that was too bad, because you'd chosen it yourself. What you should do – if you were sophisticated – was just give the glass a swirl and sniff, which would tell you whether or not the wine was off. So this was what Ollie took to doing, reducing his performance to a series of loud inhalings followed by a curt nod. Sometimes, if he thought one of the girls didn't know what he was doing, he'd go into a long explanation of why he hadn't actually tasted the stuff.

I must say Oliver ordered some pretty filthy wines those times I went out with him. I shouldn't be surprised if some of the bottles *were* corked.

But what does that matter now? The same as what does it matter whether or not I was a virgin when I met Gillian? I wasn't, as I say, though I don't delude myself that this area of my life which I kept hidden from Oliver was the story of one triumph after another. It was average, I suppose, whatever average means in this context. Sometimes it was jolly nice, sometimes it was a bit fraught, and sometimes I had to remind myself not to start thinking of other things in the middle. Average, you see. But then Gillian came along, and everything starts here. Now.

I love that word. Now. It's *now* now; it's not *then* any more. *Then* has gone away. It doesn't matter that I disappointed my parents. It doesn't matter that I disappointed myself. It doesn't matter that I couldn't ever get myself across to other people. That was then, and then's gone. It's *now* now.

I don't mean I've done a sudden transformation. I'm not a frog that's been kissed by a princess or whatever the fairy tale is. I haven't suddenly become incredibly witty and good-looking – you'd have noticed, wouldn't you? – or a high-flier with a huge family that takes Gillian into its bosom. (Do those families exist? On television you're always seeing fascinating households full of eccentric old aunts and sweet children and interestingly varied adults, who may have their ups and downs but are basically all pulling together and 'on the side of the family', whatever that means. Life never seems to be like that to me. Everyone I know seems to have a small, broken family: sometimes broken up by death, sometimes by divorce, usually just by disagreement or boredom. And *no-one* I know has any sense of 'the family'. There's just a mum they like and a dad they hate, or vice versa, and the eccentric old aunts that I've come across tend to be eccentric only because they're secret alcoholics and smell like unwashed dogs or turn out to be suffering from Alzheimer's disease or something.) No, what's happened is this. I've stayed the same as I was before but now it's all right to be what I was before. The princess kissed the frog and he didn't turn into a handsome prince but that was all right because she liked him as a frog. And if I *had* turned into a handsome prince Gillian would probably have shown me – him – the door. She doesn't go for princes, Gillian.

I was a bit nervous about meeting her mother, I can tell you. I polished my shoes and no mistake that morning. A mother-in-law (that's how I thought about her already), a *French* mother-in-law who's been deserted by an Englishman now being introduced by her daughter to the Englishman she wants to marry? I suppose I thought she'd either be fantastically frosty and sit on one of those little gilt chairs with a fancy gilt mirror behind her, or else be quite fat and red-faced and come in from the stove holding a wooden spoon and give me a huge embrace smelling of garlic and stockpot. On balance I would definitely have preferred the latter, but of course I got neither (that's families again for you). Mrs or Mme Wyatt wore patent-leather shoes and a smart brownish suit with a gold brooch. She was polite, but no friendlier than she had to be; she looked at Gillian's jeans with disapproval but without comment. We had tea and discussed everything except the two things that interested me: the fact that I was in love with her daughter, and the fact that her husband had run off with a schoolgirl. She didn't ask me what my prospects were, or how much I earned, or whether I was sleeping with her daughter – all of which I had thought of as possible avenues of conversation. She was – is – what people call a handsome woman, a phrase which has always struck me as a bit patronising. (What does it mean? It means something like: surprisingly fanciable if it was socially OK to fancy women of that age. But perhaps someone did – does – fancy Mme Wyatt. I'd like to think so.) That's to say, she had firm features and smartly cut, possibly dyed hair obviously kept under regular control, and she behaved as if she had known a time when she turned every head and expected you to be aware of this too. I looked at her a lot during that tea. Not just out of polite attention, but trying to see how Gillian would turn out. It's supposed to be a key moment, isn't it? Meeting your wife's mother for the first time. You're meant either to run a mile, or else collapse back happily: oh yes, if she turns out like *that*, I can more than handle it. (And the prospective mothers-in-law must be aware that this is going through the young man's mind, mustn't they? Perhaps sometimes they deliberately make themselves look a terrible fright to scare him away.) With Mme Wyatt, I had neither of these reactions. I looked at her face, at the shape of the jaw and curve of the forehead; I looked at the mouth of the mother of the girl whose mouth I couldn't get enough of kissing. I looked and I looked; but while I saw similarities (the forehead, the set of the eyes), while I could understand that other people might take them for mother and daughter, it didn't work for me. I couldn't see that Gillian was going to turn into Mme Wyatt. It was completely improbable, and for one simple reason: Gillian wasn't going to turn into *anyone* else. She would change, of course. I'm not so silly and in love that I don't know that. She would change, but she wouldn't change into someone else, she would change into another version of herself. And I would be there to see it happen.

'How did it go?' I asked as we were driving away. 'Did I pass?'

'You weren't being examined.'

'Oh.' I felt a little disappointed.

'She doesn't work like that.'

'How does she work?'

Gillian paused, changed gear, pursed those lips which were and yet weren't at all like her mother's lips, and said, 'She waits.'

I didn't like the sound of that at first. But later, I thought, Fair enough. And I can wait too. I can wait until Mme Wyatt sees me for what I am, understands what Gillian sees in me. I can wait for her approval. I can wait for her to understand how I make Gillian happy.

'Happy?' I said.

'Mmm.' She kept her eyes on the traffic, took her hand off the gear-stick briefly, patted my leg, then withdrew her hand to change gear. 'Happy.'

We're going to have children, you know. No, I don't mean she's pregnant, though I wouldn't mind too much if she were. It's a long-term plan. We haven't really discussed it, to be honest; but I've seen her with kids once or twice and she seems to get on with them instinctively. To be on the same wavelength. What I mean is, she doesn't seem surprised by the way they behave and how they react to things; it seems normal to her and she accepts it. I've always found children to be OK, but I've never completely worked them out. I can't read them. Why do they go on the way they do, making a huge fuss about little things and then ignoring what ought to be much more important? They walk into the corner of the TV set and you think they've broken their skull, but they just bounce off; next moment they sit down very gently on their bottoms which are padded with what looks like fifteen nappies and they burst into tears. What's it about? Why haven't they got a sense of proportion?

Still, I want kids with Gillian. It seems the natural thing to do. And I'm sure she'll want them too when the time is right. That's something women know, isn't it – when the time is right? I've already made them a promise, those kids we're going to have. I'm not going to be like my parents. I'm going to try and see the point of you, whatever that point is. I'll back you. Whatever you want to do is OK by me.

G i l l i a n   I suppose I do have one worry about Stuart. Sometimes I'm working away up here in my studio – the name's a bit too grand for the room, which is only 12 by 12, but even so – and there's music on the radio and I'm sort of on automatic pilot. Then I'll suddenly think, I hope he doesn't get disappointed. This may be an odd thing to say when you've only been married a month, but it's true. It's something I feel.

I usually don't mention the fact that I once trained as a social worker. It's another thing people tend to make crass comments about, or crass assumptions anyway. For instance, it's perfectly obvious that what I was trying to do for my clients was patch up their lives and their relationships in a way that I'd been unable to do for my parents. That's perfectly obvious to anyone, isn't it? Except to me.

And even if I was in some way trying to do this, I certainly didn't succeed. I lasted eighteen months before packing it in, and in that time I saw a lot of disappointed people. Most days I saw damage, people with huge problems, emotional, social, financial – sometimes self-inflicted, mostly just handed down to them. Things families had done to them, parents, husbands; things they'd never get over.

Then there were the other ones, the disappointed ones. And that was real damage, irreversible. The ones who began with such high hopes of the world, then put their trust in psychopaths and fantasists, invested their faith in boozers and hitters. And they'd go on for many years with incredible perseverance, believing when they had no reason to believe, when it was crazy for them to believe. Until one day they just gave up. And what could twenty-two-year-old trainee social worker Gillian Wyatt do for them? Believe me, professionalism and cheerfulness cut very little ice with these clients.

People get broken in spirit. That's what I couldn't face. And it came to me later, as I began to love Stuart, this thought: please don't let him be disappointed. I'd never felt that before with anyone. Worrying about their long-term future, how they'd turn out. Worrying what they might think when they finally looked back.

Listen, I'm not playing this . . . game. But equally there's no point sitting in the corner with a handkerchief stuffed in your mouth. I'll say what I have to say, what I know.

I went out with quite a lot of men before I met Stuart. I was nearly in love, I was proposed to a couple of times; on the other hand, I once went for a year without men, without sex – both seemed too much trouble. Some of the men I went out with were 'old enough to be my father' as they say; on the other hand, many weren't. So where does that leave us? One bit of information and people are immediately off into their theories. Did I marry Stuart because I thought he wouldn't let me down the way my father had? No, I married him because I loved him. Because I love, respect and fancy him. I didn't fancy him at first, not particularly. I don't conclude anything from that either, except that fancying is a complicated business.

We were in that hotel with schooners of sherry in our hands. Was it a cattle market? No, it was a sensible group of people taking a sensible step about their lives. It happened to work for the two of us, we were lucky. But we weren't 'just' lucky. Sitting alone with self-pity isn't a good way of meeting people.

I think that in life you have to discover what you're good at, recognise what you can't do, decide what you want, aim for it, and try not to regret things afterwards. God, that must sound pious. Words don't always hit the mark, do they?

Perhaps that's one of the reasons I love my work. There aren't any words involved. I sit in my room at the top of the house with my swabs and solvents, my brushes and pigments. There's me and a picture in front of me, and music from the radio if I need it, and no telephone. I don't really like Stuart coming up here much. It breaks the spell.

Sometimes the picture you're working on answers back. That's the most exciting part, when you take off overpaint and discover something underneath. It doesn't happen very often, of course, which makes it all the more satisfying when it does. For instance, an awful lot of breasts got painted out in the nineteenth century. So you might be cleaning a portrait of what's meant to be an Italian noblewoman, and gradually uncover a suckling baby. The woman turns into a Madonna beneath your eyes. It's as if you're the first person she's told her secret to in years.

The other month I was doing a forest scene and found a wild boar someone had painted out. This completely changed the picture. It seemed to be of horsemen having a nice peaceful ride in the wood – picnickers, almost – until I discovered the animal, when it became perfectly clear that it had been a hunting scene all along. The wild boar had been hiding behind a large and actually rather unconvincing bush for a hundred years or so. Then up here in my studio, without a word being spoken, everything came back plainly into view, as it was meant to be. All by taking off a little overpaint.

O l i v e r   Oh *shit*.

It was her face that did it. Her face as she stood outside the register office, with that big municipal clock behind her, ticking off those first glistening moments of nuptial bliss. She was wearing a linen suit the colour of pale watercress soup, with the skirt cut just above the knee. Linen, we all know, crushes as easily as timid love; she looked uncrushable. Her hair was taken back just on one side, and she smiled in the general direction of the entire human race. She wasn't clinging to the steatopygous Stu, though she held his arm, it's true. She just exuded, she glowed, she was fully there yet tantalisingly absent, withdrawn at this most public moment into some private dominion. Only I appeared to notice this, the rest thought she just looked happy. But I could tell. I went up and gave her a kiss and murmured felicitations in her one visible and lobeless ear. She responded, but almost as if I wasn't there, so I did a few gestures in front of her face – Signalman Flagging Down Runaway Express, sort of thing – and she briefly focused on me and laughed and then went back into her secret nuptial sett.

'You look like a jewel,' I said, but she didn't respond. Perhaps if she had, things would have been different, I don't know. But because she didn't respond, I looked at her more. She was all pale green and chestnut, with an emerald blaze at her throat; I roamed her face, from the bursting curve of her forehead to the plum-dent of her chin; her cheeks, so often pallid, were brushed with the pink of a Tiepolo dawn, though whether the brush was external and garaged in her handbag or internal and wielded by ecstasy, I was unable or unwilling to guess; her mouth was besieged by a half-smile which seemed to last and last; her eyes were her lustrous dowry. I *roamed* her face, do you hear?

And I couldn't bear the way she was there and not there, the way I was present to her and yet not present. Remember those philosophers' schemes according to which we only exist if we are perceived as existing by something or somebody other than ourselves? Old Ollie, before the bride's oscillating acknowledgment of him, felt all wobbly with existential peril. If she blinked I might vanish. Perhaps this was why I turned myself into some happy-snap Diane Arbus, seizing the camera and cavorting mirthfully in search of an angle which would set off Stuart's embryonically goitrous condition to a satirical T. Displacement activity. Pure despair, as you can see, fear of oblivion. Of course they never guessed.

It was my fault, and it wasn't my fault. You see, I wanted a church wedding. I wanted to be best man. They couldn't understand it at the time, and nor could I. None of us has any religious sense, there weren't any fundamentalist kinsmen to pacify: the absence of a fellow in a frilly white frock wouldn't have led to the thrust of disinheritance. But Ollie must have been prescient. I said I wanted to be best man, I said I wanted a church wedding. I rather went on about it. I started shouting. I came the Hamlets a bit. I was drunk at the time, if you must know.

'Oliver,' said Stu after a while, 'you're way out of order. This is our wedding. We've already asked you to be a witness.'

I reminded them both of the force of ancient ceremony, the ley-lines of hymeneal fortune, the gilded corrugations of the sacred text. 'Go on,' I urged in completion, 'get done by a vic.'

Stuart's plump little visage tightened as far as that was a physical possibility. 'Oliver,' he said, lapsing almost parodically at this solemn moment into the brute vocabulary of mercantilism, 'we've asked you to be a witness and that's our final offer.'

'You'll regret it,' I yelled, a captain of industry from Mitteleurop thwarted by the Monopolies Commission. 'You'll regret it.'

What I mean by prescient is this. If we'd had a church wedding, she'd have done the white-lace-and-trimmings bit, the full veil-and-trail number. I might have looked at her outside the church and seen just another assembly-line bride. And then it might never have happened.

It was her face that did it. I didn't know at the time. I thought I was just a bit hyper, like everyone else. But I was gone, sunk. Unimaginable change had happened. Fallen like Lucifer; fallen (this one is for you, Stu) like the stock market in 1929. I was also gone in the sense that I was transformed, made over. You know that story of the man who wakes up and finds he's turned into a beetle? I was the beetle who woke up and saw the possibility of being a man.

Not that the organs of perception apprehended it at the time. As we sat there at the wedding-feast I held to the pedestrian belief that the rustling jetsam at my feet was merely the accumulation of champagne foil. (I had to insist on personally opening the little non-vintage number Stuart had secured in bulk. No-one knows how to open champagne nowadays, not even waiters. Especially waiters. The idea, I have to keep telling people, is not to make the cork go jolly *pop* and thus provoke an ejaculatory *mousse* from the bottle. No, the idea is to open it without so much as a nun's fart. Hold the cork and turn the bottle, that's the secret. How many times do I have to repeat it? Forget the flourish of the big white napkin, forget two thumbs on the cork's corona, forget aiming at the bulbs in the recessed ceiling-lights. Just hold the cork and turn the bottle.) No, what blew against my ankles like tumbleweed that afternoon was not the crinkle of Mumm NV but the discarded skin of my former being, my beetle carapace, my sloughed and umber appurtenances.

Panic, that was the first reaction to whatever it was that had just happened. And it got worse when I realised I didn't know where they were going for their *lune de miel*. (How duncical, by the way, for both French and English to retain the same phrase. You would think that one of us might scurry around for a new word instead of accepting linguistic hand-me-downs. Or perhaps that's the point: the phrase is the same because the experience is the same. [*Honeymoon*, by the way, just in case you can't cut the etymological mustard, has only in recent times come to denote a nuptial holiday involving the purchase of duty-free goods and the taking of too many colour prints of exactly the same scene. Dr Johnson, in his intermittently droll *Dictionary*, was for once not attempting to stir mirth when he defined it thus: 'The first month after marriage, when there is nothing but tenderness and pleasure.' Voltaire, an altogether more sympathetic figure, who incidentally used to serve himself the best Burgundy while giving his guests *vin ordinaire*, observed in one of his philosophical tales that *la lune de miel* is followed the next month by *la lune de l'absinthe*.])

You see, I suddenly felt that I couldn't bear it, not knowing where they were going to be for the next three and a half weeks (though in retrospect I doubt whether the location of the groom much perturbed me). So when, towards the end of lunch, Stuart lurched to his feet and informed the table – why this confessional urge that comes upon people at such times? – that he was 'Just going to decant' (and the awful phrases they come up with: from which beagling divisional manager did my chum filch that one?), I slipped from my own chair without a word, kicked away the detritus of my previous life which was posing as champagne foil, and followed him to the Gents.

There we stood, side by side at those hip-high porcelain

scoops, each staring grimly ahead at some Mexican firing-squad in the way that Englishmen do, neither dropping his gaze for a squint at the other's tackle. There we stood, two rivals as yet quite unaware they were rivals, each grasping his *membrum virile* – should I offer the groom some tips as to its deployment? – and peeing virtually unamended, rebottleable Mumm NV on to a little violet cube of toilet-freshener. (How would my life change if I had a great deal of money? I return constantly to the same two luxuries: having someone to wash my hair every morning, and peeing over crushed ice.)

We seemed to be peeing more than we could possibly have drunk. Stuart gave a little embarrassed cough, as if to say, 'Don't know about you, but I'm not even halfway there.' It seemed the moment to enquire into the planned whereabouts of the hymeneal rough-and-tumble. But all I got in reply was a squinty smirk and the hiss of piss.

'No, really,' I insisted a minute or so later, as I laundered my fingers and Stuart needlessly scraped a fetid plastic comb over his cranium, 'where are you going? You know, just in case I need to get in touch.'

'State secret. Even Gillie doesn't know. Just told her to take light clothes.'

He was still smirking, so I presumed that some juvenile guessing-game was required of me. I hazarded various Stuart-esque destinations like Florida, Bali, Crete and Western Turkey, each of which was greeted by a smug nod of negativity. I essayed all the Disneylands of the world and a selection of tarmacked spice islands; I patronised him with Marbella, applauded him with Zanzibar, tried aiming straight with Santorini. I got nowhere.

'Look, something might happen . . .' I began.

'Sealed envelope with Mme Wyatt,' he replied, laying an uncharacteristic finger against his nose as if this was what he'd been to spy-school for.

'Don't be so bloody bourgeois,' I shouted. But he wouldn't tell me. Back at the table I was in crepuscular mood for a few minutes, then bent once more to the task of diverting the wedding guests.

The day after they left for their honeymoon I telephoned Mme Wyatt, and guess what? The old *vache* wouldn't tell me. Claimed she hadn't opened the envelope. I said I missed them, I wanted to telephone them. It was true, I did miss them. I may have cried down the telephone, but Mme Dragon wouldn't unbend.

And by the time they came back (yes, it was Crete: I'd guessed, but he hadn't flickered, the duplicitous bastard), I knew I was in love. I got a sun-'n'-sex postcard from Heraklion, worked out which day they'd be returning, telephoned all possible airlines and went to meet them at Gatwick. When the indicator board clacked out the information BAGGAGE IN HALL against their flight, a circle of bell-ringers in my stomach all heaved on their ropes at the same time, and the terrible clangour they set off in my skull could only be stilled by a couple of stiff ones at the bar. Then I waited at the barrier, the motley flesh around me all pulsing with welcome.

I saw them before they saw me. Stuart had typically picked a trolley with one locked wheel, and he emerged from the tender scrutiny of the *douaniers* in a comic curve, his uncertain course hymned by Gillian's indulgent laughter and his trolley's maundering squeak. I adjusted the chauffeur's cap I'd borrowed, hoisted a rudely lettered sign reading 'Mr & Mrs Stewart Hughes' (the misspelling was a tad masterly, I thought), took a deep breath and prepared to face the glittering turmoil that my life would become. As I watched her before she became aware of me, I whispered to myself, Everything begins here.

6: Stave Off
Alzheimer's

Stuart   It's really rather awful you know. I keep on feeling sorry for Oliver. I don't mean I shouldn't – no, I've got lots of reasons now – it's just that I'm uncomfortable with it. This isn't what I should feel for him. But I do. Have you seen those cuckoo clocks which have little weathermen as part of the mechanism? The clock goes off, the cuckoo goes *cuckoo*, and then a little door opens and either the good-weather weatherman comes out, all grinning and dressed for the sunshine, or else another door opens and it's the bad-weather weatherman who comes out with an umbrella and a raincoat and a grumpy expression. The point is, only one of the two can come out of his little door at any one time, not just because that would make impossible weather, but because the two little men are joined together by a metal bar: one has to stay in if the other one is out. That's how it's always been with Oliver and me. I've always been the one with the umbrella and raincoat, forced to stay indoors in the dark. But now it's my time in the sun, and that seems to mean that Oliver's going to have less fun for a bit.

He looked a real mess at the airport, and I don't think we helped matters. We'd had these super three weeks in Crete – marvellous weather, nice hotel, swimming, really got on – and even though the flight was delayed we were still in a terrific mood when we got to Gatwick. I waited at the carousel, Gillie fetched a trolley, and by the time she got back the bags had already come up. I loaded them on, and when she tried to push she found out she'd got a trolley with a wonky wheel. It wouldn't go in a straight line and kept squeaking, as if it was trying to draw the attention of the customs officers to the person pushing: 'Hey, take a look at this chap's bags.' That's what I thought the trolley sounded like as we went through the green channel. I'd joined in trying to control the thing by now as Gillian found she couldn't manage curves on her own.

So it wasn't really surprising that we didn't recognise Ollie when we got into the arrivals hall. No-one knew we were on this flight, and we only had eyes for one another, frankly. So when someone emerged from the scrum of drivers meeting various flights and waved a sign in our face, I sort of pushed him away. I didn't really look at him, though I immediately smelled alcohol on his breath, and thought, that firm isn't going to last long if it's sending out drunken drivers to pick up clients. But it was Oliver, dressed in a chauffeur's cap and carrying a sign with our names on it. I pretended to be glad to see him, though my first thought was that Gill and I wouldn't be alone on the train back to Victoria. We'd have Oliver with us. Isn't that unkind? You see what I mean about feeling sorry for him?

And he was in a terrible state. He seemed to have lost weight, and his face was all white and drawn, and his hair, which he normally keeps quite neat, was getting straggly. He sort of stood there, and then, after we'd recognised him, he threw himself on us both, hugging and kissing us. Not typical behaviour at all, because it was more pathetic than welcoming. And he did smell of drink. What was that about? He said our flight had been delayed and he'd spent the time in the bar, and then added, rather unconvincingly, that some woman had insisted on 'plying Phaeton with liquor' as he put it, but there was a hollowness in the way he said it, and I don't think either Gill or I believed him for a moment. And here's another odd thing: he didn't ask us about our honeymoon. Not till much later. No, the first thing he launched into was a harangue about how Gillian's mother wouldn't tell him where we were staying. I wondered if we should let him drive, given the state he was in.

Later, I found out what it was all about. You'll never guess what's happened. Oliver has gone and lost his job. He's managed to get himself sacked from the Shakespeare School of English. Now that has to be a first. I don't know how much Oliver's told you about the Shakespeare School, but take it from me that place is tacky: how it got its registered status I shudder to think. I went there once. It's in what was obviously quite a nice terrace at one time, early Victorian or something, with big fat columns holding up the porches and railings on the street and steps leading to the basement. But the whole area's gone terribly downhill. The telephone boxes are all covered with prostitutes' phone numbers, the street-sweepers probably haven't been since 1968, and there are left-over hippies in attics playing mad music all the time. You can imagine the sort of area. *And* the Shakespeare School is in the basement. *And* the Principal looks like a serial killer. *And* Ollie managed to get himself sacked from the place.

He didn't want to talk about it, and muttered that he'd resigned over a matter of principle concerning next year's timetable. As soon as he said this, I didn't believe him. Not that it's impossible – indeed, it's rather the sort of thing Oliver might do – but I've somehow stopped believing most of what he says. That's rather awful, isn't it? He is my oldest friend. And it's not made any better by feeling sorry for him. A year or two ago I would have believed him, and maybe the truth would have come out a few months later. But now I instinctively thought, Oh no you didn't Ollie, you didn't resign, you got sacked. I suppose it's something to do with me being happy, being married, knowing where I am: I can see things more clearly now than I used to.

So when I next got Oliver alone, I said to him quietly, 'Look, you can tell me, you didn't resign, did you?' He went all quiet and un-Oliver-like and admitted that he'd got the sack. When I asked him what for he gave a sad sigh and then a sort of bitter grin and looked me in the eye and said, 'Sexual harassment.' Apparently there'd been this girl, Spanish or Portuguese I think, and Ollie had been giving her private lessons at his flat, and he thought she fancied him, and he'd had a couple of Special Brews at the time and thought she was just shy, and then he tried kissing her, and it's the old, old, sordid story, isn't it? Turned out the girl was not just a devout Catholic who was only interested in improving her English but also the daughter of some big-shot industrialist with lots of connections at the Embassy . . . The girl told her father, and one phone-call later Oliver was out in the gutter with the styrofoam burger boxes and not even any severance pay. He got quieter and quieter as the story unfolded, and I believed every word of it. He also couldn't face me. Towards the end I realised he was crying. When he finished he looked up at me, and there were tears all down his face, and he said to me, 'Lend us a quid, Stu.'

Just like at school. Poor old Oliver. This time I simply wrote him a decent-sized cheque and told him not to worry about repaying it.

'Oh, but I will. I've got to.'

'Well, let's talk about that another time.'

He wiped his face, then he picked up the cheque again, and his wet thumb smudged my signature. God, I felt sorry for him.

You see, it's now my job to look after him. It's as if I'm repaying him for looking after me at school. All those years ago after we'd been friends for a couple of months or so (and he'd borrowed quite a bit more money off me), I confessed to him that I was being persecuted by a thug called Dudley. Jeff Dudley. The *Edwardian* informed me recently that he'd been appointed trade attaché in one of our Central American embassies. Perhaps that means he's a spy nowadays. Why not? At school his best subjects were lying, stealing, extortion, blackmail, and gang-leadership. It was a fairly civilised school, so Dudley's gang consisted of only two: himself and 'Feet' Schofield.

I would have been safer if I'd been better at games or cleverer. I didn't have a protective big brother: all I had was a small sister. Also, I wore glasses and didn't look capable of jujitsu. So Dudley picked on me. The usual things – money, services, pointless humiliations. I didn't tell Oliver at first because I thought he'd despise me. He didn't; instead, he sorted them out in two weeks flat. First he told them to lay off me, and when they sneered and said what would happen if they didn't, he merely replied, 'A series of inexplicable misfortunes.' Well, that's not how schoolboys talk, so they sneered some more and waited for Oliver to challenge them to a formal fight. But Oliver never played things by the rules. A series of indeed inexplicable misfortunes, none of them obviously traceable to Oliver, then occurred. A master found five packs of cigarettes in Dudley's desk (one was a beating offence at that time). Schofield's sports kit was discovered half burnt in the school incinerator. Both the saddles off my persecutors' bikes disappeared one lunchtime, and they had to ride home, as Oliver put it, in 'discomfort bordering on danger'. Shortly afterwards Dudley tried to waylay Oliver after school, and was probably about to suggest meeting behind the bike sheds with knuckledusters at noon when Oliver punched him in the throat. 'Another inexplicable misfortune,' he said, as Dudley lay on the ground choking. After that, the two of them left me alone. I offered my thanks to Oliver, and even suggested some debt restructuring by way of gratitude, but he just shrugged it off. That's the sort of thing Oliver does.

What ever became of 'Feet' Schofield? And where did he

get his nickname? All I can remember is that it had nothing to do with his feet.

G i l l i a n   You don't know exactly when you fall in love with someone, do you? There isn't that sudden moment when the music stops and you look into one another's eyes for the first time, or whatever. Well, maybe it's like that for some people, but not me. I had a friend who told me she fell for a boy when she woke up in the morning and realised he didn't snore. It doesn't sound much, does it? Except it sounds true.

I suppose you look back and select one particular moment out of several and then stick to it. Maman always said she fell for Daddy when she saw how precise and gentle he was with his fingers while filling his pipe. I only ever half-believed her, but she always told it with conviction. And everyone has to have an answer, don't they? I fell in love with him *then*, I fell in love with him *because*. It's a sort of social necessity. You can't very well say, Oh, I forget. Or, it wasn't obvious. You can't say that, can you?

Stuart and I went out together a few times. I liked him, and he was different from other boys, not at all pushy, except pushy to please I suppose, but even that was sweet in a way – it made me want to say, it's all right, don't fret so much, I'm having a perfectly nice time, slow down. Not that it was slow down in the sense of Don't go too fast physically. If anything, the opposite was the case. He tended to stop kissing me first.

What I'm trying to tell you about is this. He offered to cook me dinner one evening. I said I'd like that. I went round to his flat at about 8.30, and there was a nice smell of roasting meat and candles on the table which were lit even though it wasn't yet dark, and a bowl of those Indian bits and pieces for beforehand, and flowers on the coffee table. Stuart was wearing the trousers of his work suit, but he'd changed his shirt, and he had an apron over the top. His face seemed to be divided into two: the bottom half was all smiling and pleased to see me, the top half was frowning with anxiety about the dinner.

'I don't cook much,' he said, 'but I wanted to cook for you.'

We had shoulder of lamb, frozen peas, and potatoes roasted round the meat. I said I liked the potatoes.

'You par-boil them,' he said solemnly, 'then you scrape them with a fork and that puts ridges on them and then you get more crispy bits.' It must have been something he'd seen his mother do. We had a nice bottle of wine, and whenever he poured it he put his hand over the price-tag which he'd forgotten to remove. I could see he was doing that deliberately, out of embarrassment. He thought he should have taken the price off. Do you see what I mean, he was *trying*?

Then he wouldn't let me help clear away. He went off into the kitchen and came back with an apple pie. It was a warm spring evening and the food was winter food, but that didn't matter. So I had a slice of pie and then he put the kettle on for coffee and went to the loo. I got up and took the pudding plates into the kitchen. As I was putting them down I saw a piece of paper leaning against the spice-rack. Do you know what it was? It was a timetable:

    6.00   Peel spuds

    6.10   Roll pastry

6.20 Switch oven on

6.20 Bath

and it went on like that . . .

8.00 Open wine

8.15 Check potatoes browning

8.20 Put on water for peas

8.25 Light candles

8.30 G arrives!!

I hurried back to the table and sat down. I was trembling. I also felt bad about reading it because I'm sure Stuart would have thought I was spying. But it just got to me, each item more than the last. *8.25 Light candles.* It's all right, Stuart, I thought, I wouldn't have minded if you'd left that till after I arrived. And then *8.30 G arrives!!* Those two exclamation marks really did for me.

He came back from the loo and I had to stop myself telling him what I'd found out and that it didn't seem silly or neurotic or hopeless or anything, but just very thoughtful and touching. Of course I didn't say anything, but I must have reacted in some way and it got through to him, because he seemed more relaxed from that point on. We spent a long time on the sofa that evening, and I would have stayed the night if he'd asked me but he didn't. And that was all right too.

He worries a lot, Stuart. He really wants to get things right. Not just for himself, and for us. He's terribly bothered about Oliver at the moment. I don't know what's happened to him. Or rather, I do. He tried to molest some poor girl at the

Shakespeare School and got thrown out. Well, that's reading between the lines of what Stuart told me. Stuart was leaning over backwards to see Oliver's point of view. Leaning so far, in fact, that we had this ridiculous disagreement. Stuart said the girl must have been leading Oliver on and being provocative, I said she was probably shy and terrified by these advances from her teacher, until we both realised neither of us had set eyes on the girl or knew what had happened. We were just guessing. But even just guessing has rather put me off Oliver at the moment. I don't exactly approve of teacher-pupil relationships, for reasons that don't need filling in. Stuart said he'd given Oliver some money, which I thought was quite unnecessary, not that I said so. After all, Oliver's a healthy young man with a university degree. He can find another job. Why should he get some of our money?

Still, it's true he's a mess at the moment. It was awful at the airport. Just the two of us. I remember thinking as we stood in the baggage hall, this is a bit like the rest of life. Two of us in a great mass of strangers, and various things to do that you've got to get right, like follow signs and collect your luggage; then you get looked over by the customs, and no-one particularly cares who you are or what you're doing there so the two of you have to keep one another cheerful . . . I know, it probably sounds sentimental but that's what it felt like to me at the time. And then we get through customs, and the two of us are having a laugh because we're safely back, and suddenly this drunk in a chauffeur's cap throws himself at us and nearly puts out my eye with a cardboard sign and treads on my foot into the bargain. And guess what? It's Oliver. Looking like death. He obviously thought it was funny, what he was doing, but it wasn't at all. It was pathetic. That's the trouble with people like Ollie, I think: when they come off they're really good company, and when they don't they miss by a mile. Nothing in the middle.

Anyway, we pulled ourselves together and pretended to be pleased to see him, and then he drove us back to London like a maniac, keeping up a stream of gibberish which after a while I stopped listening to. Just put my head back on the seat and closed my eyes. The next thing I remember was being jerked to a stop outside the house and Oliver saying in a rather odd voice, 'A propos de bottes, how was the lune de miel?'

O l i v e r   Have a cigarette? You don't? I know you don't – you've told me that before. Your disapproval still flashes in neon. Your frown is worthy of the mother-in-law from *Katya Kabanova*. But I have puckish news for you. I read in the paper this morning that if you smoke you're less likely to develop Alzheimer's disease than if you don't. A hit, a veritable hit? Go on, have one, kipper your lungs and keep your brain intact. Isn't life bedizened with jaunty contradictions? Just when you think you've got it straight, along comes the Fool with his pig's bladder and whops you on the nose.

By the way, I'm no idiot. I could tell Gillian and Stuart weren't thrilled to see me at the airport. I can sense a *piccolo faux pas* when I make one. Ollie, old son, I said to myself, your puppyish fraternising is misplaced. Put that couple down at once, stop licking their faces. Except, of course, it wasn't really puppyish, or particularly fraternal. I met them because I'm in love with Gillian. All the rest was just an act.

It was odd, that drive back to London. Odd? Rather, spectacularly *sui generis*. Gillian sat in the back and soon dropped off to sleep. Every time I looked in the mirror – and I can be a *very* careful driver if I want to be – I saw the languid bride with shuttered eyes and hair adrift. Her neck rested on the top curve of the seat and this lifted her mouth as if for kissing. I kept looking in the mirror but not, you understand, for traffic. I *roamed* her face, her sleeping face.

And there was plump, placid, erotically drained Stuart beside me, looking so fucking . . . *blithe*, pretending it was nice to be met at the airport, and probably thinking about how he was going to claim back some Danegeld on the unused half of their return *billets* from Gatwick to Victoria. Stuart, I warn you, can be a major nickelfucker. When he goes abroad, he always buys a return ticket to the airport a) because he thinks this will save three milliseconds in a fortnight's time; b) because he knows he's coming back; and c) in case fares go up in the interval. Oliver always buys a single. Who can predict what Brazilian carnival queen might not cross his path? Who cares about the possible queue a week next putative Saturday at the Gatwick *guichet*? I once read a case in the newspaper about a man who jumped in front of an Underground train. At the inquest they said he probably hadn't intended to kill himself because he had a return ticket in his pocket. Well, excuse me, M'Lud, there are other explanations. He could have bought a return ticket because he knew that inserting a scintilla of doubt would spare the feelings of those close to him. Another possibility is that he could have been Stuart. If Stuart decided to give a train driver six weeks compassionate leave or whatever the allowance is, he'd buy a return ticket.

Because he'd be thinking, what if I don't kill myself after all? What if I decide against it at the last minute? Think of those awful queues before the ticket machines at Tottenham Court Road. Yes, I'll take a return just in case.

You think me unfair? Listen, too much has been going on in my head of late. I am in stark need of a febrifuge. The cerebellum is positively bursting with over-activity. Imagine: I was a bit pissed for a start, the object of my complete love was nesting in my rear-view mirror, the corpulent groom – my best friend – who had spent three weeks pleasuring her in the Hellenic sunshine was sitting beside me with a clank of duty-free between his calves, I'd lost my job, and the other drivers on the road were all tuning up for Formula One. I'm meant to be calm? I'm meant to be fair?

What I did in the circumstances was go off into an Ollieish riff about *je ne sais quoi*, keeping Stu achortle without waking the fair Gillian. Every so often I'd have to grip the wheel tightly because what I really wanted to do was interrupt my drollery, pull over on to the hard shoulder, turn to my passenger and say, 'By the way, Stuart, I'm in love with your wife.'

Is that what I'll say? I'm terrified, I'm awed, I'm megafuckstruck. I'll have to say something like that before long. How will I tell him? How will I tell *her*?

You think you know people, don't you? OK, you've got a best friend, he gets married, and the day he gets married you fall in love with his wife. How will your best friend react? There aren't many benign possibilities, I'd guess. 'Oh I can quite see your point of view' is not a reaction that is on the agenda, quite frankly. Out with the Kalashnikov more likely. Banishment the minimum sentence of the law. Gulag Ollie, they'll call me. But I won't be banished. You see? I won't be banished.

What has to happen is this. Gillian has to realise she loves me. Stuart has to realise she loves me. Stuart has to step down. Oliver has to step up. Nobody must get hurt. Gillian and Oliver must live happily ever after. Stuart must be their best friend. That's what has to happen. How high do you rate my chances? As high as an elephant's eye? (That cultural allusion is for you, Stu.)

Oh, *please* take that disapproving look off your face. Don't you think I'll have enough of that coming my way in the weeks and months and years ahead? Give us a break. Put yourself in my *pantoufles*. Would you renounce your love, slip gracefully from the scene, become a goatherd and play mournfully consoling music on your Panpipes all day while your heedless flock chomp the succulent tufts? People don't *do* that. People never did. Listen, if you go off and become a goatherd you never loved her in the first place. Or you loved the melodramatic gesture more. Or the goats. Perhaps pretending to fall in love was merely a smart career move allowing you to diversify into pasturing. But you didn't *love* her.

We're stuck with it. That's the long and short of the matter. We're stuck in this car on this motorway, the three of us, and someone (the driver! – me!) has leant an elbow on the button of the central locking system. So the three of us are in here till it's resolved. *You're* in here too. Sorry, I've clunked the doors, you can't get out, we're all in this together. *Now* what about that cigarette? I'm smoking, and I wouldn't be surprised if Stuart took it up quite soon. Go on, have one. Stave off Alzheimer's.

7: Now Here's a Funny Thing

S t u a r t   Now here's a funny thing. I was on my way to work this morning. I probably haven't explained that there are two ways of walking to the station. One takes me along St Mary's Villas and Barrowclough Road, past the old municipal baths and the new DIY and wholesale paint centre; while the other means cutting down Lennox Gardens, taking that street whose name I always forget into Rumsey Road, then past the row of shops and back into the High Street. I've timed both ways and there isn't any more than twenty seconds in it. So some mornings I go one way, and some mornings the other. I sort of toss up as I leave the house over which direction to take. I tell you this as background information.

So, this morning I set off down Lennox Gardens, the Street with No Name, and then into Rumsey Road. I was looking about a lot. You know, that's one of the many differences since Gill and I have been together: I start seeing things I never would have noticed before. You know how you can walk along a street in London and never raise your eyes above the top of a bus? You go along, and you look at the other people, and the shops, and the traffic, and you never look up, not really *up*. I know what you're going to say, if you did look up you'd probably step in a pile of dog turds or walk into a lamp-post, but I'm serious. I'm serious. Raise your eyes just that little bit more and you'll spot something, an odd roof, some fancy bit of Victorian decoration. Or lower them, for that matter. The other day, one lunchtime in fact, I was walking up the Farringdon Road. All of a sudden I noticed something I must have walked past dozens of times. A plaque set in the wall at shin height, painted cream with the lettering picked out in black. It says:

These Premises
Were Totally Destroyed
by a
ZEPPELIN RAID
During the World War
on
September 8th 1915

John Phillips
Rebuilt 1917   Governing Director

I thought that was interesting. Why did they put the plaque so low down, I wondered. Or perhaps it's been moved. You'll find it at Number 61, by the way, if you want to check up. Next door to the shop that sells telescopes.

Anyway, what I'm trying to say is that I find myself looking around more. I must have passed that florist's in Rumsey Road several hundred times and never really looked at it, let alone into it. But this time I did. And what did I see? What was my extraordinary reward at 8.25 on a Tuesday morning? There was Oliver. I couldn't believe it. Oliver of all people. It's always been quite hard getting Oliver up to this end of town – he jokingly claims he needs a passport and an interpreter. But there he was, going round the flower shop, accompanied by this assistant who's picking out great armfuls of flowers.

I knocked on the window but neither of them turned round, so I went in. They were standing at the desk by now and the girl was working on the bill. Oliver had his wallet out.

'Oliver,' I said, and he turned round and looked really surprised. He even started to blush. That was a bit embarrassing – I'd never seen him blush before – so I decided to have a joke. 'So this is how you spend all the money I've lent you,' I said, and do you know what – he really did blush at that. Completely scarlet. Even his ears went bright red. I suppose on reflection it wasn't a very kind thing to say, but he really reacted oddly. He's obviously in a bad way at the moment.

'*Pas devant*,' he finally said, indicating the girl in the shop. '*Pas devant les enfants*.' The girl was staring up at the two of us, wondering what was going on. I thought the best thing to do was spare Oliver's blushes, so I murmured something about getting off to work.

'No,' he said, and got hold of my sleeve. 'No.' I looked

at him, but he didn't say anything more. With his free hand
he started shaking his wallet until the money began to fall out
on to the desk. 'Haste, haste,' he said to the girl.

He held onto my suit while she added up the bill (more
than £20, I couldn't help noticing), took his money, gave him
change, wrapped the flowers and poked them under his arm.
He picked up his wallet with his free hand, and sort of tugged
me to the door.

'Rosa,' he said as we got out on to the pavement. Then he
let go of my sleeve as if he'd confessed what it was he had to
confess.

'Rosa?' He nodded but couldn't look at me. Rosa was
the girl from the Shakespeare School, the one he got the sack
over. 'They're for her?'

'She's living up here. Her Pater threw her out. All Ollie's
fault as per usual.'

'Oliver.' I suddenly felt much older than him. 'Is this
wise?' What on earth was going on? What *would* the girl
think?

'Nothing's *wise*,' he said, still not looking at me. 'You can
grow a beard waiting to do something *wise*. Party of baboons
with typewriters working for a million years wouldn't come
up with anything *wise*.'

'But ... you're going round there at this time of the
morning?'

He glanced up at me, dropped his eyes again. 'Was there
last night.'

'But Oliver,' I said, trying to make some sense of the
story, and also trying to make a bit of a joke of it at the
same time, 'Isn't it traditional to give flowers to a girl when

you arrive rather than after you've left?'

Unfortunately, this didn't seem to be the right thing to say either. Oliver started gripping the flowers hard enough to snap their stems. 'Terrible bosh,' he finally said. 'I made a terrible bosh of it. Last night. Like trying to ease an oyster into a parking meter.'

I wasn't sure I wanted to hear any more, but Oliver had got hold of my sleeve again. 'The body can be a hideous betrayer,' he said. 'And the Latin races are arguably less accustomed to first-night nerves. And therefore on the unforgiving side.'

This was all rather embarrassing, from about six different angles. Apart from anything else, I was on my way to work. And it was the last sort of confession I'd ever have expected from Oliver. But I suppose if you lose your job, and your dignity . . . and he'd probably been drinking too much, which they say doesn't help. Oh dear, the wheels really do seem to be coming off Ollie at the moment.

I didn't know what to do or say. I didn't feel I should suggest a doctor, just like that, standing there on the pavement. Eventually Oliver let go of my sleeve.

'Have a good day at the office, dear,' he said, and sloped off.

I didn't read my newspaper on the train at all this morning. I just stood there thinking of Oliver. What a recipe for disaster – going back to that Spanish girl who'd got him sacked in the first place, and then . . . I don't know. Oliver and girls – it's always been a trickier subject than he likes to make out. But this time he does seem to have hit rock bottom. The wheels really have come off.

Oliver   *Ouf! Paf! Bof!* Wow! Call me the Great Escapologist. Call me Harry Houdini. Hail Thalia, Muse of Comedy. Oh boy I need a round of applause. Oh boy I need a *poumon*ful of Gauloise. You can't deny me one after that.

OK, OK, I feel a bit bad, but what would you have done? I know, you wouldn't have been there in the first place. But I was, and that's always going to be the brute difference between us, isn't it? Still, did you cop the panache? I have to hand it to myself, I really do. And what about the Ancient Mariner sleeve-tugging aspect? That worked out really well, didn't it? I've always said, if you want to outwit an Englishman, touch him when he doesn't want to be touched. Hand on the arm plus emotional confession. They can't bear that, the Anglos, they'll cringe and shiver and swallow whatever you tell them. 'Like trying to ease an oyster into a parking meter.' Did you see Stuart's face when I left him? What a cameo of tender concern.

I'm not really gloating, well only a *soupçon*, I'm more relieved: that's the way it comes out with me. And I probably shouldn't be telling you all this if I want to keep your sympathy. (Have I got it in the first place? Hard to tell, I'd say. And do I want it? I do, I do!) It's just that I'm too involved in what's happening to play games – at least, to play games with you. I'm fated to carry on with what I have to do and hope not to incur your terminal disapproval in the process. Promise not to turn your face away: if *you* decline to perceive me, then I really *shall* cease to exist. Don't kill me off! Spare poor Ollie and he may yet amuse you!

Sorry, getting a bit hyper again. *So.* So there I am in some *terra incognita* by the name of Stoke Newington, which

Stuart assures me is the next district where house prices are due to display tumescence, but where for the moment there dwelleth men whose heads do grow beneath their shoulders. And why am I there? Because I have to do something very simple. I have to go round to the wife of a man – a man! my best friend! – whom I have just left trogging off to the tube station; I have to go round to his wife of six weeks and tell her I love her. Hence the shrubbery of blue-and-white under my left arm, whose ineptly-wrapped stems have bedewed my *pantalon* in a manner suggesting the splatter of micturition. How not inappropriate: for when the shop-bell heralded the earnest banker I really thought I was going to pee myself.

I walked around a bit to let my trousers dry and practised what I was going to say when Gillian opened the door. Should I hide the flowers behind my back and produce them like a conjuror? Should I lay them on the doorstep and vamoose before she responded to the bell? Perhaps an aria would be appropriate – *Deh vieni alla finestra* . . .

So I strolled amid the base huts sheltering those far-flung operatives of commerce, waiting for the heat of the day to draw the moisture from my 60/40 silk/viscose trouser mix. That's what I feel like myself, and rather too often, if you must know: 60 per cent silk and 40 per cent viscose. Sleek but inclined to rumple. Whereas Stuart is 100 per cent man-made fibre: hard to crush, easy to wash, simple to drip-dry, stains merely lift out. We are cut from a different cloth, Stu and I. And on *my* cloth, if I didn't hurry, the water-stains would soon be replaced by sweat-marks. God I was nervous. I needed some valerian tea; either that or a monster Manhattan. A febrifuge or a mega-snort, one or the other. No, what I really needed was a handful of beta-blockers. Do you know about them? Propranolol is one of their various soubriquets. Developed for concert pianists suffering from nerves. Controls the flutters without interfering with the performance. Do you think they work for sex? Perhaps Stuart will get me some after hearing about my *nuit blanche* with Rosa. It would be just like him to salve the fractured heart with chemicals. But what *I* needed them for was to deliver the heart, rubescent and entire, to the woman about to answer the bell at number 68. Is there a dusky dealer lounging in a doorway with slick grin and open palm? 40 mg of propranolol, my man, and sharp about it, here's my wallet, here's my Rolex Oyster, take everything . . . no, those are *my* flowers. Take everything except my flowers.

But now they're hers. And when *le moment suprême* glowed (let me translate that briefly into Stuartese: when push came to shove), there was no difficulty. You may find Ollie rather baroque, but that's only the facade. Penetrate inside – stay awhile with guidebook raised – and you will find something calmly neoclassical, something wisely proportioned and cool. You are inside Santa Maria della Presentazione, or Le Zitelle, as the information brochures prefer. The Giudecca, Venice, Palladio, O ye tourists of my soul. That's what I'm like on the inside. Any tumultuous exterior I offer is merely to draw the crowds.

So what happened was this. I rang the door-bell, holding my flowers spread across both outstretched forearms. I did not want to appear like a delivery man. Rather I was a simple, a frangible petitioner, assisted only by the goddess Flora. Gillian opened the door. This was it. This was it.

'I love you,' I said.

She looked at me, and alarm put to sea in her tranquil eyes. To calm her, I handed over my bouquet, and quietly repeated, 'I love you.' Then I left.

I've done it! I've done it! I'm out of my skull with happiness. I'm joyed, I'm awed, I'm poo-scared, I'm mega-fuckstruck.

M i c h e l l e (16)   You get some real posers. That's the trouble with the job. It's not the flowers, it's the people that buy them.

Like this morning. If only he hadn't opened his mouth. When he walked in I thought, You can take me dirty dancing any day of the week. Really tasty, long black hair, brilliant, the suit was brilliant as well. Bit like Jimmy White if you know what I mean. He doesn't come up to the desk straightaway, but gives me a nod and starts looking at the flowers, really closely, like he really knew about them. I have this game with myself, me and Linzi both play it, you decide how fanciable someone is. If they're not very fanciable, you say, 'He's only a Tuesday,' meaning if he asked you out you'd only keep one night of the week free for him. The best is to call someone 'Seven Days of the Week', which means you'd keep every day free if he asked. So this boy is looking at the irises and I'm doing the VAT on a multiple despatch but I'm also looking out of the corner of my eye and thinking, 'You're a Monday to Friday.'

Then he makes me go round the shop with him and pick out flowers that are blue or white, nothing else. I point out some nice pink stocks and he does this huge shudder and goes 'Uuuuuugggh.' Who does he think he's impressing? Like those boys that come in for a single rose as if nobody's ever done that before. Some boy give me a single red rose and I'd say, What you done with the other four, given them to your other girls?

Then we're at the desk and he leans over all cocky like and actually gets hold of my chin and says, 'Why so glum, my fair one?' I pick up the scissors because I'm alone in the shop and if he touches me again he'll leave without something he came in with, when the bell goes on the door and this other boy in a city suit comes in, boring yuppie sort. And the poser's dead embarrassed because this other boy knows him and he's just spotted him trying to get off with a girl in a shop, not his sort of style at all, and he blushes all over, scarlet, even his ears, I noticed the ears.

Then he goes all quiet and throws some money at me and tells me to hurry up and can't wait to get the other boy out of the shop. So I take my time, not asking if he wants Cellophane gift-wrapping but just doing it really slowly and then I say I done the VAT wrong. And all the time I'm thinking, What did you open your mouth for? You were a Monday to Friday till then. Now you're just a tosser.

I like flowers. But I won't stay here long. Linzi won't neither. We can't stand the people that buy them.

G i l l i a n   Something strange happened today. Something very strange. And it didn't stop after it had happened, if you see what I mean. It went on being strange in the afternoon, and then in the evening too.

I was sitting in front of my easel at about quarter to nine, doing preliminary tests on a little panel-picture of a City church; Radio 3 in the background was churning out something by one of those Bachs who weren't Bach. Then the bell went. As I was putting down my swab, it went again, straightaway. Probably kids, I thought, they're the only ones to ring like that. Wanting to clean the car. Either that or they're finding out if someone's home before going round the back and breaking in.

So I went all the way down to the door slightly irritated, and what did I see? A huge bunch of flowers, all blue and white in a Cellophane wrapping. 'Stuart!' I thought – I mean, I thought they had come from Stuart. And when I saw Oliver holding them I still believed that was the most probable explanation – Stuart had sent Oliver round with the flowers.

'Oliver!' I said. 'What a surprise. Come in.'

But he just stood there, trying to say something. White as a sheet, and holding his arms out as rigid as a shelf. His lips moved, and some noises came out but I couldn't make sense of them. It was like in films when people have a heart attack – they mumble something which seems very important to them but which no-one can understand. I looked at Oliver and he seemed to be in genuine distress. The flowers had dripped all down his trousers, his face was frighteningly lacking in colour, he was trembling, and his lips seemed to be sticking together as he tried to speak.

I thought it might help if I took the flowers off him, so I reached out and lifted them carefully, holding the stem ends away from me. Just instinct, because I had my painting clothes on and a bit of water wouldn't have done any harm.

'Oliver,' I said. 'What is it? Do you want to come in?'

He still stood there with his arms sticking out, like a robot butler without a tray to carry. Suddenly, and very loudly, he said,

'I love you.'

Just like that. Well, I laughed, of course. It was quarter to nine in the morning and it was Oliver speaking. I laughed – not scornfully or anything, but just as if it was a joke which I'd only half got.

I was waiting for the other half when Oliver fled. He just turned on his heel and fled. I mean it. He ran, and I was left there on the step with this huge bunch of flowers. There didn't seem anything else to do except take them inside and put them in water. There were huge quantities of them, and I ended up filling three vases and a couple of Stuart's beer-mugs. Then I went back to work.

I finished the testing and started cleaning the sky, which is where I always begin. It didn't need much concentration, and all through the morning I kept getting interrupted by the thought of Oliver standing there not being able to say anything, and then practically shouting what he did. He's definitely in an extremely jumpy mood at the moment.

I suppose it was because we know he's been highly strung lately – his peculiar behaviour at the airport, for a start – that it took longer than it should have done for me to think over properly what had happened. And when I did I found I couldn't concentrate on my work at all. I kept imagining conversations that evening with Stuart.

'I say, what a lot of flowers.'

'Mmm.'

'Got a secret admirer, have we? I say, there *are* a lot.'

'Oliver brought them.'

'Oliver? When was that?'

'About ten minutes after you left for work. You must have just missed him.'

'But why? I mean, why did he give us all these flowers?'

'They're not for us, they're for me. He says he's in love with me.'

No, I couldn't have this conversation. I couldn't have anything approaching this conversation. In which case, I would have to get rid of the flowers. My first thought was to put them in the dustbin. Except what if Stuart took something out there? What would you think if you found your own dustbin stuffed full of completely fresh flowers? Then I thought of going across the road and throwing them in a skip – except that this would look very peculiar. We don't as yet have any friends in the street, but we're on Hello terms with a few neighbours, and frankly I wouldn't want them to see me putting all these flowers on a skip.

So I stuffed them down the waste-disposal unit. I took Oliver's flowers, and fed them petal-first into the grinder, and in just a few minutes I had reduced his gift to a sludge which the cold water was washing away down the waste-pipe. A strong scent came from the unit for a while, but then gradually died away. I scrumpled up the Cellophane, went to the dustbin and pushed it into a cereal box we'd thrown out. Then I washed and dried the two beer-mugs and the three vases, and put them back in their normal places, as if nothing had ever happened.

I felt I had done what was necessary. Oliver might well be having some sort of breakdown, in which case he'd need us both to be right on his side. One day I'll tell Stuart about the flowers and what I did with them and I expect we'll have a good laugh with Oliver as well.

Then I went back to my panel-picture and worked until it was time to start the supper. Something made me pour myself a glass of wine before Stuart returned at his usual hour of 6.30. I'm very glad I did. He said he'd been wanting to ring me all day but didn't want to interrupt my work. He said he'd met Oliver in the florist's round the corner on his way to the station. He said Oliver was extremely embarrassed, as well he might have been, because he was buying flowers to make his peace with a girl he'd gone to bed with the night before and been impotent with. What's more, the girl in question was the Spanish girl who'd been the cause of his being sacked by the Shakespeare School. It seems she's been thrown out by her father and is living not far from us. She'd invited him round the previous evening and things hadn't gone at all as he'd hoped. That's what Stuart said that Oliver said.

I don't think I reacted to this story in the way Stuart expected. I probably didn't appear to be concentrating. I took sips of my wine and carried on with the supper, and at one point I went across to the bookcase and idly picked up a petal that was lying there. A blue petal. I put it in my mouth and swallowed it.

I'm thoroughly confused. And that's putting it mildly.

8: OK, Boulogne It Is

Oliver I have a dream. I heeeeeeevvv aaa dreeeeeaa-
aaammm. No I don't. I have a plan. The transfiguration
of Oliver. The prodigal son will feast with harlots no more. I'm
buying a rowing machine, an exercise bicycle, a Langlauf
podium, a Bullworker. No, I'm not, but I'm doing the equivalent. I'm planning a mega-turnaround as per the advertisement. No Pension at 45? Which Is Your Type of Baldness?
Shamed By Your English? I'm getting that pension, having that
crown-weave. And I'm not shamed by my English, so that's one
fewer fomenter of *cafard*. But in all other respects – it's the
30-day life-transformation plan. Just you try and stop me.

I've farted around too much, that's the *triste* truth. You're
allowed to do that for a bit, as long as you finally discern that
pctomania is not a profession. Put a plug in it, Ollie. Shape up.

Decision time.

First, I'm giving up smoking. Correction: I have given up smoking. You see how *serious* I am? For how many years have I not defined, or at least decorated, myself by means of the fronded fragrances of the tobacco leaf? From the first cravenly petit-bourgeois Embassy all those years ago, to the predictable monogrammed-slippers appeal of Balkan Sobranie, via the posturings of menthol and the hideous austerity of low-tar, through the Rive Gauche authenticity of fat-thumbed hand-rolling (with or without aromatic additions) and its brusque mechanical equivalent (those Stakhanovite mangles, that floppy deck-chair of rubber I could never quite subdue), all leading to the current confident plateau, the *équilibré* intake of Gauloise and Winston, alloyed occasionally by the fierce kick-start of a little Swedish number named after *hoi polloi*'s Alsatian, Prince. Woof, woof! And I'm giving all this up. No, I have given all this up. Just now, a moment ago. I didn't even ask her. I just suspect she'd want me to.

Second, I'm going to get myself a job. I can do it. I did not flee the toxic Shakespeare School of English without abstracting a certain amount of their blushlessly chauvinistic writing-paper, and now have a series of pretty testimonials to my ability, each weighted to tickle the gonads of a different prospective employer. Why did I resign? Alas, my mother died, and I had to mastermind the discovery of an old folkery for my father. And if anyone is callous enough to check on that story then I wouldn't want to work for them anyway. My mother's always dying, it's been such a help over the years, and poor Papa frequently demands a change of geriatric vista. How he longs to gaze wistfully out at a breaking wave of woodland.

How he loves to recall the far-off days before the Netherlandish beetle savaged the English elm, before the uplands were girdled with Christmas trees. Through his picture-window my Pater peers into the past. *Tap-tap-tap* goes the ancient forester with his trusty axe, runically carving a cleft in a knotted trunk to warn his fellow-woodsmen of a noxious toadstool which groweth hereabouts. And lo! how doth the brown bear frolic upon a bank of sempiternal moss! It was never like this, and my father was an Old Bastard if you must know. Remind me to tell you about him one day.

Third, I'm going to pay back Stuart. Guglielmo the Betrayer I am not. Simplicity and probity shall be my offerings. My clownish mask no longer cloaks a breaking heart, so away with it. I shall doff my slippered pantaloon, if that's what one doffs. In other words, I'm going to stop fucking well camping around.

Stuart   I've been thinking. We've got to try and help Oliver in some way. It's our duty. He'd do the same for us if we were in trouble. It was really pathetic, meeting him like that in the flower shop. He's got no job. He's got no confidence – and Oliver, even from the earliest days, was always someone who had confidence. He would take on anyone – even that father of his. I suppose that's where it started. If you're a kid of fifteen with a father like that and you take him on, then why should the world scare you? But it does scare Oliver now. This terrible business with the Spanish girl. The old Oliver wouldn't have had any . . . trouble like that, and if he did he'd just have danced away from it. He'd have thought up some joke, or turned it to his advantage. What he wouldn't have done is gone out and bought the girl loads of flowers the next morning and then get caught by me doing it. It's like saying, please don't tell, please don't broadcast it to the world, I can get hurt. He'd never have been like that in the old days. And the pathetic way he expressed himself. 'I made a terrible bosh of it last night.' That's schoolkids' talk. The wheels are coming off, if you ask me. We've got to try and help him.

Gillian   I'm not sure about any of this. I feel deeply apprehensive. Stuart came home last night in his usual cheerful mood, gave me a kiss, put his arm round me and made me sit down as if he had something important to say.

'What about a holiday?' he asked.

I smiled. 'That's nice. Of course, we *have* only just got back from our honeymoon.'

'That was years ago. Four weeks at least. Five. Holiday?'

'Mmm.'

'Thought we might take Oliver along with us. Cheer him up.'

I didn't reply, not at first. Let me tell you why. I had a friend – well, I still do, it's just that we're temporarily out of touch – called Alison. She was at Bristol with me. Her family were nice, lived somewhere down in Sussex, a normal middle-class country family. They loved one another; *her* father never ran off. Alison got married right out of university. She was only twenty-one. And do you know what her mother said to her the night before her wedding? Her mother said to her, quite seriously, as if this was advice handed down in the family from mother to daughter since time immemorial, her mother said: 'It's always a good idea to keep them on the hop.'

I laughed as well at the time, but it stuck with me. Mothers telling daughters how to manage their husbands. Necessary truths passed down the female line over centuries, and what does the accumulated wisdom amount to? 'It's always a good idea to keep them on the hop.' That depressed me. I thought, Oh no, when I marry, if I marry, things have got to be straight, out in the open. I'm not going to play games or have secrets. But it seems to be starting already. Perhaps it's inevitable. Do you think the institution doesn't work otherwise?

What should I have done? If I were trying to keep things straight, I should have told Stuart about Oliver's appearance at the door and what I did with his flowers. But then should I also have said that Oliver rang up the next day and asked if I'd liked them? That I told Oliver I'd put them down the waste-disposal and the phone went silent, and when I finally said, 'Are you still there?' he just answered, 'I love you,' and hung up. Should I have told Stuart all that?

No, presumably. So I made a joke about the holiday suggestion. 'Bored with my company already?' – which not surprisingly Stuart took the wrong way. He thought I was cross, so he got flustered and started telling me how much he loved me, and *that* wasn't what I wanted to hear either, though of course in one way it's what I always want to hear.

I'd made a joke of it. I'm not keeping him on the hop, but I am making a joke of things. This soon?

Stuart   I don't think Gillian took too kindly to my suggestion that the three of us go on holiday together. I was about to explain when she sort of cut me off. Nothing she said, just a way she has of slightly turning and doing something else and not replying as quickly as she might. It's funny, but I seem to have known that little habit for the whole of my life already.

So the holiday idea's been dropped. Or rather, changed. Just a long weekend, just the two of us. Take the car down to Dover first thing on Friday morning, then head off into France. Monday's a holiday, so we've got nearly four days. Find a little hotel somewhere, see the early autumn colours, go to a market and buy lots of strings of garlic which will start going mouldy before we can possibly use them up. No need to plan anything – and I'm someone who likes planning things, or rather gets worried if things aren't planned. Perhaps this is a sign of Gill's effect on me – that nowadays I can say something like, 'Why don't we just take off?' And it's not *far*, I know, or for long, and the chances of all the hotels in northern France being booked solid are pretty slim, so I'm not really worrying. Even so, it's a start for me. It's a start. I'm practising being spontaneous. That's a joke, by the way.

Oliver seemed upset when I told him. It shows how really fragile he is at the moment, I suppose. We met for a drink. I told him we were heading off to France for the weekend. His face sort of fell, as if we were abandoning him. I wanted to add, 'It isn't for long', or something like that, but you don't exactly say that between friends, do you?

He didn't answer at first, then asked where we'd be staying.

'I don't know. We'll find somewhere.'

At this he seemed to liven up, and went back to being

Oliver. He put his hand on my forehead as if I was running a fever. 'Are you well?' he asked. 'This isn't like you. Whence this new spirit of recklessness? Haste thee to the druggist for a febrifuge.'

This sort of banter went on for a while. He wanted to know which ferry we were taking, whether we were going via Calais or Boulogne, which direction we were heading, when we were coming back, etc., etc. It didn't seem particularly odd at the time, I suppose, but looking back I was surprised he didn't say anything like, 'Have a nice trip.'

When we parted, I said, 'I'll bring you some duty-free Gauloises.'

'Don't bother,' he said.

'What do you mean? It's no trouble.'

'Don't bother,' he repeated, sounding almost ratty.

O l i v e r   Jesus, I had this panic attack. We met in a pub, some crepuscular burrow where Stuart is a regular little furry creature, where he can crouch happily in the reconstructed inglenook (imitation Norman Shaw) and quaff his ale as his yeoman forefathers have so quaffed since antiquity. God I hate pubs. I especially hate pubs since I've given up smoking (the spurning of which addiction went completely unnoticed by our friend Stuart). Oh, and I also hate the word crepuscular. I think I'll stop using it for a bit. Tip me the wink if I lapse, won't you?

So we were sitting there, in this horrible place where the 'glass of white' is even more noxious than the yeoman's brew, and their selection of Highland malts is less than the finest, and I'm getting these pancreas-piercing whiffs of other people's nicotine (hit me with a gasper, go on, do it to me – I'll betray my country for a Silk Cut, I'll betray my friends for a Winston) when Stuart, with a creepily smug look on his face, suddenly announces, 'We're taking off, you know.'

'What do you mean?'

'We're taking off on Friday. Dover. First ferry and then you won't see us for dust.'

I panicked, I admit it. I thought he was taking her away for ever. I saw them driving and driving. Strasbourg, Vienna, Bucharest, Istanbul, not stopping, not looking back. I saw her tossing newly gauffred curls as the open roadster headed east, away from Ollie ... Temporarily I managed to re-erect my jocular facade, but inside I was panicking. He could take her away, I thought, he could just do that, he has such power to hurt me, this little furry creature who hasn't even noticed that I've given up the weed. He has such a capacity for unreflecting cruelty now. And I've given him that.

But of course it turns out that the blithe *estivant* was only planning what he doubtless terms a Weekend Break. *Aestivate*, used *esp.* of animals, to spend the summer in a state of torpor. And the autumn. And most of his life. He has such sudden power to hurt, this Stuart.

He promised to send me a card. He promised to send me a fucking picture postcard.

Gillian   This is how the conversation went.

'Can we go shopping some time?'

'Shopping? Of course. What do you want to buy?'

'Shopping for you.'

'For me?'

'Clothes.'

'Don't you like what I wear, Oliver?' I tried to keep my tone light.

'I want to clothe you.'

I thought the best thing to be, before this went any further, was brisk. 'Oliver,' I said trying to sound like his mother (or at least like mine), 'Oliver, don't be ridiculous. You haven't even got a job.'

'Oh I know I can't afford to *pay*,' he said sarcastically. 'I know I haven't got any *money*, like Stuart.' Then there was a pause, and his tone changed. 'I just want to clothe you, that's all. I could help. I want to take you shopping.'

'Oliver, that's very sweet of you,' I said. Then, brisk again, 'I'll bear it in mind.'

'I love you,' he said.

I put the phone down on him.

That's what I'm going to do, what I've decided to do. Be brisk, polite, and put the phone down. It's ridiculous. He's obviously in a mess at the moment. And he's probably, without knowing it of course, jealous of our happiness. We went around together, the three of us, but then Stuart and I got married, and he feels excluded. Instead of three, it's now two plus one, and he feels it. It's quite normal in a way, I suppose. I'm sure he'll get over it.

In any other circumstances I wouldn't have minded going shopping with Oliver. Stuart isn't much use, to be honest, not because he doesn't enjoy shopping, but because he likes everything I try on. He says I look terrific in all colours and all styles. If I came out of the changing-room with a bin-liner round my waist and a lampshade on my head he'd say that they suited me. Which is sweet and touching, as you can imagine, but not really much practical help.

Oliver   I'm not being fanciful. For once. No doubt you were imagining what you take to be my imaginings about Gillian's vestments: a sable swirl out of *Boris Godounov*, colours by Rimsky, light summer prints by the infant Rossini, gay accessories by Poulenc . . . No, sorry. I'm neither a salivating cheque-signer (how could I be?), nor an orchidectomised walker; I just happen to know that my eye, my sense of colour, my *nous* about fabric are all superior to those of both Stuart and Gillian combined. Squared, cubed. At least, if one judges by results. Even people who don't care about clothes look better in something that's cut properly. And even people who say they don't care how they look care how they look. Everyone does. It's just that some people think they look their best by looking terrible. It's a kind of arrogance, of course. I look like shit because my mind is on higher things, because I'm so busy I don't have time to wash my hair, because if you really love me you'll love me like this as well. Not that Gillian is anywhere near this category. On the contrary. It's just I'd like to *make her over*.

Make over. To refashion. But also, in Stuart's mind, a term from the termitic world of business and finance. To make over: to transfer possession (of an object, a title) to someone else. Verb transitive.

S t u a r t We had a wonderful weekend break. Headed off down the motorway from Calais. Turned left when we felt like it, found ourselves somewhere near Compiègne. Stopped at a village as it was getting dark. A half-timbered family hotel with rooms off a creaky wooden balcony running round two sides of a courtyard. Of course we went to a little market and naturally we bought a couple of plaited strings of garlic which will go mouldy before we've finished them. So we'd better give some away. The weather was a bit damp, but who cares?

It wasn't till we were on the boat that I gave Oliver a thought, to be honest. I remembered him and suggested buying him some Gauloises. Gillian told me he'd given up smoking. How very odd. And untypical.

G i l l i a n I don't know where to begin. I also don't know where this is going to end, or how it's going to end. What's happening? It's not my fault, but I feel guilty. I *know* it's not my fault in any way, and still I feel guilty.

I don't know if I did the right thing, either. Maybe I shouldn't have done anything. Maybe what I did was an act of complicity, or looked as if it could have been. Perhaps everything – not that there *is* anything – should just have been allowed to come out into the open at that point. Why not? And yet . . . we'd had such a good few days I suppose I wanted to keep the mood going.

The first time it stopped raining was on the ferry back from Boulogne. That was ironic. That's what made it happen in a way.

Going out, we crossed Dover–Calais. Then we drove hard

down the autoroute. We chose an exit from the motorway almost at random. We chose a village to stay in almost at random – it was the place we got to as the evening was drawing in. We left after breakfast on the Monday and stopped for lunch near Montdidier. Then on towards Amiens with the windscreen wipers going flip-flop as we drove past sodden barns and soaking cattle. Somewhere beyond Amiens I had a memory of the car-ferry docks at Calais. First they send you all round the town and then you get processed into a system with thousands of other people and it doesn't feel at all like driving to a town on the coast and just getting on a boat. I mean, that's what it ought to feel like, oughtn't it? So I suggested to Stuart that we go to Boulogne instead. He was a bit against this at first because there aren't as many ferries from Boulogne. On the other hand it would save us driving 30-odd extra kilometres in the rain, and anyway I said if we get there and there isn't a ferry for hours we can just carry on to Calais. I've made this sound like an argument but it wasn't anything like that. It was a happy discussion and then an easy decision. That's how things are with us. Stuart never makes me feel his pride is riding on whether we do what I suggest or what he suggests. That was something I found attractive from the beginning. If you propose a change of plan to most men they take it – even if not consciously, and that's often worse – as some sort of insult or criticism. They can't bear you to have different ideas about relatively unimportant things. But as I say, Stuart's not like that. 'OK, Boulogne it is,' he said, as another Renault flashed past and blinded the windscreen with spray.

The point is this. No-one knew where we'd gone. No-one

knew where we decided to stay. We set off, stopped at random, pottered around, changed our plans, and got the first crossing from a port we hadn't arrived at. And Oliver was on the boat.

It had rained. It rained solidly every single day in fact, and it didn't stop as we were queuing to drive on to the ferry. All the insides of the boat seemed damp as well, the steps and the handrails. We sat in one of those lounges that are part of a huge bar area and the windows were misted up with condensation; when you rubbed them you still couldn't see much because of all the rain dripping down outside. About half way across the Channel a man in a plastic mackintosh came back to a nearby table and announced that the rain had finally stopped – just our luck, he added. When Stuart and I heard this we got up and looked for the nearest exit. You know how it is on ferries – you get a bit disoriented, you never know if you're on A deck or B deck, or which bit of the outside you're getting to when you go through a door – the front, the stern, or the sides. So we had chosen an exit at random, and I stepped over one of those high door-frames which are presumably intended to stop the sea water from sloshing into the saloon. We were halfway along one side of the ship, and as I looked to the left I saw Oliver about fifteen feet away, staring out into the Channel. I saw him in profile. He wasn't looking at me.

I turned away at once, and pushed back against Stuart.

'Sorry,' I said, and went back inside. He followed. I said I'd felt queasy suddenly. He said didn't I need fresh air then. I said it was the sudden fresh air that had done it. We sat down again. He was very solicitous. I said it would be all right. I half kept my eye on that exit.

After a few minutes, when he thought I was OK, Stuart

stood up.

'Where are you going?' I asked. I had a horrid premonition. I had to stop him going out on deck.

'Just thought I'd get Oliver some Gauloises,' he said. 'Duty free.'

I wasn't sure I was controlling my voice. 'He doesn't smoke,' I said. 'He's given up.'

Stuart patted me on the shoulder. 'I'll get him some gin, then,' he said, and wandered off.

'Oliver doesn't smoke,' I found myself whispering after him.

I watched the door. I waited for Stuart to come back. We had to escape without being spotted. I felt as if our happiness depended upon it. I made a fuss about being first in the queue going down to the car-decks. The stairs were just as wet and dangerous as when we'd got on. Stuart had bought some Gauloises anyway. He said he'd put them away for a bit and give them to Oliver when he started smoking again.

What's happening?

O l i v e r   I got them home safely. That was all I wanted. Perhaps you foresaw some clangorous maritime encounter, with streaming sou'westers and a vessel torn symbolically between pitch and roll? But in any case, the sea was calm, and I got them home safely. I got *her* home safely.

9: I Don't Love You

S t u a r t   Something's come over my friend Oliver recently. He says he's taken up running; he says he's given up
smoking; he says he's planning to pay back the money I
lent him. I don't really believe any of this, but the fact that
he even says it means that something's come over him.

That business about the phones, for instance. Suddenly,
the other evening, he starts asking me about all the new sorts
of mobile phone on the market — how they work, what their
range is, how much they cost. I suppose he's planning to put a
carphone into that skip he drives. It's the last thing I'd expect
of Oliver. He's so . . . retro. I don't think you've grasped how
retro he is. He probably comes across as arty and a bit careless,
but it's much worse than that. I don't think he's equipped for
the modern age, quite frankly. He doesn't understand about

money or business or politics or machines; he thinks black vinyl gives a better sound than CDs. What can you do with someone like that?

Oliver   I have to be near her, do you understand? I have to win her, I have to earn her, but first I have to be near her.

I think I know how those farouchely stubborn seekers of popular approval feel, as they endure the pedestrian trudge that leads finally to the green leather benches of the Palace of Westminster and the right to hawk insults at one another. House to house, like the Fuller's brush salesman or carbon-crusted chimney-sweep of yore. Except that such creatures have long since departed our streets, along with the yodelling muffin man, the taciturn knife-grinder and the smiling Wolf Cub offering a Job for a Bob. How the picturesque old trades, the pack of Happy Families, are withering. Who comes calling at your door nowadays? Only the ardent burglar seeking your absence; the fretting fundamentalist demanding your conversion before Judgement Day; the swaddled housewife in trainers assaulting the letter-flap with a sheaf of Tenpence Offs, a miniature sample of fabric conditioner and the calling-card of some fly-by-night cabby; these, and the prospective MP. May I count on your vote? Fuck off, fartface. Oh, how interesting. If you've got a moment I'd love to explain our party's view on the matter. Slam! Then on to the next house where they slyly accept a poster and bin it as soon as your back is turned; and then to the next where support is promised if only your party in exchange guarantees to persecute, imprison and preferably execute certain categories of non-white-skinned people. How do they do it? Why do they go on?

At least the constituency in which I sought election was a small one, and the varieties of available humiliation were limited. I was received as a thief, a well-mannered rapist, bucketless car-washer, double-glazing runner, not to mention corrupt informant that some of them tiles is loose, Ma'm, and we just happen to be in the area with a long ladder so why not call it eighty quid? Yet I was no more than a modest petitioner for lodgment. Just a room for occasional use over a few months, cash in advance of course, sorry no baby-sitting. A couple of funny looks later and I realised I also had to head off the perception that I wanted to hire a sex cave for *outré* rumpy pumpy with a slew of bimbo victims. Screen-writer, you see, demands of studio, absolute solitude essential, come and go as I please, often not there, vagaries of genius and its errant locomotion, several forged references available from heads of Oxbridge colleges, principals of Shakespeare Schools, even one on House of Commons paper. Not a vagrant, not a burglar, just fucking Orson Welles, that's who you'd be helping, Missus, and I won't need to use the phone ever.

It nearly worked at number 67, which would have been ideal. But she offered me a nice sunny room under the eaves at the back. So I affected to quail before Mr Sol's power-drill rays. My tender talent needed the succour of northern light. Any chance of the front . . . ? But no. And so I trailed my plodden way to number 55, where a monkey-puzzle tree twirled in the front garden and the windows suffered painfully from glaucoma. The lych-gate creaked and left its prickly signature of rust upon the palm (I'll get it fixed, Ma'm!); the bell rang not at all unless obliquely pressed by a nor'-nor'-westerly thumb. Mrs Dyer was tiny; her head sat on her spine like a sunflower on its stalk; and her hair had passed through its albid phase and was now the colour of a Gitaned forefinger. She had a room, north-facing; she used to enjoy 'the films' herself until her eyesight got poorly; she didn't want any money in advance. I couldn't bear it. Half of me wanted to say, Don't trust me, you don't know me, it's dangerous for you to take people at their word, you so frangible, me so robust; the other half wanted to say, I love you, come away with me, sit on my knee, I'll always remember you. You so full of your past, me so full of my future.

Instead, I said, 'I'll fix your gate if you like.'

'There's nothing wrong with it,' she replied rather firmly, and I felt unspeakable tenderness towards her.

So here I am, a week later, aloft in the canopy of my monkey-puzzle tree, staring out across the darkening street, waiting for my love to come home. She'll soon be here with her stocks of quilted kitchen towel, her milk and butter, jams and pickles, loaves and fishes; with her verdant washing-up liquid and a jumbo pack of Stu's repugnant breakfast cereal which he will shake jauntily each morning like a pair of maracas. *Sh-chug-a-chug. Sh-chug-a-chug-chug.* How shall I hold myself back? How stop myself swinging down through the branches to help unload her little car?

Loaves and fishes. I bet Stuart sees her basically as a good little shopper. Whereas for me she works miracles.

Gillian   I was unpacking the car when the phone went. I could hear it in the house. I had a carrier bag in each hand, some bread under my arm, the house keys in my mouth, the car keys still in my pocket. I kicked the car door shut, put down a bag, locked the car, picked the bag up, ran up the path, stopped at the door, dropped the bread, couldn't find my house keys, put down my bags, remembered the keys were in my mouth, opened the door, ran in, and the phone stopped.

I didn't really mind. What used to irritate me doesn't so much any more, and even quite boring things, like doing the shopping, are almost fun. Shall we try this? I wonder if Stuart likes sweet potatoes? And so on. Ordinary stuff.

The phone went again. I picked it up.

'Sorry.'

'I beg your pardon?'

'Sorry. Oh, it's Oliver.'

'Hello, Oliver.' Little Miss Brisk again. 'What are you sorry about?'

There was a silence, as if I had asked him a very profound question. Then he said, 'Oh, er, I thought you must be busy. Sorry.'

Suddenly there was a burst of crackle on the line and some juddering. He sounded a long way off. I thought he might have run away, and was ringing to apologise for his previous calls.

'Oliver, where are you?'

Again, a long silence. 'Oh, I could be anywhere.'

Suddenly I had this vision of him having taken an overdose and phoning to say goodbye. Why should I think that?

'Are you all right?'

Then his voice became clear again. 'I'm fine,' he said. 'I'm better than I've been for a long time.'

'Good. Stuart's been worrying about you. We both have.'

'I love you. I'll always love you. It won't ever stop.'

I put the phone down. What would you do?

I keep trying to think whether I've ever encouraged him. I never intended to. Why do I feel guilty? It's not right. I haven't done anything.

I put him off the idea of going shopping with me. Or rather, I just told him it wasn't on. Now he says he wants to come and see me working. I told him I'd think about it. I'm going to be very firm and straightforward and businesslike with Oliver from now on. Then he'll see there's no point fooling around and pretending to be in love with me. But I won't tell Stuart. Not yet, I've decided, maybe never. I think he'd be . . . dashed by it. Or he'd think about it too much. And if Oliver wants to see me – which might be a good idea if I can talk some sense into him – then I'll only do so if I've cleared it with Stuart first.

There. That's what I'll do. That's my decision.

But I know why I feel guilty. Perhaps you guessed. I feel guilty because I find Oliver attractive.

Mrs Dyer   He's a very pleasant young man. I like to have young people about the house. I like a bit of coming and going. He's writing something for the films, he says. Promised me a free ticket for the opening. They've got their lives before them, the young, that's what I like about them. He offered to fix the gate, but there's no point in that. It'll see me out.

I was coming back from the shops the other day when I saw him get out of his car. I was in Barrowclough Road, near the baths. He got out of his car and locked it and set off ahead of me. When I got home he was already in his room, whistling away cheerfully. I wonder why he left his car in Barrowclough Road. It's two streets away, and there's lots of parking outside the house here.

Perhaps he's ashamed of that car of his. Even I could see it was rusting away.

O l i v e r   I was a tad mogadonic, but that was on account of being poo-scared. Still, I did it, I proved it!

I had them to dinner at my principal residence, having prepared a *tagine* of lamb with apricots, which I teased with a husky Australian Shiraz from the Mudgee River. Quite a frisky combination – friskier than Stu and Gill, that's for sure. Faced with this living miscegenation, I had spells of getting all minimalist, which rendered things a bit tense. I felt like Eugene Onegin listening to that tiresome Prince hymn his Tatyana. Then Gillian blabbed to Stuart that I wanted to come and watch her at work.

'Hush, my treasure,' I urged, '*pas devant!*'

But Stuart is so effervescent, so bloody *méthode champenoise* nowadays that I could have gone down on my knees to his wife and he would have accepted my explanation that I was tacking up her hem. 'Jolly good idea,' he said. 'Always meant to do that myself. Very tasty this,' he went on (not alluding to the succulent Gill). 'Is it veal?'

After coffee I announced myself eager for the fleecy crook of Morpheus' shoulder, and they buggered off. I gave them a three-minute start then Bogartishly gunned my heap. (In truth I had to coax and canoodle a reluctant spark from my grumpy and costive engine block. But then, isn't life just like motoring?) Now Stuart, you should know, is rancidly smug about finding his way through London without so much as crossing a bus-route — his driving is all Kilburn cut-throughs and dinky dives along back-streets tumescent with sleeping policemen. Whereas Ollie happens to have spotted that nowadays there is no such thing as a short-cut in London: all the back roads are clogged up by master cartologists such as Stu, petrol-pinching aficionados of kink and gully who spin their Oldsmobile Mantras into canny U-turns like instructors on the skid-rink. All of whom have been second-guessed by Ollie, who romps his plodmobile (definitely not a Lagonda!) gaily down the Bayswater Road, barrels up Piccadilly, even throttles back on the vacant Euston Road to give the competition a sporting chance.

I had time to seminarise Mrs Dyer on the lesser masterpieces of Norman Wisdom before skipping to my room, whistling like one struck by sudden nocturnal inspiration. Then I turned out the light and settled at the window amidst the bottle-brush fronds of monkey-puzzle. Where were they? Where were they? Had the tortoise turned turtle in some sulphurous cul-de-sac? If he . . . But ah, there's the gunmetal glint I seek. And there's her profile, so heart-rendingly unaware . . .

The car stopped. Stuart jumped out and pattered plumply round to Gillian's door. As she got out he burrowed into her like some nesting beast.

A sight to deliquesce the bowels. I bantered little with myself as I drove home later that night.

Gillian   He was very calm. I was jumpy. I suppose I expected him to pounce or something. He saw the radio propped on the little stool and asked me if I played it while I worked. I said I did.

'Play it, then,' he said quietly.

There was a Haydnish sonata, a gentle piano tracking up and back in patterns which you could half anticipate even if you'd never heard the piece before. I began to relax a bit.

'Tell me what you're doing.'

I stopped and turned.

'No,' he said. 'Just talk to me as you do it.'

I went back to the picture. It was a little winter scene – the Thames frozen from bank to bank, people skating, and children playing round a bonfire on the ice. Quite jolly, and quite filthy, having hung in the banqueting hall of a City guild for centuries.

I explained about doing tests under the line of the frame, about beginning with spit on a tiny swab and working your way up through various solvents, about finding the right solvent for the glaze. How the glaze may vary across the picture. How some pigments come off more easily than others (reds and blacks always seem more soluble when I'm cleaning with ammonia). How I tend to start with the boring bits like the sky and then reward myself later with an interesting part like a face or a patch of white. How all the enjoyment is in the cleaning and almost none in the retouching (this surprised him). How old paint cures, so that a 17th-century painting is in fact much easier to clean than a 19th-century one (this also surprised him). And all the time I was talking I rolled my swabs back and forth over the frozen Thames.

After a while the questions ceased. I carried on working. Rain fell quietly on the window. The piano made its patterns in the air. The bar on the electric fire buzzed from time to time. Oliver sat behind me, silent, watching.

It was very peaceful. And he didn't once tell me he loved me.

Stuart   I think it's a really good idea for Oliver to see Gillie occasionally like this. He needs someone to calm him down. I expect he can talk to her in a way he can't talk to me.

'I suppose he calls round after he's been to see Rosa,' I said.

'Who?'

'Rosa. The girl he got sacked because of.' Gill didn't reply. 'I mean, doesn't he talk to you about her? I assumed that's what he did.'

'No,' she said. 'He doesn't talk to me about Rosa.'

'Well, you should ask. He probably wants to but can't bring himself to.'

Oliver   It's wonderful. I go and sit there while she works. The hungry eye hoovers up her stout jugful of brushes, her bottled solvents – xylene, propanol, acetone – her jars of vivacious pigment, her special picture restorer's cotton wool which with teasing banality turns out to be mere Economy

Pleat from Pretty. She sits in a soft curve at her easel, gently swabbing away three centuries from a grumpy London sky. Three centuries of what? Of jaundiced varnish, wood-smoke, grease, candle-wax, cigarette smoke and fly-shit. I kid you not. What I deconstructed as distant birds dotted into a sullen sky by a brief wrist declining detail turned out to be – fly-shit. The solvents listed above, you might care to know, make no impress on *mouche* excrement, so when confronted by this problem in your own home life use sputum or ammonia, and if that fails you must pick the droppings off with a scalpel.

I had imagined the cleaning to be a routine trundle and the retouching a source of joy, but apparently it's *vice versa* and *tête-bêche*. I probed Gillian further as to the wellsprings of her professional satisfaction.

'Finding something you didn't know was there, when you take off overpaint, that's the best. Watching something two-dimensional gradually turn into something three-dimensional. Like when the modelling in a face begins to emerge. For instance, I'm looking forward to doing *this* bit.' With the tip of her swab she indicated the figure of an infant sliding on the ice with hands trepidatiously grasping a chair.

'Do it, then. *Aux armes, citoyenne.*'

'I haven't earned it yet.'

You see how everything makes sense nowadays, how everything resounds in this world? It's the story of my life. You discover what you didn't know was there. Two dimensions give way to three. You appreciate the modelling in faces. But you have to have earned it all. Very well, I shall earn it.

I asked her how she would know when all her dabbing and rolling with Economy Pleat from Pretty would have fulfilled its purging task.

'Oh, this should take me about another fortnight.'

'No, I mean how can you *tell* when you've finished?'

'You can sort of tell.'

'But there must be a point . . . when you've hosed off all the muck and the glaze and the bits of overpainting and your musks of Araby have done their work and you get to the point when you *know* that what you see before you is what the chap would have seen before him when he stopped painting all those centuries ago. The colours just as he left them.'

'No.'

'No?'

'No. You're bound to go a little bit too far or not quite far enough. There's no way of knowing *exactly*.'

'You mean, if you cut that picture up into four – which would be a distinctly pro-life act if you want my opinion – and gave it to four different restorers, they'd each stop at a different point?'

'Yes. I mean, obviously they'd all get it roughly back to the same level. But it's an artistic rather than a scientific decision, when to stop. It's something you feel. There's no "real" picture under there waiting to be revealed, if that's what you mean.'

It is, oh it is. Isn't that wonderful? Oh effulgent relativity! *There is no 'real' picture under there waiting to be revealed.* What I've always said about life itself. We may scrape and spit and dab and rub, until the point when we declare that the truth stands plain before us, thanks to xylene and propanol and acetone. Look, no fly-shit! But it isn't so! It's just my word against everybody else's!

Mrs Dyer   And another thing he does. He talks to himself in his room. I've heard him. They say these creative people can be a bit potty. But he's got bags of charm. I said to him, if I was fifty years younger. And he gave me a smacker on the forehead, said he'd keep me up his sleeve if he never made it to the altar.

Oliver   I told you, I'm sorting out my life. That stuff about exercise was a bit of a fibette, I admit – I'm sure I'd collapse from jogger's nipple climbing into my Nikes. But in other respects . . . Look, I have to do two things. One, make sure I have every afternoon, Monday to Friday, free in case she will let me be with her. Two, earn enough money to support both my Babylonian apartment in the West and my Spartan hiring in the North. And the answer – *sapristi!* – is: I work at weekends. Apart from anything else, that takes my mind off the wombat of Stoke Newington and his tufty little dormitory.

I've changed my job. I now work at Mr Tim's College of English. Something about the title unleashes upon one the suspicion that Mr Tim is not, himself, as it were, English. But I take the humanitarian line that this permits Mr Tim to engage in full imaginative sympathy with those tongues of Babel who throw themselves on his mercy. As yet, the College is not an officially recognised English Language School – Mr Tim is so o'erburdened with pastoral responsibilities that he keeps failing to apply for a thumbs-up from the British Council (even the base Shakespeare School had achieved recognition). As a result, our classes are not overrun with Saudi princelings. Do you know how some of the kids afford the fees? They walk up and down the teeming thoroughfares of Central London distributing to lookalikes and doppelgangers a leaflet advertising Mr Tim's College of English. The fish feeds upon its own tail. Mr Tim, by the way, does not acknowledge the modern concept of the language laboratory; nor does he cleave to the antique idea of the library of books; still less does he believe in separating students of different ability. Do you detect a touch of moral fervour rippling its unsightly way across the normally limpid Weltanschauung of Oliver Russell? Perhaps you do. Perhaps I'm changing more than my job. EFL, by the way. Nobody sees the joke. English as a Foreign Language. No? Let me put it into a sentence: 'I'm teaching English as a Foreign Language.' Look, the point is, if that's how it's being taught, it's not surprising that most of our alumni can't buy a bus-ticket to Bayswater. Why don't they teach English as English, that's what I want to know.

Sorry. Didn't mean to blow off like that. Anyway, I merely had to dangle my aromatically forged reference from the Hamlet Academy before Mr Tim and there I was, unleashed upon the cosmopolitan *virginibus puerisque* couchant before their desks. The gold moidore factor is not quite what it was, since Mr Tim is a major nickelfucker. £5.50 an hour oozed reluctantly from his wallet, as against the munificent £8 of the Shakespeare School. At this rate poor Ollie will end up a Mr Mopp.

Why, Mr Tim enquired, his accent a silky simulacrum of an Inuit chewing a Berlitz tape, did I want the afternoons off? So poor old Pater rode to the rescue once again. Close as Achilles and Patroclus, the two of us (knowing that the raunch

of the reference would evade Mr Tim). Have to find him yon
old folkery with the picture-window looking on to the stand
of immemorial beeches, the dingle dell, the plashing brook,
the wishing-well, the verdant sward . . . May the Old Bastard
discover that Bosch was not exaggerating, that his *Triumph of
Death* was a pastel cartoon compared to the real thing. But
don't let me get started on *that, please*.

And in the afternoons, when she lets me, I go and sit with
her. The swab of the rag, the tickle of the brush, the buzz of
the fire (I'm so sentimental about that electric bar already),
the serendipity of Radio 3, and her quarter-profile as she sits
turned away from me, hair hooked back behind one lobeless
ear.

'It's not true about Rosa, is it?' she asked yesterday.

'What isn't?'

'That she lives somewhere round here and you go and
see her?'

'No, it's not true. I haven't seen her since . . . since then
. . .' I couldn't say any more. I was embarrassed – a state
of mind which, you might have observed, transpires in the
psyche of Oliver Russell about as frequently as the passage
of Halley's Comet. I didn't like to recall that squalid gavotte
of erotic incomprehension I had once danced, didn't like to
compare – to imagine Gill comparing – my being in a room
with *her here* and my being in a room with *another there*. I
was . . . embarrassed. What more can I say? Except that this
condition clodhopped into view only because I intend to tell the
unlipsticked truth to Gill. Look, no make-up! Ollie's Honour,
cross my heart and hope to become a Girl Guide.

It's infectious. I go there, and I sit in her room, and

we are very quiet, I don't fucking camp around, I never
smoke, and we tell one another the truth. Nn-nn-*nnn*. Do I
hear violins? The lilting scrape of the zigeuner tune, the con-
veniently passing flower-seller, the sad candle-lit smile of the
softly envious match-girl? Go on, embarrass me some more,
Ollie can take it, he's getting used to it.

Look, I know I have a reputation for serving up the truth
with more than the traditional British accompaniments. Two
veg and Oxo gravy is not my style. But with Gillian, things
are different.

And I've discovered this really tasty metaphor. Fashions
in the universe of picture restoration – I speak from recent
but devoted authority – tend to change. One moment it's out
with the Brillo pad and scour, scour, scour. Another moment
it's retouch with a decorator's brush, load every rift with pigment, and so on. The current talismanic concept is *reversibility*.
This means (you don't mind if I simplify matters a tad?) that
the restorer should at all times do only what she knows
may be undoable later by others. She must appreciate that
her certainties are only temporary, her finalities provisional.
So: your Uccello has been skewered by an assegai-wielding
sociopath convinced that some noxious item of legislation
will be reversed once he Goths a valuable masterpiece. Here
in the art hospital the slash is mended, the pits and ruts are
Polyfilled, and the retouching is about to begin. What does
the restorer do first? She uses an *isolating varnish* to ensure
that the paint she applies can be removed without trouble at
some later date – when, for example, the fashion might be to
display the historical vicissitudes of the painting as well as its
aesthetic freight. This is what we understand by *reversibility*.

Don't you see how it all applies? Isn't it tasty? You will help spread the word, won't you? Text for today: *We shall undo those things which we ought not to have done, and there is health in us.* Reversibility. Already I am organising supplies of isolating varnish to all churches and register offices.

When she said it was time to go, I told her I loved her.

G i l l i a n   This has got to stop. It's not what I thought would happen. He was meant to come round and tell me his troubles. But it turns out that *I'm* doing most of the talking. He just sits there, very quietly, and watches me work and waits for me to talk.

Usually I have the radio on in the background. You can ignore it if you need to concentrate. I never thought I could work with someone like Oliver there, but I can.

Sometimes I wish he'd just pounce. Right, Oliver, out you go, Stuart's best friend, right that's it, *out.* But he doesn't, and I'm less and less convinced I'd react like that if he did.

As he was saying goodbye today, I saw him open his mouth and look at me in that way.

'No, Oliver,' I said, Little Miss Brisk. 'No.'

'It's all right. I don't love you.' His expression didn't change, though. 'I don't love you. I don't adore you. I don't want to be with you all the time. I don't want to have an affair with you. I don't want to marry you. I don't want to listen to you for ever.'

'Out.'

'I don't love you. It's all right.' He began to close the door. 'I don't love you.'

Talking It Over

Oliver The monkey-puzzle tree brandishes its knobbly fingers at the evening sky. Rain falls. Cars swish by. I stand at the window. I watch and wait. I watch and wait.

10: I'm Not Sure I Can Believe This

Stuart   I'm not sure I can believe this. I'm not exactly sure what 'this' is, to begin with.

Is it 'nothing' (as Gill assures me), or is it 'everything'?

What do they say, those bloody know-alls whose wisdom is handed down from generation to generation? The husband is always the first to suspect and the last to know.

Whatever happens ... whatever happens, I'm the one that's going to get hurt.

By the way, would you like a cigarette?

Gillian   The other two, they each want one thing, for me to be with them. I want two things. Or rather, I want different things at different times.

God, yesterday I looked at Oliver and I had this strange thought. I want to wash your hair. Just like that. I suddenly got embarrassed. His hair wasn't dirty – it was all clean and flyaway in fact. It's wonderfully black, Oliver's hair. And I just saw myself washing it while he sat in the bath. I've never thought of doing that to Stuart.

I'm the one in the middle, the one that's being squeezed every day. I'm the one that's going to get hurt.

Oliver   Why do I always get the blame? Ollie the heart-breaker, Ollie the marriage-breaker. Wild dog, blood-sucker, snake in the grass, parasite, predator, vulture, dingo. It isn't like that. I'll tell you what I feel like. Don't laugh. I'm a fucking moth bashing its head against a fucking window. Bash, bash, bash. The soft yellow light which looks so gentle to you but which sears my guts.

Bash, bash, bash. I'm the one who's going to get hurt.

11 : Love, &c.

O l i v e r　I've been calling her every day to tell her I love her. Now she's stopped putting the phone down on me.

S t u a r t　You will have to bear with me. I do not have the flashing brain of my friend Oliver. I have to work things out step by step. But I get there in the end.

You see, the other day I came home from work earlier than usual. And as I turned into our street – *our* street – I saw Oliver in the distance, coming towards me. I waved, sort of instinctively, but he had his head down and didn't see me. He was about forty yards away, and hurrying along, when he suddenly fished a key out of his pocket and turned into a house. A house on the other side of the road from ours, the one with a monkey-puzzle tree in front. Some old biddy lives there. By the time I got level – it was number 55 – the door had shut. I carried on home, let myself in, gave my habitual cheery View Halloo, and started to think.

The next day was a Saturday. I know Oliver gives lessons at home on Saturdays. I put on a sports jacket, found myself a clipboard and biro, then went across to number 55. I was, you understand, from the local council, just tidying up our records for the new community charge or poll tax, and verifying the occupants of each residence. The little old lady identified herself as Mrs Dyer, freeholder.

'And there's a . . .' – reading from my clipboard – 'Nigel Oliver Russell living here?'

'I didn't know he was called Nigel. He told me he was called Oliver.'

'And a Rosa . . .' I gabbled a foreign name, trying to sound vaguely Hispanic.

'No, there's no-one of that name.'

'Oh, I'm sorry, my eye must have slipped a line. So there's just you and Mr Russell?'

She agreed. I started down the path. She called after me, 'Don't worry about the gate. It'll see me out.'

Right. That was the start. Oliver was not letting himself in to Rosa's flat the other evening.

Now we have to eliminate the next possibility. On Sunday morning Gillian went back upstairs to work, as she's promised the museum she'll let them have that scene of the frozen Thames back by the end of next week. (Have you seen it, by the way? It's quite pretty, I think, just what a picture should be.) Now there is no phone jack in her studio. We deliberately didn't have one put in so she wouldn't be disturbed up there. Downstairs, two storeys away, I called Oliver. He was in the middle of a conversation class, as he put it – which means having some poor student round for a cup of coffee, chatting to her about the World Cup or something, and relieving her of a tenner. No, not the World Cup, knowing Oliver. He probably asks them to translate a pictorial guide to sex.

Anyway, I got down to business straightaway, and said how it had slipped our minds, how we hadn't been half hospitable enough, but when he was next up in our neck of the woods visiting Rosa, would he like to bring her round for a meal?

'*Pas devant,*' came the reply, '*C'est un canard mort, tu comprends?*' Well, I can't remember exactly what he said, but no doubt it was something bloody irritating like that. I did my Pedestrian Old Stuart number, and he felt obliged to translate. 'We're not seeing so much of one another nowadays.'

'Oh, sorry about that. Foot in mouth time again. Well, just yourself then, sometime soon?'

'Love to.'

And I rang off. Have you noticed the way people like Oliver always say *We*'re not seeing so much of *one another* nowadays? What a thoroughly dishonest phrase. It always sounds like such a civilised arrangement, whereas what in fact it means is: I dropped her, she stood me up, I was bored anyway, she'd rather go to bed with someone else.

So that was Stage Two complete. Stage Three followed over supper, where I made concerted enquiries about the well-being of our mutual friend Oliver, with the implication that Gillian saw a fair bit of him. Then I asked, 'Is he sorting things out with Rosa? I thought we might have them both round one evening?'

She didn't answer at once. Then she said, 'He doesn't talk about her.'

I let it pass, and instead offered congratulations on the sweet potatoes, which Gillian had never cooked before.

'I wondered if you'd like them,' she said. 'I'm glad you do.'

After dinner we took our coffee into the sitting-room and I lit up a Gauloise. It's not a thing I do very often, and Gillian gave me an enquiring glance.

'Shame to waste them,' I said. 'Now that Oliver's given up.'

'Well, don't make it a habit.'

'Did you know,' I replied, 'that it has been statistically proved that smokers are less vulnerable to Alzheimer's disease than non-smokers?' I was rather pleased with this obscure item of information, which I'd picked up from somewhere.

'That's because smokers all die before they're old enough to get Alzheimer's,' said Gill.

Well, I had to laugh at that. Thoroughly outmanoeuvred in one respect.

Often, we make love on Sunday nights. But I wasn't feeling like it for some reason. For a particular reason: I wanted to think things over.

So. Oliver is discovered early one morning buying flowers in Stoke Newington for Rosa, with whom he has had a sexual fiasco the night before. Oliver, who is in a bad way, is encouraged to visit Gillian any time he's up in the area calling on Rosa. He does therefore visit regularly. Except that Oliver isn't seeing Rosa. Indeed, we have no evidence that Rosa lives up here. On the other hand, we do have evidence that Oliver lives up here. He has hired a room from Mrs Dyer at number 55, and sees Stuart's wife during the afternoon when Stuart is safely at work earning money to pay the mortgage.

WHERE DO THEY DO IT? AT HIS PLACE OR AT HERS? DO THEY DO IT IN THIS BED, THIS VERY BED?

Gillian   The fact is, sometimes I put the telephone down and I can still hear Oliver's voice in my ear telling me he loves me, and . . . No, I'm not sure I can tell you the rest.

Stuart   I'm not going to ask. It may not be true. If it isn't true it's a terrible thing to say. And if it is true?

I really didn't think there was anything wrong with our sex-life. I didn't. I mean, I don't.

Look, this is silly. It's *Oliver* who says he's got the sex problems. Why should I assume – why should I even suspect – he's having an affair with my wife? Unless he said he had a sex problem so that I wouldn't get suspicious. And it worked, didn't it? What was that old play Gillian and I once went to, where some bloke pretends to be impotent and everyone believes him and all the husbands let him visit their wives? No, that's ridiculous. Oliver isn't like that, he isn't calculating. Unless . . . how could you have an affair with your best friend's wife without being calculating?

Ask her, ask her.

No, don't ask her. Leave it alone. Wait.

How long has it been going on?

Shut up.
We've only been married a few months.
Shut up.
And I gave him a large cheque.
Shut up. Shut up.

Oliver   She's got this comb. This comb with its tender mutilations.

When she works, she first of all puts her hair back. There's a little comb which she keeps on the stool where the radio stands. She takes this comb, and pulls her hair back over her ears with it, first the left side then the right, always that way round, and after she's finished pulling back each side she puts a tortoise-shell grip in her hair, just behind the ear.

Sometimes, when she's working, a strand or two of hair will come loose, and then, without breaking concentration, she will reach instinctively for the comb, take out the grip, pull her hair back, put the grip back in, and return the comb to the stool, all without taking her gaze from the canvas.

That comb has some teeth missing. No, let's be precise. That comb has fifteen teeth missing. I've counted them.

This comb, with its tender mutilations.

Stuart   Oliver has had quite a few girlfriends over the years, but if you want my opinion he's never been in love. Oh, he's *said* he's in love, lots of times. He's made corny old comparisons between himself and characters in

Grand Opera, he's done things which people are supposed to do when they're in love, like mope a lot, and blab to their friends, and get drunk when things are going wrong. But I've never believed he's *actually* been in love.

I never told him, but he reminded me of those people who are always claiming to have the flu when all they've got is a heavy cold. 'I had that nasty three-day flu,' they'll say. Oh no you didn't, you had a runny nose and a bit of a headache and your hearing went funny, but that wasn't flu, that was only a cold. Just as it was the previous time. And the time before that. Nothing more than a heavy cold.

I hope Oliver hasn't got the flu.

Shut up. Shut up.

O l i v e r   'Punctuality is the virtue of the bored.' Who said that? Someone. Some hero of mine.

I whisper it to myself, Monday to Friday, between 6.32 and 6.38, sitting in my bottle-brush canopy, as steatopygous Stu comes trundling home. 'Punctuality is the virtue of the bored.'

I can't stand to see him coming home, either. How dare he come home and end my happiness? Of course I don't want him to fall under a tube train (clutching his return half in his raincoat pocket!), I just can't bear the gloom I feel as he turns the corner with his briefcase in his hand and a mugwump smile on his face.

I've taken to doing something I probably shouldn't. It's Stuart's fault, he set me off, mugwumping home like that to his little tufty nest, all smug and snug, while I sit up here in my unlighted room pretending to be Orson Fucking Welles. When he turns the corner, some time between 6.32 and 6.38, I press number 1 on my absurd matt-black leather-encrusted portable telephone which would live much more happily in that stocky briefcase of Stu's. It has all sorts of nifty ploys, this phone, as the vendor throbbingly explained to me. One of the more basic of these – which even I was deemed able to comprehend – is called a Storage Facility. In other words, it remembers numbers. Or in my case, it remembers one number. Hers.

As Stuart turns his shining sunset face toward home, Oliver presses 1 and waits for her voice.

'Yes?'

'I love you.'

She puts the phone down.

Stu reaches for the handle of his gate.

My phone pops, buzzes, and offers its expectant dialling tone up to my ear.

Gillian   He touched me today. Oh God, don't say it's started. Has it started?

I mean, we've touched each other before. I've taken his arm, ruffled his hair, we've hugged, kissed cheeks, the usual between friends. And this was less, less than any of those, and yet much more.

I was at my easel. My hair came loose. I reached out my hand towards the comb I keep on my stool.

'Don't move,' he said, very quietly.

I went on working. I felt him come across. He took the grip out of my hair, the hair fell loose, he combed it back behind my ear, slid the grip into place, clicked it shut, put the comb back on the stool, went and sat down. Just that, no more.

Luckily I was working on a straightforward patch. I just continued automatically for a minute or two. Then he said, 'I love that comb.'

It's unfair. Comparisons are unfair, I know. I shouldn't make them. I never gave that comb of mine a thought. I've always used it. One day, soon after we met, Stuart was in my studio and saw it. He said: 'Your comb's broken.' A couple of days later, he gave me a new one. He'd obviously gone to some trouble because it was the same size as the old one, and tortoise-shell too. But I didn't use it. I kept the old one. It's as if my fingers have got used to feeling for those missing teeth and know where they are.

Now Oliver just says, 'I love that comb,' and I feel lost. Lost and found.

It isn't fair on Stuart. I say to myself, 'It isn't fair on Stuart', but the words don't seem to have the slightest effect.

O l i v e r   When I was a boy, The Old Bastard used to take *The Times*. No doubt he still does. He vaunted his skill at the *mots croisés*. For my part, I used to look at the Obituaries and work out the average age at which Old Bastards had died that day. Then I'd work out how long there was to go statistically for the Old Bastard Crossword Solver himself.

There was also the Letters Page, which my father would scrutinise for dank prejudices dripping with the correct amount of pond-weed. Sometimes the Old Bastard would give a deep, almost colonic grunt as some pachydermatous *déjà pensée* – Repatriate All Herbivores to Patagonia – miraculously accorded with his own, and I would think, Yes, there really are a lot of Old Bastards out there.

The thing I remember from the Letters Page in those antique days was the way the OBs signed off. There was Yours faithfully, Yours sincerely, and I have the honour to be, sir, your obedient servant. But the ones I always looked for – and which I took to be the true sign of an Old Bastard – simply ended like this: *Yours etc.* And then the newspaper drew even more attention to the sign-off by printing it: *Yours &c.*

Yours &c. I used to muse about that. What did it mean? Where did it come from? I imagined some bespatted captain of industry dictating his OB's views to his secretary for transmission to the Newspaper of Record which he doubtless referred to with jocund familiarity as 'The Thunderer'. When his oratorical belch was complete, he would say, 'Yours etc,' which Miss fffffolkes would automatically transcribe into, 'I have the honour to be, sir, one of the distinguished Old Bastards who could send you the label off a tin of pilchards and you would still print it above this my name,' or whatever, and then it would be, 'Despatch this instanter to The Thunderer, Miss fffffolkes.'

But one day Miss fffffolkes was away giving a handjob to the Archbishop of York, so they sent a temp. And the temp wrote down Yours, etc, just as she heard it and *The Times* reckoned the OB captain of industry a very gusher of wit, but decided to add their own little rococo touch by compacting it further to *&c*, whereupon other OBs followed the bespatted lead of the captain of industry, who claimed all the credit for himself. There we have it: *Yours &c.*

Whereupon, as an ardent damp-ear of sixteen, I took to the parodic sign-off: *Love, &c.* Not all my correspondents unfailingly seized the reference, I regret to say. One *demoiselle* hastened her own de-accessioning from the museum of my heart by informing me with *hauteur* that use of the word *etc.*, whether in oral communication or in carven prose, was common and vulgar. To which I replied, first, that 'the word' *et cetera* was not one but two words, and that the only common and vulgar thing about my letter – given the identity of its recipient – was affixing to it the word that preceded *etc.* Alack, she didn't respond to this observation with the Buddhistic serenity one might have hoped.

Love, etc. The proposition is simple. The world divides into two categories: those who believe that the purpose, the function, the bass pedal and principal melody of life is love, and that everything else – *everything* else – is merely an *etc.*; and those, those unhappy many, who believe primarily in the *etc.* of life, for whom love, however agreeable, is but a passing flurry of youth, the pattering prelude to nappy-duty, but not something as solid, steadfast and reliable as, say, home decoration. This is the only division between people that counts.

Stuart   Oliver. My old friend Oliver. The power of words, the power of bullshit. No wonder he's ended up giving conversation lessons.

O l i v e r   I don't think I've made myself clear. When I closed the door the other day and sought to evade the delicious tickle of Gillian's mock-severity, I said to her (oh, I remember, I remember – there is a black box in my skull and I keep all the tapes): 'I don't love you. I don't adore you. I don't want to be with you all the time. I don't want to have an affair with you. I don't want to marry you. I don't want to listen to you for ever.'

Did you spot the odd one out?

S t u a r t   Cigarette?

O l i v e r   And I'm having an AIDS test.

That surprises you/that doesn't surprise you? Delete one only.

But don't jump to conclusions. Or at any rate, not to those conclusions: contaminated needles, Hunnish practices, the bathhouse factor. My past may in some respects be more lurid than the next man's (and since the next man is likely to be Stuart Hughes, squire, banker and mortgagee, then it's certain to be more lurid), but this isn't confession time. 'Listen With Mother' plus 'Police Five' this is not.

I want to lay my life before her, don't you see? I'm starting over, I'm clean, I'm *tabula rasa*, I'm not fucking camping around, I'm not even smoking any more. Isn't that the dream? Or at least, one of the two dreams. The first goes: here I am complete, full, capacious, ripe, find what you will in me, use all that is there. The other goes: I am empty, open, nothing but potentiality, make of me what you will, fill me with what you want. Most of my life has been spent pouring dubious substances into the tanks. Now I'm draining them, hosing them down, sluicing them out.

And so I'm taking an AIDS test. But I may not even tell her.

Stuart   Cigarette?

Go on, take one.

Look at it this way. If you help me out with this pack, then I'll smoke fewer and be less likely to die of lung cancer and may even, as my wife pointed out, survive long enough to succumb to Alzheimer's. So take one, it's a sign that you're on my side. Put it behind your ear and keep it for later if you like. On the other hand, if you don't take one . . .

Of course I'm drunk. Wouldn't you be?

Not very drunk.

Just drunk.

Gillian   I don't want anyone to think that I married Stuart out of pity.

It happens. I know, I've seen it. I remember a girl at college, a sort of quiet, determined girl called Rosemary. She was half going out with Simon, a huge, lanky boy whose clothes always seemed a bit odd because he had to go to a special shop for them. High and Mighty, I think it was called. He'd made the mistake of telling someone this, and the girls used to laugh at him behind his back. Nothing much at first. 'How's Mr High and Mighty then, Rosemary?' But sometimes it got a bit worse.

There was a small sharp-faced girl with an evil tongue who said *she'd* never go out with him because she'd never know what her nose would be bumping into next. Mostly, Rosemary seemed to go along with this, as if she was being teased as well. Then one day – it wasn't any worse than usual either – the girl with the tongue said very slowly and slyly I remember, 'I wonder if everything's in proportion?' Lots of girls had a good laugh, and Rosemary sort of joined in, but she told me later it was at that very moment she'd decided to marry Simon. She hadn't even been particularly in love with him up till then. She just thought, 'He's got that coming to him all his life, and I'm bloody well going to be on his side.' And she was. She went out and married him.

But I didn't do that. If you marry someone out of pity, then you probably stay with him or her out of pity, too. That's my guess.

I've always been able to explain things. Now none of the explanations seem to fit. For instance, I'm not one of those people who's automatically dissatisfied with what I get; nor am I the sort who only wants what she can't have. I'm not a snob about looks; if anything, it's the other way round – I distrust good-looking men. I've never run away from relationships; generally I've stuck in too long. And Stuart is the same, Stuart I fell in love with last year – there haven't been any of those nasty discoveries some women make. *And* (just in case you're wondering) there's absolutely nothing wrong with our sex-life.

So what I have to understand is this: despite the fact that I love Stuart, I seem to be falling in love with Oliver.

It's every day now, every evening. I wish it would stop.

No I don't. I can't, otherwise I wouldn't answer the phone. Just about half-past six. I'm waiting for Stuart to come home. Sometimes I'm in the kitchen, sometimes I'm finishing up in the studio and have to run downstairs. The phone goes, I know who it is, I know Stuart will be back soon, but I rush and answer it.

I say, 'Yes?' I don't even give the number. It's as if I can't wait.

He says, 'I love you.'

And do you know what's started happening? As I put the phone down I feel wet. Can you imagine it? God, it's like phone pornography or something. Stuart puts his key in the door and I'm feeling wet from the voice of another man. Shall I pick up the phone tomorrow? Can you imagine it?

M m e W y a t t   *L'Amour plaît plus que le mariage, pour la raison que les romans sont plus amusants que l'histoire.* How would one translate that? Love pleases more than marriage, in the same way as novels are more amusing than history. Something like that. You English do not know Chamfort enough. You like La Rochefoucauld, you find him 'very French'. You have some idea of the polished epigram being a culminating point of the 'logical mind' of the French. Well, I am French, and I do not so much like La Rochefoucauld. Too much cynicism, and also too much . . . polish if you like. He wants you to see how much work he has put into appearing to be wise. But wisdom is not like that. Wisdom has more life in it, wisdom has humour rather than wit. I prefer Chamfort. He said this as well: *L'hymen vient après l'amour, comme la* *fumée après la flamme.* Marriage comes after love as smoke comes after fire. Not as obvious as it first seems.

I am called Mme Wyatt and I am supposed to be wise. It comes from this, my little reputation. From being a woman of a certain age, who after being left by her husband some years ago and having never remarried still retains her sanity and her health, who listens more than she talks, and offers advice only when it is solicited. 'Oh, how right you are, Mme Wyatt, you are so wise', people have said to me, but the prelude to this is usually an extended display of their own stupidity or error. And therefore I do not feel so wise. Or at least, I know that wisdom is a comparative matter, and that in any case you should never offer all you have, all you know. If you show everything, you interfere, you cannot be of help. Although sometimes it is very difficult not to show everything.

My child, my daughter Gillian, comes to see me. She is miserable. She is afraid she is falling out of love with her husband. Someone else says he is in love with her and she is afraid she may be falling in love with him. She does not say who it is, but naturally I have my ideas.

What do I think of that? Well, I don't think very much – I mean, I have no opinion of such a situation in general, I only think that such things happen. Of course, in the actual case of my own child, I have opinions, but they are not opinions except for her.

She was miserable, I was miserable for her. It is not like changing cars, this business, after all. She cried, and I tried to comfort her, by which I mean I tried to help her to understand her own heart. That is all you can do. Unless there is something terrible in the marriage to Stuart, which she assures me there is not.

I was sitting with my arms around her and listening to her tears. I remember how grown-up she was as a child. When Gordon abandoned us, it was Gillian who was the one who comforted me. She used to embrace me and say, 'I'll look after you, Maman.' There is something heartbreaking about being comforted by a child of thirteen, you know. This memory almost made me cry myself.

Gillian was trying to explain how she felt frightened by the idea that she could stop loving Stuart so soon after starting to love him, as if she was defective. 'I thought it was later, the dangerous time, Maman. I thought I was safe for a few years.' She had half-turned in my arms and was looking up into my face.

'It is always the dangerous time,' I said.

'What do you mean?'

'It is always the dangerous time.'

She looked away and nodded. I knew what she was thinking. I had better explain that my husband Gordon at the age of forty-two, when we had been married — oh, it does not matter how long — ran off with a schoolgirl of seventeen years. Gillian was thinking that she had heard of the seven-year itch, as you call it, and had seen in her father the fifteen-year itch, and was now discovering for herself that there was even another before the seven-year one. She was also thinking that I too must be remembering Gordon, and I must be reflecting on the similarity between father and daughter, and how this must be painful for me. But I was not thinking that, and I could not say what I was thinking.

Oliver   Do you want to know something funny? G and S didn't meet in that wine bar as they always pretended. They met in the Charing Cross Hotel at one of those stand-up *partouzes* for Young Professionals.

Some moment of svelte intuition made me bring up with Gillian the supposed encounter at Squires Wine Bar with or without the apostrophe before the *s*. At first she didn't reply. She sputumed her swab and rolled it across her picture some more. Then she told me. Observe that I didn't have to ask. So it must be working the other way round as well: she's decided not to have any secrets from me either.

Apparently there are these locations for the amatoriously parched to which you can repair four times on successive Fridays, all for the sum of £25. I was shocked – that was my first reaction. Then I thought, well, don't ever underestimate furry little Stu. Trust him to go about the business of L'Amour like a market researcher.

'How many times did you have to go before you met Stuart?'

'That was my first time.'

'So you got him for £6.25?'

She laughed. 'No, I got him for £25. They didn't give refunds.'

What a dulcet swoop of wit. 'They didn't give refunds,' I repeated, and the giggles hit me like swamp-fever.

'I didn't tell you that. I shouldn't have told you any of that.'

'You didn't. I've forgotten already.' And I duly reined in my jocosity.

But I bet Stuart went back for his refund, major nickelfucker that he is apt to be at times. Like claiming the return half of his ticket when I met them at Gatwick. And I bet he succeeded. So he cost her £25 and she cost him £6.25. What would he take for her now? What's his mark-up?

And speaking of the gold moidores: Mrs Dyer, with whom I might be inclined to elope were not my heart bidden elsewhere, informed me yesterday that I was on the poll tax register. They don't hang about, those guys, do they? Hoovering up every groat and drachma. Do you think there are humanitarian exceptions? Surely Oliver must be a special case under some grim subsection?

G i l l i a n   He does it every time now. My hair doesn't even have to come loose, he just takes the comb and undoes the clip and pulls the hair back and smoothes it down and puts the grip back in. And I'm burning.

I got up and kissed him. I opened my mouth straight into his, and stroked his neck and pushed down into the flesh of his shoulders and held my body so that he could touch me anywhere he wanted. I stood there kissing him, my hands up on his neck, my body waiting for his hands, even my legs apart. I kissed and I waited.

I waited.

He kissed me back, in my open mouth, and still I waited.

He stopped. My eyes were on him. He put his hands on my shoulders, turned me, and led me back to my easel.

'Let's go to bed, Oliver.'

Do you know what he did? He pushed me down on my chair and actually put a swab back in my hand.

'I can't work. I can't work *now*.'

The thing about Oliver is, he's different when he's alone

with me. You wouldn't recognise him. He's much quieter, and he listens, and doesn't talk in that show-off way. And he doesn't seem at all as confident as he probably appears to others. I know what you're expecting me to say next. 'Oliver's really quite vulnerable.' So I'm not going to say it.

'I love you,' he said. 'I adore you. I want to be with you all the time. I want to marry you. I want to listen to your voice for ever.' We were on the sofa now.

'Oliver, you'd better make love to me. You really had.'

He got up. I thought he was getting up to take me to bed, but he just started walking around. Up and down my studio.

'Oliver, it's all right. It's all right if . . .'

'I want all of you,' he said. 'I don't want part of you. I want the lot.'

'I'm not up for sale.'

'I don't mean that. I mean, I don't want to just have an affair with you. Affairs — affairs are — I don't know — like buying a time-share apartment in Marbella or something.' Then he froze in mid-stride and glanced wildly over as if expecting me to be cross at the comparison. He looked almost desperate. 'It's very nice, actually, Marbella. Much nicer than you'd think. There's a little square, I remember, with orange trees in it. There were workmen picking the oranges when I was there. It was February I think. Of course you have to go off-season.'

He was panicking, you know. When it comes down to it, Oliver's probably got less self-confidence than Stuart. Not so deep down, either.

'Oliver,' I said. 'We're agreed I'm not a time-share apart-

ment in Marbella. And stop walking about like that. Come
and sit here.'

He came and sat down very quietly. 'My father used
to beat me up, you know.'

'Oliver . . .'

'It's *true*. I don't mean he used to spank me as a child.
He did that, of course he did *that*. What he really liked doing
was hitting me across the back of the legs with a billiard cue.
That was my punishment. It's quite painful, actually. "Thighs
or calves?" he used to ask. And I'd have to choose. There's
not much difference, actually, in the pain.'

'I'm sorry.' I put my hand on his neck. He began to cry.

'It was worse after my mother died. He sort of took
it out on me. Perhaps I reminded him of her too much, I
don't know. Then, one day, I suppose I was about thirteen
or fourteen, I decided to stand up to the Old Bastard.
"Thighs or calves?" he asked as usual. I don't know what I'd
done. I mean, I was always doing things, things he thought
deserved punishing. This time I said, "You're stronger than
me now. But you aren't always going to be, and if you ever
hit me again, I promise you that when I'm strong enough I'll
beat you to a pulp." '

'Yes.'

'I didn't think it would work. I mean, I was trembling,
and smaller than him, and as I said it I thought *beat you to a
pulp* was a really stupid way of putting it, and he'd just laugh
at me. But he didn't. He stopped. He stopped for ever.'

'Oliver, I'm sorry.'

'I hate him. He's old now and I still hate him. I hate him
for being here, in this room with us. What's he doing *here*?'

'He isn't. He's gone. He's got a time-share apartment in Marbella.'

'Christ, why can't I do it? Why can't I say the right things, I mean, *now* of all times?' He got up again. 'I'm not saying any of this very well.' He put his head down and wouldn't look at me. 'I love you. I'll always love you. It won't ever stop. I'd better go now.'

About three hours later he called me.

'Yes?' I said.

'I love you.'

I put the phone down. Almost at once Stuart's key scraped at the lock. I was burning. The front door closed. 'Anyone ho-ome?' Stuart shouted, with a sort of yodel he puts in his voice so that it will carry all the way up the house. 'Anyone ho-ome?'

What should I do?

O l i v e r   Argumentation against affairs, written down by one who has had more than his share of them:

1) Vulgarity. Everyone's doing it. I mean, *everyone*. Priests do it, the Royal Family does it, even hermits find a way of doing it. Why aren't they constantly bumping into one another on their damp passage from bedroom to bedroom? Bonk, bonk – who's there?

2) Predictability. Courtship, Conquest, Cooling, Crack-up. The same dreary little plot-line. Dreary, but no less horribly addictive. After each failure, the quest for another

failure. Make the world fresh again!

3) Time-sharing. I thought I put that rather well to
Gillian. How can you enjoy your holiday when you
know the owners are waiting to move back in? And
fucking against the clock is not my style; though in
certain circumstances it can have its wily addictions.

4) Lying. A direct result of 3) above. Affairs corrupt
– and I speak as One Who, etc. It's inevitable. First you
lie to one partner and then, very soon afterwards, you lie
to the second. Oh, you say you won't, but you will. You
scoop out a little duck-pond of emotional integrity with
a great bulldozer of *mensonges*. Watch the track-suited
husband go off jogging with a pocketful of change for
the telephone. Jingle, jingle. 'Might need a soft drink on
the way, darling!' Jingle, jingle, the sound of lies tinkling.

5) Betrayal. How satisfied everyone is with small betrayals. What juice they provide. Roger the Dodger gets
away with it again, part 27 – when getting away with it
is really not very difficult. Stuart is my friend – yes he is –
and he is going to lose his wife to me. That's a Big Betrayal,
but then I think people can handle Big Betrayals better than
small ones. An affair would be a small betrayal, and I don't
think Stuart could handle that as well as the Big Betrayal.
You see, I do think about him as well.

6) I haven't yet had the result of my AIDS test.

Now, I didn't put it like this to Gillian, not exactly, no. In fact, to tell the truth, I think I made a terrible bosh of it.

G i l l i a n   On the way to the station, just on the corner at the other end of Barrowclough Road, there's a greengrocer's shop. It's where I bought the sweet potatoes. Or rather, I bought the SWEET POTATO'S. The man who runs it does these price labels which he hand-letters in sort of italic capitals. And very carefully, without ever missing, he puts an apostrophe into everything he sells. APPLE'S PEAR'S CARROT'S LEEK'S – you can buy them all there – SWEDE'S TURNIP'S and SWEET POTATO'S. Stuart and I used to find this funny and a bit touching, this chap doggedly getting it wrong all the time, every single time. I walked past the shop today and suddenly I didn't find it at all funny any more. CAULI'S COX'S SPROUT'S. I just found it so sad it went right through me. Not sad because he couldn't spell, not that. Sad because he got it wrong, and then he went on to the next label and got that wrong, and then he went on to the next one and got that wrong too. Either someone's told him and he didn't believe it, or else in all the years he's been a greengrocer, nobody's told him. I don't know which is sadder, do you?

I think about Oliver all the time. Even when I'm with Stuart. Sometimes I can't bear it that Stuart seems cheerful. Why can't he see what I'm thinking about, *who* I'm thinking about? Why can't he read my mind?

Stuart   Sit down. Do you like Patsy Cline?

> Two cigarettes in an ashtray
> My love and I in a small café
> Then a stranger came along
> And everything went wrong
> Now there's three cigarettes in the ashtray

Poor Patsy, she's dead. And you've still got that ciggy behind your ear, by the way. Why don't you smoke it?

> I watched her take him from me
> And his love is no longer my own
> Now they are gone
> And I sit alone
> And watch one cigarette burn away

Good old Stuart, he's so reliable. You know where you are with Stuart. He puts up with things. He trundles along. He turns a blind eye. We can take him for granted. He'll always be the same.

Ask no questions and they'll tell you no lies. But that only takes you so far. Oliver's coming over in a few minutes. He thinks we're all three off to the cinema together like best old friends. But Gillian has gone to see her mother, so Oliver will have to make do with me. I'll ask him some questions and he'll tell me some lies.

Just before she left, I was sitting here with my headphones on listening to a tape of Patsy. Gillian came in to say goodbye, so I pressed the pause button and lifted one ear-piece away from the side of my head.

'How's Oliver?' I asked.

'Oliver? Oh, he's fine, I think.'

'You're not having an affair with him by any chance?' I said it in a light-hearted way, of course. What, me, worry?

'Christ. Christ, no.'

'Oh, well, that's all right, then.' I pulled the ear-piece down again, closed my eyes to avoid Gill's face, and moved my lips along to Patsy's. I felt Gillian give me a kiss on the forehead and nodded in response.

Now we'll see what he's got to say for himself.

O l i v e r   It will not have escaped you that my friend Stuart is not a man of broad culture. If you were to ask him the name of Proust's girlfriend, he'd brood for a quinquennium, then start to glower at you like a samurai, decide it's a trick question, and finally answer, with a *petite* pout of aggression, 'Madeleine. Everyone knows that.'

So I wasn't anticipating, oh, Schreker's *Die Gezeichneten* when he answered the door, beckoned me inside with fervent child-molester eyes, and scrabbled a questing paw at his tape-deck. Mayhap he had just discovered the 1812 Overture and enjoyed singing along to the cannon and fireworks. Or were we in for the Enigma Variations, accompanied by much toilsome reading of the sleeve-note about one of music's least vital mysteries, namely the identity of the Friends Portrayed Therein? Oh, and did you know Dorabella apparently had a little speech impediment, which is why the music seems to hesitate, to go hip-hip-hop, in her Variation? Have a choc-ice,

Maestro. But hie me to the vomitorium, pronto.

He played me this song. It seemed to last about 3 hours
47 minutes, though he assured me it was less. So that's what
they call 'country music', is it? Then I'm so glad I live in the
town. It has at least this rarity, this sophistication: that of being
unparodiable – for the simple reason that it parodies itself as
it goes along, like a lawn-mower picking up its own clippings.
There's no room for an old man with a rake, and equally no
room for a young man with a mock. Hiddly-up, please Daddy,
I'm lonesome again, Hiddly-up . . . No point in trying. And the
singers, they wear rhinestones – and rhinestones, you see, are
already parodies of diamonds, so you can't parody rhinestones.
Ah, and here comes wizened Walter coaxing a gout of cadenza
from his wizened violin. You still sho' can show'em all Walt,
whine, chug-a-chug, Hiddly-up, please Daddy . . .

'What did you think?'

What did I think? For some reason he was positively
scowling at me. He couldn't, surely, be asking me for a
musical analysis of the piece?

As I scrabbled in the loose scree of my cortex for something
that didn't inevitably include Stuart within the dragnet of my
contempt, he got up and chubbily poured us both a drink.

'So what did you think, then, Oliver?'

At the last moment the Muse of Tact scooped me up. 'I
don't think *ashtray,*' I said, 'is a wholly satisfying rhyme for
ashtray.'

That seemed to placate him.

My rather brutal *viva voce* had briefly expelled from my
head what I had planned to do on my arrival. I handed Stuart
an envelope. How much English I had taught as a Foreign

Language to recuperate one quarter of the loan Stuart had advanced me!

Whereupon he became unexpectedly bellicose, and cast the dosh back at me like Alfredo in *Traviata*.

'You'll need that for your poll tax,' he said. I just looked at him. Why is everyone suddenly going on at me as if I had some spectroscopic interest in the digestive processes of local government finance? 'The poll tax you'll have to pay on your *second home*' – he pronounced those unlovely words with what thousands would call a sneer – 'over the road at number 55.'

As I find myself repeating nowadays until it becomes a catch-phrase, don't underestimate our furry friend. And from that point on the evening, I have to admit, did not unravel as I had been led to believe it would. We did not patronise the kinematograph. Gillian was 'Away Visiting Her Mother'. Stuart's atonement for this absence of lustre consisted in a bottle of duty-free whisky, and there seemed no point in not Being Manly with him. For it was a starless night when the virtuoso of vault and till had upon him the mildness of Titus Andronicus.

'Are you and Gill having an affair?'

You see what I mean? What lorry-like directness. And how uncharacteristic. One who habitually clung to the *outré* back streets when crossing London was now sailing down Haymarket.

I was taken aback, I admit. Many a time and oft have I been called upon to deny that I was having an affair when I was. But to deny that I was having an affair when I wasn't – this seemed to demand a new skill. I swore I wasn't. I looked around for something to swear on, but objects of shared veneration are quaintly unobtainable nowadays. I could only think of Gillian's heart, her life, the hair on her head, none of which seemed wholly appropriate to the case, nor liable to milk some of the bullishness from Stuart's deportment.

We drank quite a lot of the whisky, and as we did so the possibility that the two of us might philosophically exchange rival accounts of our perception of the external world rather came and went; indeed there were moments of distinctly Neanderthal backsliding from Stu. At one point he cut into my admittedly sinuous line of argument with nothing less than a shout.

'Lend us a quid, Give us your wife.'

This observation did not seem germane to what I was seeking to establish. I looked at Stu.

'Lend us a quid, Give us your wife. Lend us a quid, Give us your wife.'

This rhetorical device is, I believe, known as repetition.

'What I tell you three times is true,' I murmured, not expecting the allusion to be fly-fished from the waters of my discourse.

However, Stuart's 'interruption' – to supply its alternative rhetorical name – did offer me, if not a doorway, then at least a humble cat-flap into what I had been planning to say.

'Stuart,' I began, 'I assure you that Gillian and I are not having an affair. We are not even, as the diplomats say, having talks about talks.' He grunted in hesitant comprehension of the worldly reference. 'On the other hand,' I continued, and his prickly brows began to coalesce furiously at the realisation that more was to come, 'as one friend to another, I have to tell you that I am in love with her. Don't admonish me, not yet, let me first register with you that I am as *bouleversé* by it all as you are. Had I the slightest control over it, I would not have fallen in love with her. Not now. I would have fallen in love with her when I first met her.' (Why didn't I? Was it some stub of loyalty, or the fact that she wore 501s with trainers?)

This didn't seem to be going down too well with Stuart, so I hastened on to the nub of the matter, where I hoped his professional training would assist him towards personal insight. 'We live in an era of market forces, Stuart' – I could see that this arrested him – 'and it would be naïve or, as they used to term it, romantic not to realise that market forces now apply in whole areas where hitherto they were deemed inapplicable.'

'We're not talking about money, we're talking about love,' he protested.

'Ah, but there are such parallels, Stuart. They both go where they wist, reckless of what they leave behind. Love too has its buy-outs, its asset stripping, its junk bonds. Love rises and falls in value like any currency. And confidence is *such* a key to maintaining its value.

'Consider also the element of good fortune. You have told me yourself at some point how the great entrepreneurs need to be lucky as well as audacious and skilful. What could be more fortunate than your meeting Gill first time off at the Charing Cross Hotel, or my good fortune that *you* had had the good fortune to have met her?

'Money, as I further understand it, is morally neutral. It can be put to good use, it can be put to bad use. We may criticise those who deal in money, as we may criticise those who deal in love, but not the substances themselves.'

I could sense I might be losing him, so I sought to summarise at this point. I poured both of us the last of the whisky to aid comprehension. 'It's market forces, Stu, that's what you've got to get hold of. And I'm going to take her over. My offer will be accepted by the broad, I mean the board. You may become a non-executive director – otherwise known as a friend – but I'm afraid it's time to hand back the chauffeur-driven car.

'Of course, I can see the paradox as plainly as you do. You are a creature of the market-place, yet you seek to reserve this one domestic area of your life and declare that it is not to be influenced by the great forces known to you between 9 and 5 every working day. I, on the other hand, a – how shall we put it? – classical humanist of artistic bent and romantic nature, reluctantly admit that human passions operate not according to some gracious rule-book of courtly behaviour, but following the gusts, the veritable hurricanoes of *le marché*.'

It was at about this time that the accident occurred. Stuart was, as I recall, giving me a light (I know – but at moments of stress a certain nicotine recidivism does beckon), and we stood up for some reason, when an unfortunate clash of heads occurred which quite stunned us both. Luckily he had his lenses in; otherwise he might have broken his glasses.

Mrs Dyer was extremely kind. She washed the blood off my clothes and said that in her opinion, even though her eyes weren't what they had once been, she thought the cut needed stitching. But I frankly did not care to attempt pilotage of my vehicle at that time of night, and retired upwards to my tree-house.

If you're drunk, you don't feel pain. And if you wake up with the worst hangover since Silenus' 21st-birthday hoolie, you don't feel it then either. Whether this system works equally well for all I leave to the experimenting individual.

Stuart   I admit it was probably wrong to head-butt him, but I was just submitting to market forces, don't you see?

The fact of the matter is, I often don't listen to what Oliver says. Or rather, I know what he's saying even if I only attend half the time. It must be some filter mechanism that's developed over the years, which sorts out things it's relevant for me to know from all the waffle surrounding them. I can sit there, nursing my drink, even singing a song to myself inside my head, and still pick the bones out of the waffle.

Of course they're having an affair. Oh, don't *you* give me that look as well. The husband is always the first to suspect and the last to know, as I said, but when he knows, he *knows*. And shall I tell you how I know? Because of what she told him, what she told him about us. I can just about – *just about* – believe the cover story, that he's in love with her, that he calls round every afternoon, that he's hired a room because his aching bloody heart has to be near her, but that they aren't up to any monkey business. But what made me sure, what convinced me that it wasn't his aching bloody heart but his aching bloody prick that needed attending to, was something he didn't even notice he'd said. It was about Gill and me meeting at the Charing Cross Hotel. We went to so much trouble at the time. Gill and I agreed we wouldn't tell anyone – but we most of all agreed we wouldn't tell Oliver – about how we met. We were embarrassed, OK, I admit it. We were both a bit embarrassed. That's not something you forget. But she forgot it. She went and blabbed to Oliver. That's the proof that she's having an affair with him – she betrayed me. And the proof that *he's* having an affair with her is the way he dropped it into the conversation as if it were just an unimportant fact everyone agreed on. If he *wasn't* having an affair with her, then he'd have made a big fuss and dance and gone in for what he thinks of as teasing but which increasingly strikes me as activity indicating some lack of psychological balance.

He hasn't changed, Oliver. Lend us a quid, give us your wife. He's basically a parasite, do you see? A work-shy snob and a parasite.

One of the things I didn't listen to was a whole lot of stuff about What Holds Couples Together and What Holds Society Together. Oliver doing one of those clever little essays he was so good at writing when we were both at school. Why having a bit on the side is like the French Revolution – I used to be impressed by that sort of thing before I grew up. And then as I remember we went on from there to a whole piece of piss about market forces. I listened with slightly more attention at this point, because Oliver making a complete fool of himself is always a bit more interesting than Oliver making half a fool of himself. And so I studied his complex argument and weighed all the evidence, and what it came down to – correct me if I'm oversimplifying – is that it's because of the *Market* that I'm diddling your wife. Oh, so that's why. I thought it was because you're in love with her, or you hate me, or both, but if it's because of the *Market*, then of course I, as a humble cog in the machine, understand why you're doing what you're doing.

It makes me feel so much better.

At that moment he put another cigarette in his mouth (his ninth of the evening – I was counting) and discovered he'd finished his matches.

'Give us a Dutch fuck, old chum,' he said.

The expression was new to me, and probably offensive, so I didn't reply. Oliver leaned towards me, reached out and took the cigarette I was smoking from my hand. He knocked off some ash, blew on the end until it glowed red, then lit his cigarette from mine. There was something repulsive in the way he did it.

'That's a Dutch fuck, old chum.' And he gave me a horrible, leering smile.

It was at this point that I decided I'd had enough. The 'old chum' didn't help, either. I stood up and said, 'Oliver, have you ever had a Glasgow kiss?'

He obviously thought we were discussing the use of language, and may even have thought I was advising him on how to have sex with my wife. 'No,' he said, interested. 'I've never been to Sporransville.'

Dutch fuck, Glasgow kiss. Dutch fuck, Glasgow kiss. 'I'll show you.' I stood up, and motioned him to do the same.

He rose rather unsteadily. I took him by the sweater and looked into his face, that horrible sweaty face that had fucked my wife. When? When last? Yesterday? Two days ago?

'This is a Glasgow kiss,' I said, and butted him in the face. He fell over, and at first was sort of half-laughing, as if I must have been going to show him something else but had slipped. Then it became clear that it hadn't been a mistake, and he ran away. He's not exactly one of life's bare-knuckle fighters, our Oliver. In fact, he's a complete physical coward. Won't go into a pub unless it's ladies' night, if you see what I mean. He always claimed he had an abhorrence of violence because his father used to beat him when he was a small boy. What with? A rolled-up sweet paper?

Oh, look, I don't want to talk about Oliver any more. *Any more.* I feel terribly exhausted after last night, and the imbecile bled on the carpet as well.

You want to know how I feel? All right, I'll tell you. When we were at school we used to have to play at being soldiers. The Combined Cadet Force. And this is how you cleaned a rifle. You took a piece of cloth, a 4 x 2, and folded it into one end of a pull-through, and dropped the other end down the barrel of the rifle, and then pulled the cloth all the way through the barrel, which was quite difficult actually, as the folded cloth fitted very tightly. You pulled it all the way from the breech to the snout. And that's what I feel like. Someone's pulling a piece of 4 x 2 on a wire all the way through my body, from my arsehole to my nose, over and over and over again. From my arsehole to my nose. That's how I feel.

Look, just leave me, if you don't mind. I've got to be left alone. Thank you.

> Two cigarettes in an ashtray
> My love and I in a small café
> Then a stranger . . .

Of course, *you* know if they're really fucking, don't you? *You* know. So tell me. Go on, tell me.

12: Spare Me Val.
Spare Yourselves Val.

Stuart

> I stop to see a weeping willow
> crying on his pillow
> maybe he's crying for me
>
> And as the skies turn gloomy
> nightbirds whisper to me
> I'm lonesome as I can be

That's Patsy. Well, you wouldn't not recognise the voice, would you? It's from her song 'Walking After Midnight'.

I played the song to Gillian. I asked her what she thought of it.

'I haven't really got an opinion,' she said.

'Very well, then,' I said, 'I'll play it you again.'

I played it her again. In case you are unfamiliar with this song, which I personally rate as one of Patsy's masterpieces, it's about a woman who has been forsaken by her man and goes out walking – 'after midnight' – hoping to come across him and perhaps persuade him to come back to her.

When the song had finished, I looked up at Gillian, who was standing there with an expression of, well, indifference, I suppose: as if she'd left something on the stove but it really didn't matter one way or the other whether it got burnt. She also didn't say anything, which not surprisingly I found a bit irritating. I mean, I'm sure I would have some comment to make on one of her favourite pieces of music.

'I'll play it you again then.'

So I did.

> And as the skies turn gloomy
> nightbirds whisper to me
> I'm lonesome as I-I can be . . .

'So what do you think?' I asked.

'I think,' she said, 'that it's riddled with nauseating self-pity.'

'Well, wouldn't you be?' I shouted. 'Wouldn't you be?'

Not very drunk.

Just drunk.

Mme Wyatt   What I mean is this. They will tell you that from the point of view of statistics this happens, that happens. Sure, all right. But for me, the dangerous time is always. I have seen a lot of marriages, long, short, English, French. It is a dangerous time after seven years, for sure. It is a dangerous time after seven months.

What I could not tell my daughter was this. I had an affair a year after I married Gordon. Nothing to do with how we were getting on: we were in love. But I had a brief affair all the same. 'Oh, how French,' I hear you say. *Oo-la-la*. Well, not so much. I have an English friend, a woman, who had an affair six weeks after getting married. And is this so surprising? You can feel happy and you can feel trapped at the same time. You can feel security and you can feel panic, this is not new. And in a way the beginning of the marriage is the most dangerous time because – how can I say this? – the heart has been made tender. *L'appétit vient en mangeant.* Being in love makes you liable to fall in love. Ah, I am not setting up in competition with Chamfort, you understand, that is just my observation. People think it has to do with sex, that someone is not doing his duty in bed, or her duty in bed, but I think this is not the case. It has to do with the heart. The heart has been made tender, and that is dangerous.

But you can see why I cannot say this to my daughter? Ah, Gillian, I quite understand. I had an affair a year after I married your father, this is quite normal. I could not impose that tyranny upon her. I am not ashamed of my affair, and have no reason to keep it secret except that it would be harmful to tell. The girl must find her own destiny, it is cruel to let her imagine she is suffering a terrible imitation of her mother. I must not impose such a tyranny of knowledge upon my daughter.

So I only say, 'It is always the dangerous time.'

Of course I knew immediately that it was Oliver.

Gillian   He said: 'Please don't leave me yet. They'll think I haven't got a prick.'

He said: 'I love you. I'll always love you.'

He said: 'If I catch Oliver inside this house, I'll break his fucking neck.'

He said: 'Please let me make love to you.'

He said: 'It's quite cheap to get someone killed nowadays. It hasn't at all kept up with the rate of inflation. Market forces must be to blame.'

He said: 'I've only felt alive since I met you. Now I'll have to go back to being dead again.'

He said: 'I'm taking a girl out to dinner tonight. I may fuck her afterwards, I haven't decided yet.'

He said: 'Why did it have to be Oliver?'

He said: 'Can I still be your friend?'

He said: 'I don't ever want to see you again.'

He said: 'If Oliver had had a proper job this would never have happened.'

He said: 'Please don't leave me. They'll think I haven't got a prick.'

Mme Wyatt   And there was one other thing my daughter said to me, which I found terribly poignant. She said, 'Maman, I thought there were *rules*.'

She didn't mean rules of behaviour, she meant something more than that. People often imagine that if they get married that will 'solve things', as they say. My daughter of course is not so naïve as to think that, but she did, I believe, hope or perhaps just feel that she would in some way be protected – at least for a while – by something which we could call the immutable rules of marriage.

I am now more than fifty years of age, and if you ask me what are the immutable rules of marriage, I can think of only one: a man never leaves his wife for an older woman. Apart from that, anything that is possible is normal.

Stuart   I went over to number 55 yesterday evening. The little old lady who lives there, Mrs Dyer, answered the door.

'Oh, you're that man from the Council,' she said.

'That's right, Madam,' I said. 'I'm sorry to disturb you so late, but it is a Council responsibility to inform all landlords – and landladies – as urgently as possible if their tenants have been positively tested for AIDS.'

'You've been drinking,' she said.

'Well, it's a very stressful job, you know.'

'All the more reason why you shouldn't drink. Especially if you have to operate machinery.'

'I don't operate machinery,' I said, feeling we were getting off the point.

'Then try and have an early night.' And she shut the door in my face.

She's right, of course. I might have to operate machinery. For instance, I might have to run my car backwards and forwards over Oliver's body. Bump, bump, bump. That would be a task I would have to be sober for.

I don't want you to get me wrong. I don't just sit around getting drunk and listening to Patsy Cline tapes. Well, I do that a bit, it's true. But I'm not going to spend more than a certain percentage of my time wallowing in – what did Gill call it? – yes, 'nauseating self-pity' was the phrase. I'm also not going to give up, do you see? I love Gill, and I'm not going to give up. I'm going to do whatever I can to stop her leaving me. And if she does leave me, I'm going to do everything I can to get her back. And if she won't come back . . . well, then I'll think of something. I'm not going to take this lying down.

I didn't mean it about running over Mrs Dyer's tenant with my car, of course. It's just something you say. You don't get any practice in these situations beforehand, do you? All of a sudden they're on you, and you have to deal with them. So you say things you don't mean, and things you can imagine someone else saying suddenly come out of your own mouth. Like for instance when I told Gill I was taking a girl out to dinner and I might fuck her afterwards if I felt like it. That's just stupid, trying to hurt Gill. The person I took out to dinner was a woman, it's true. But it was Val, who's an old friend from way back, and the person I want to make love to is Gill. No-one else.

Oliver   I let myself in and unleashed the bison's cough I've developed to let Mrs Dyer know I'm leaving the pedal imprint on her parquet. She came out of the kitchen, turning her sunflower head sideways to squint up at me.

'I'm sorry to hear you've got the AIDS,' she said.

My mind did not, at that instant, have quite the solidity of Soviet monumental sculpture in the Stalin-to-Brezhnev era. I pictured Mrs Dyer mistakenly opening a brown envelope from the clinic. Except that I'd said I'd call them. Except that they didn't have this address.

'Who told you so?'

'The gentleman from the Council. The one who came about the poll tax. The one who lives over the road. I've seen him. He's got a nice-looking wife.' She waved in the direction . . . and all fell into place.

'It was a joke, Mrs Dyer,' I said. 'A sort of joke.'

'I think he thought I didn't know what the AIDS was.' I looked at her as if I was a touch *bouleversé* myself that she did. 'I read the leaflets,' she said. 'Anyway, I told him you were very clean and we had separate toilets.'

My heart was suddenly a sog of tenderness. Extend a cautious foot into my *coeur* and you'd go in right over the wellie. 'Mrs Dyer,' I said, 'I hope you won't think me too forward, but would you consider becoming my wife?'

She gave a quiet cackle. 'Once is enough for any woman,' she said. 'And besides, young man, you've got the AIDS.' She gave another skirl of amusement, and disappeared back into her kitchen.

I sat at my window behind the monkey-puzzle tree and thought of Stuart at the breakfast table shaking his packet of cereal: *Sh-chug-a-chug, Sh-chug-a-chug-chug*. And then – the mind is such a bluebottle, such a jumping-jack – I thought of Stuart in bed with Gillian. I bet it's the same. I bet he goes *Sh-chug-a-chug, Sh-chug-a-chug-chug*. It hurts, oh it hurts.

Stuart   I don't mean everything I say at the moment, but I did mean what I said about Oliver not having a proper job. What would be the most effective cure for sexual immorality, for wife-stealing? Full employment, with every adult male working the same hours, 9.00 to 5.30. Oh, and Saturdays as well, let's get back to the six-day week. Not popular with the unions, of course, and there'd have to be exceptions made for airline pilots and so on. Of course, airline pilots and their crews are notoriously immoral. What other professions are full of immorality and wife-stealing? University lecturers, actors and actresses, doctors and nurses . . . You see what I mean? None of them work regular hours.

And Oliver is a liar, of course. That helps. I've always thought that over the years I'd learned how much to allow for his exaggerations, but maybe I was way out all along. For instance, the story about his father beating him up. I wonder if that's true. He's always made a big thing about it – how his dad started beating him up after his mum died when he was six. How he took a billiard cue to him because Oliver looked like his mum and so his dad was in effect punishing her for leaving him by dying (do people really behave like this? Oliver assured me they do). How the abuse went on for years and years, until one day, when he was fifteen (though sometimes it's sixteen, sometimes thirteen), Oliver turned round and thumped his father. After that it never happened again, and now Dad lives in some old folks' home and Oliver every so often goes to visit hoping to find some spark of affection in these closing years, but always comes back sad and disappointed. Which is a great sympathy-winner, not least with women.

No-one's heard his dad's version, needless to say. I met

him briefly a couple of times, when I went to call on Oliver, and he never tried to beat *me* up. After hearing Oliver's stories I expected him to have vampire teeth and carry a pair of handcuffs; but he struck me as a nice enough old boy with a pipe. Oliver certainly hates him, but there may be other reasons for that, like he eats his peas off a knife or doesn't know that Bizet wrote *Carmen*. Oliver is a snob, as you might have noticed.

He's also, I can't help pointing out, a coward. Or at least, put it this way. The big event in Oliver's childhood is the moment when he turns on his violent dad and gives him such a whipping that the Old Bastard – as Oliver refers to him – slinks away with his tail between his legs. Now, I'm quite a bit smaller than Oliver, but when I gave him a little poke in the face with my head, how did he react? He ran away squealing and blubbing. Is this the behaviour of the famous tamer of bullies? Oh yes, and what about that billiard cue? Oliver once told me that he and his father only had one thing in common: they both hated sport.

Gillian   Oliver needed five stitches in his cheek. He told the hospital he'd tripped over and gashed it on the corner of a table.

He said the expression of violence on Stuart's face had to be seen to be believed. He said he thought Stuart wanted to kill him. He suggested I put water in the whisky bottle. He begged me to leave at once.

Stuart

> And as the skies turn gloomy
> Nightbirds whisper to me
> I'm lonesome as I-I can be . . .

Gillian   You know, in all the time Stuart and I were together he never once asked me why I was at the Charing Cross Hotel that evening. I mean, he asked about it in one sense, and I replied that I'd seen the ad in *Time Out*, but he never asked me *why*. He was always very careful in his finding-out about me. I think it was partly that he didn't mind what had happened before: here I was, and that was all Stuart was interested in. But it was a bit more than that. Stuart had his idea of what I was like, he'd decided upon it, and he didn't want to hear anything different.

Why I was there is easily told. A married man: he wouldn't leave his wife, I couldn't give him up. Yes, that old story, the one that keeps dragging on. So I took steps to stop it dragging on. You've got to be responsible for your own happiness – you can't expect it to come flopping through the door like a parcel. You've got to be practical in these matters. People sit at home thinking Some Day My Prince Will Come. But that's no good unless you've got a sign up saying Princes Welcome Here.

Oliver couldn't be more different. For a start, he wants to know everything about me. I sometimes feel I'm letting him down by not having had a more exotic past. I've never been pearl-fishing in Tahiti. I didn't sell my virginity for a sable coat. I've just been me. On the other hand, that *me* isn't settled and

decided in Oliver's mind the way it was in Stuart's. And that's
. . . nice. No, it's more than nice. It's sexy.

'You know, I bet Stuart basically thinks of you as a good
little shopper.' This was a few weeks ago.

I don't like Stuart being criticised. In fact, I won't have it.
'I *am* a good little shopper,' I replied (though that's not how
I think of myself). At least, I'm much better than Oliver, who
tends to go into a trance over a green pepper, if you know
what I mean.

'Sorry,' he said quickly. 'What I *meant* is merely that
for me you are someone of well, endless possibility. I do not
stake out and fence in what is taken to be your approved and
registered nature.'

'That's very sweet of you, Oliver.' I was teasing him a
little, though he didn't seem to notice.

'It's just that – not to say a word against – Stuart's
never actually *seen* you.'

'And do you – *see* me?'

'3-D specs. Eyes for nothing else.'

I smiled and kissed him. Later, I wondered: but if two
such different people as Stuart and Oliver can both fall in
love with me, what sort of *me* is it? And what sort of *me*
falls in love first with Stuart and then with Oliver? The same
one, a different one?

Harringay Hospital
Accident & Emergency Department

Surname	RUSSELL
First Name(s)	OLIVER DAVENPORT
	DE QUINCEY
Address	55, St Dunstan's Road, N16
Occupation	Screenwriter
Place of Accident	Home
Time of Arrival	11.50
GP's Name	Dr. Cagliari (Sicily)

NOTES
    <u>says</u> old duelling scar reopened by walking
        into monkey-puzzle tree
    smells of alcohol + +
    no L.O.C.
    last tetanus > 10 years ago
    O/E 3cms laceration (R) cheek
    X-R → no # seen
    sutured c̄ 10 x 50 Nylon
    tet tox
    R.O.S. here 5/7   *J. Davis*
                                                        16.00

Oliver   I never thought I might have the AIDS, as Mrs
Dyer so arrestingly refers to the matter. But it shows my
intentions are serious, doesn't it? *Tabula rasa,* starting from
scratch.

    And I don't have to pay the poll tax twice, because I don't
really live at number 55, and I'm not going to be there much

longer anyway. I have this fantasy about asking Mrs Dyer to be a bridesmaid. Or a matron-of-honour, perhaps.

Some things get to you. I wish I hadn't thought of Stuart going *Sh-chug-a-chug*. You see, I used to have this joke with myself. Some book I read when barely post-pre-pubescent contained the words: *he made free with her narrow loins*. I admit, almost without shame, that for years this phrase hung from a string in my skull like some Christmas decoration, gilded and talismanic. So that's what they're up to, dirty beasts, I'd think. Me too, soon. Then, for many years, reality effaced phraseology. Until the words came back to me with Gill. I'd sit aloft in my monkey-puzzle tree and whisper to myself (not *wholly* seriously, I trust you comprehend), '*I shall make free with her narrow loins*'. But I can't do that any more, because of some cerebral hitch, some jammed ganglion. Because every time I hear the words they are followed by the sound of Stuart going *Sh-chug-a-chug, Sh-chug-a-chug-chug*, like a tubby tender behind a slinky locomotive.

I hope to God they're not still doing it. I hope to God they're not even sleeping in the same bed still. I can't ask. What do you think?

After *la lune de miel* comes *la lune d'absinthe*. Who'd have thought that Stuart would turn violent in his liquor?

Stuart

> I stop to see a weeping willow
> cryin' on his pillow
> maybe he's cryin' for me . . .

Not very drunk.

Just drunk.

Gillian   And I know there's a question I've got to answer. You've a right to ask it, and I can't be surprised if there's a sceptical tone to your voice, or even a bit of a sneer. Go on, ask it.

Look, Gill, you've told us how you fell in love with Stuart – getting soppy when you saw his cooking timetable – so what about telling us how you fell in love with Oliver? You saw him filling in his pools coupon, doing The Times crossword?

Fair enough. I'd probably be a bit dubious in your position. But I'd just like to say this. I didn't choose what happened. I didn't manipulate things, suddenly decide that Oliver was a 'better deal' or something than Stuart. It happened to me. I married Stuart, then I fell in love with Oliver. I don't feel complacent about that. Some of it I don't even like. It just happened.

But 'that moment' – the one people I don't even know yet are going to ask me to remember. We were in a restaurant. It's supposed to be French but it isn't. I think half the waiters are Spanish and half are Greek, but they look Mediterranean enough and the chef puts anchovies and olives in everything and they call the place Le Petit Provençal, which seems to fool most people, or if not fool them, at least satisfy them.

We were there because Stuart was away for the night and Oliver insisted on taking me out to dinner. First of all I didn't want to go, then I said I'd pay, then I suggested going Dutch, but we got into the usual male pride bit, and the way *that* works is that it's harder for them to accept you paying half if they're short of money. So there I was, half-reluctant, half-bullied, in a restaurant I didn't much like but which I'd chosen because I thought it was cheap enough for him to take me to. None of this seemed to affect Oliver. He was very relaxed, as if all the negotiations it had taken to get us there had never occurred. I suppose I was also apprehensive in case he started slagging off Stuart, but quite the opposite. He said he didn't remember much about school any more, but all the nice things were to do with Stuart. There was some gang they defeated all by themselves, just the two of them. There was someone they called 'Feet' because he had big hands. There was the time the two of them went hitch-hiking to Scotland. Oliver said it took them weeks to get there because he was such a snob about cars at that time he would actually turn down lifts when someone had stopped because he didn't like the upholstery or the hub-caps. And then it rained all the time so they sat in bus-shelters and ate oat-cakes. Oliver said he'd already started to get interested in food so Stuart gave him a blind-fold test. Oliver closed his eyes and Stuart fed him alternately little bits of damp oat-cake and little bits of damp torn-up packaging. Stuart had claimed that Oliver couldn't tell the difference.

It was all ... surprisingly easy, I suppose, and Oliver grunted approvingly at the food even though we both knew it wasn't up to much. As we were finishing our main course, he stopped a waiter who was passing our table.

'Le vin est fini,' Oliver said to him. He wasn't showing off or anything, just assuming that the waiters at somewhere called Le Petit Provençal were French.

'Sorry?'

'Ah,' said Ollie. He turned his chair slightly, and tapped the wine bottle as if teaching at that awful Shakespeare School of English. 'Le vin . . . est . . . fini,' he repeated, articulating carefully and with a rising note at the end, indicating that there was more to come. 'The . . . wine . . .' he went on in a thick non-English accent, '. . . comes . . . from . . . Finland.'

'You want another bottle?'

'Si, signor.'

I'm afraid I just hooted, which wasn't very fair on the waiter, who went and got us another bottle rather grumpily. As he was pouring it into my glass, Ollie murmured, 'A rather pleasant Chateau Sibelius, I think you'll find.'

And that set me off again. I laughed till I coughed. Then I laughed till it hurt. And the thing about Ollie is he knows how to make a joke run. I don't want to make comparisons, but Stuart isn't very good at jokes and if he makes one he just leaves it there, as if he's shot a rabbit or something and that's the business done. Whereas Oliver keeps at it, and if you aren't in the mood it could be tiresome, but I guess that evening I was in the mood.

'And with the coffee, Modom? A little Kalevala? A Suomi on the rocks? I know, a glass of Karelia?' I just got incapable at that point, and the waiter didn't know what the joke was. 'Yes, I think a finger of Suomi for my friend,' said Ollie. 'What brands do you have? Do you have Helsinki Fivestar?'

I waved my hands at him to stop, which the waiter thought meant something different. 'Nothing for the lady. And for you sir?'

'Oh,' said Ollie, pretending to come down and suddenly

looking serious. 'Ah. Yes. I'll just have a small Fjord, please.'
Then we took off again, and when I came out of it my sides
were aching, I was looking across at Ollie, his eyes were glistening, and I thought to myself, God this is dangerous, this is
really beyond dangerous. Then Ollie went quiet, as if he'd felt
it too.

You don't find this as funny as I did? That's all right.
I'm only telling you because you asked. And we did leave
a large tip in case the waiter thought we were laughing at
him.

Stuart

> And as the skies turn gloomy
> Nightbirds whisper to me . . .

Gillian   The first time I met Oliver I asked him if he
was wearing make-up. That was a bit embarrassing – I mean,
to remember this afterwards as almost the first thing you said
to someone you fell in love with – but it wasn't so far out. I
mean, sometimes it *is* as if Oliver wears make-up with people.
He likes to be dramatic, he likes to shock them a bit. Only he
doesn't with me. He can be quiet, he can be himself, he knows
he doesn't have to act up a storm to impress me. Or rather,
that if he did he wouldn't.

It's a bit of a joke between us. He says I'm the only
person who sees him without make-up. But there's truth in
that.

Oliver says it's not surprising either. He says that's what I'm like. I spend my days cleaning the gook off pictures, so naturally I do with him too. 'Spit and rub,' he says. 'No harsh solvents necessary. Just spit and rub, and soon you're down to the real Oliver.'

And what's that like? Gentle, truthful, not very sure of himself, a bit lazy and very sexy. You can't see that? Give him time.

Now I'm sounding like my mother.

... (f e m a l e , b e t w e e n 25 a n d 35)   If you ask me, there's a simple explanation. Maybe not simple, actually, but I've come across it before. The point is . . .

What? What did you say? You want my credentials. YOU want MY credentials? Look, if anyone's got to provide documentation it should be you. What have *you* done to qualify for *my* opinions? What's your authority, incidentally? Just getting this far doesn't allow you to come on like the Old Bill.

You'd *believe* me more? Look, as far as I'm concerned it's a cream bun to a twopenny fuck whether or not you believe me. I'm giving you an opinion, not an autobiography, so if you don't like the deal, stroll on stranger. In any case I'm not hanging around, so there's no need to come the old-fashioned stuff with me. I understand, sure I do. You want to know whether I'm Ginny the genial GP, Harriet the haughty Harley Street headshrinker, Rachael the raunchy rock star or Nathalie the nuzzling night-nurse. My credibility depends upon my professional or social position. Well, excuse me. Or rather, fuck off. And if you desperately crave an identity, I'll give you one. Maybe I'm not really a girl after all, I just look this way. Perhaps I went to the universities of Casablanca and Copacabana. Postgraduate work in the Bois de Boulogne.

OK, I'm sorry. You just got on my wick. Also, you caught me in a bad mood. (No, *that's* none of your business, either.) Christ, look, I'll just tell you what I think and then I'll fuck off myself. You can make up your own mind. I'm not exactly flavour of the month around here at the moment, so you won't be seeing me after this.

And of course I'm not a transsexual. You can ask Stuart if you like, he'll confirm it, he's seen the evidence. Sorry, shouldn't laugh at my own jokes, it's just that you seem so disapproving. OK, look, I know those two boys from way back. I remember Oliver when his idea of opera was Dusty Springfield coming out of both speakers in the back of a Cortina. I remember Stuart when he wore glasses with bits of elastic wire round the ears. I remember Oliver in string vests and Hush Puppies, Stuart when he used to put dry shampoo on his hair. I've been to bed with Stuart (sorry: no press release) and I've also turned down Ollie for that matter. *Those* are my credentials. Plus having Stuart bend my ear about the whole story over little half-secret lunches and dinners for the past weeks and months. At first, to be honest, I thought he was after something else. Yeah, Miss Mugg all over again, I know, story of my life. I thought Stuart wanted to see *me*. Pretty stupid, I admit. He just wanted a fucking great ear to pour his troubles into. I sat there and he'd never once ask what I'd been up to, and then at the end of the evening he'd apologise for going on so much about his own life, and then we'd meet again and he'd do exactly the same. He's obsessed, that guy, to put it mildly, and I don't need it. I really don't need it, not at this point in my life. Another reason for getting out of all this.

I think Oliver is queer for Stuart. I've always felt that. I don't know how queer he is generally, but I'd say he's queer for Stuart. That's why he's always put Stuart down, laughing at how shabby and boring he is. He puts Stuart down so that neither of them will have to admit what's always been there, what might be there if they didn't play the game of Stuart being shabby and boring and such an unlikely companion for flash Oliver.

OK, you'd got there already. I'm not so surprised. But the thing I've got to say, the only thing really, is this. The *reason* Oliver wants to fuck Gillian is because it's the nearest he can ever get to fucking Stuart. OK? You read me? Harriet the haughty Harley Street headshrinker would call it by some proper name, but I'm not her. I just believe that for Oliver, fucking Gillian is a way of fucking Stuart.

Think about it. I'm off now. You won't be seeing me again, not unless there's a real turn-up for the book.

S t u a r t   Oh no. Not Val. Spare me Val. Spare yourselves Val. We really don't need her around. She's trouble. Trouble with a T, as Oliver used to put it.

She's the one who wouldn't tell you her name (what is it these people have about names?). I knew her a long time ago, as no doubt she's told you. Have you noticed that when anyone says they've known a person for a really long time, it almost always means they're going to say something nasty about them? Oh no, you don't know them *really*, not like

I do, why *I* remember . . .

Val's big line about me is that she knew me when I used dry shampoo on my hair, a million years ago. Now, let's get this straight, if you can bear a little tedium. Once, many years ago, someone, one person, once, told me that there was this powder stuff which you squirted on your hair between wet washes and you rubbed it in then brushed it out and it looked as if you've washed your hair. All right? So I bought some – this, I have to point out in my defence, was after I'd read somewhere that wet-washing your hair too often could be bad for it – and I used it one evening for the first and only time and was having a drink in a pub when this incredible screech comes from behind me. 'Stu, you've got *terrible* dandruff!' – and it was Val of course, thank you very much, always one to put you at your ease. And since I've never had dandruff, I felt my hair and then said, 'It's dry shampoo,' whereupon Val informed the whole pub that it wasn't dandruff but dry shampoo and what on earth was that and so on and so on. Not surprisingly, in view of this incident, when I got home I threw away my little puffer-tube of dry shampoo and have never used it from that day to this.

She insists on having a claim on you, that girl. Or rather, woman. She's 31, as I expect she didn't tell you, and after a glittering career selling cut-price holidays is now working as office manager in a small printing firm off Oxford Street. The sort that does party invitations and has a couple of photocopiers in the front, only one of which ever works. I don't say this to put her down, you understand, but merely to dispel any Woman of Mystery stuff she may have tried on you. This is who you're dealing with. Val from Pronto Printa.

O l i v e r   She *what?* She said *that?* It's outrageous, it's
scurrile, it's the dreariest *mensonge* she could have thought
up. That girl is trouble. Trouble with a T and that rhymes
with B and that stands for Bitch.

She turned me down in the matter of rumpy pumpy? *She*
turned *me* down, right? Project, therefore, on to that curvous
screen inside your forehead the following animated pictures,
and press your pinkie on the Dolby switch lest subtleties of
dialogue evade you. Once upon a sunbeam, Oliver, despite
vociferous New Year's Resolutions to the contrary, finds
himself yet again at one of those slovenly events attend-
ed by lumpen frolickers bearing miniature beer-kegs under
their arms, where all the girls ferociously inhale Silk Cut as
if beneficial to health (I speak as no priggish reformee – but
if you're going to smoke, *smoke*), and where you fear that at
any moment you will be seized from behind by some chintzy
pair of hands seeking to enlist you in that never-fail lithium-
inducer, the drabble-tailed conga. It was – you've guessed! –
a party.

As I recall, Stuart had begged me into attendance, in
picayune exchange, no doubt, for all those lustrous double-
dates into which I had led the plumply quivering one. Steering
my way between pipkins of Old Skullsplitter and opaque
palm-tree-bedecked bottles of liver-lancing Caribbean spirit, I
settled down beside a methuselah of Soave in some half-hearted
attempt to get pissed out of my noddle. I was drinking the
stuff through a twirly-whirly party straw and making quite
good headway when dread hands clamped themselves on my
shoulders.

'Eheu, the gout!' I cried, fearing involvement in the most

suburban of bacchanales. For the frenzy of the dance was not upon me that evening.

'Ollie, you've been avoiding me,' said the Hands, where-upon the Bum attempted a vertical landing on the arm of my chair, a manoeuvre beyond the piloting skills of the deciduous Val, who cascaded therefrom into my lap.

There passed between us over the next few minutes one of those routine flows of courtliness and badinage, but only the most inventive of text-scourers, only the most brusque denier of intentionality, would have construed the exchange as indicating either 1) that I preferred the company of Val to that of the gallon of Italian white; or 2) that I would for a moment have deprived my friend Stuart of what the young folk nowadays – no doubt unconsciously evoking the camel-hump of desire, the oasis of slaked thirst – oft refer to as 'his date'.

So we parted, on civil terms as I understood it, she to the conga and I to svelte reverie. Without so much as a *boff de politesse*.

Val   There are two types of men who slag you off, I find: the ones you've slept with, and the ones you haven't.

Stuart and I were having an affair and Oliver tried to get off with me. Stuart married that boring little goodie-goodie wife of his and Oliver got off with her. Is this a pattern or isn't it?

What bugs Stuart is that I spotted his dry shampoo, and what bugs Oliver is that I wasn't ready to leap into bed with him. Now don't you find that odd? I mean, odd that this is what bugs them? Neither of them turns a hair at the idea that Oliver's fucking Gillian because what he really wants to do is fuck Stuart. What do you make of that?

And if I were you I'd take a closer look at Gillian. Isn't she just a heroine, isn't she such a little *coper*? Daddy runs off with his bit of gym-slip and Gillie heroically survives. She even comforts her grieving mother. How unselfish, how grown-up. Next Gillian gets trapped in a Love Triangle and guess which of the three comes out the best? Well, it's Little Miss Who. Caught in the middle and still keeping her head above water while doing the right thing – which means shredding Stuart and keeping Oliver on a string.

She tells Stuart (who tells me) that some things – like seducing your husband's best friend – 'just happen', and you have to do your best from there on in. Well, that's an easy theory, isn't it? Listen, nothing 'just happens', especially not in a situation like this. What those two boys don't realise is that it's *all about Gillian*. The quiet sensible ones who claim that things 'just happen' to them are the real manipulators. Stuart's eating guilt already by the way, which isn't a bad achievement, is it?

Oh and why did she give up wanting to be a social worker? Was she too fucking sensitive to the pain of the world? Wrong way round: if you ask me, the pain of the world wasn't sensitive enough to *her*. All those damaged people and fucked-up families didn't appreciate the astonishing privilege they were being granted of having their troubles treated by Miss Florence Nightingale herself.

And another question. When do you think she decided to make a play for Oliver? I mean, when *exactly* did she start giving him the come-on without him realising that she was doing it? Because that's her trick. She hasn't been doing it to you, has she?

Oliver   Well, we are playing rough, aren't we? And the virtuous Val presenting herself like Susannah, she who suffered from the horny-pawed Elders. Well permit me to blow off a little at that thought. If Val ever found herself spied upon in her nakedness by a couple of respectable dotards, they'd both be in a necklock before they could count her moles and she'd be charging them a tenner a grope.

I expect brief acquaintance makes you underestimate the pungent earthiness of the female witness before you. If Herod's troops were on a house-to-house search for ambiguity they would not sojourn long at La Maison de Val. She is the type of being for whom the phrase 'Would you like to come in for coffee?' is gnomic to the point of incomprehensibility, and who would find the apothegm 'Is that a pine-cone in your pocket?' worthy of the Tantric masters. So Ollie might not be ungallant if he still retained a vivid memory of exactly who tried to get off with whom at that party.

And in punishment for my shrinkingness before her gummed palms (although I confess that chivalry towards Stuart was laggardly as a motive, coming a long way second to nerves, good taste, aesthetic considerations, *und so weiter*), Val announces to you out of the cerulean that I have biological designs – had, have, will have – upon the tapir-like form of Stu-baby, and that spurned in my Uranian ambitions I squander my seed upon the most congruent surrogate I can find, namely Gill.

Now, I have to point out that anyone whose cerebral cortex indicated Gillian as an erotic substitute for Stuart would be advised to call the padded van immediately. I further wish to note that your informant Val is a dedicated habituée of that fetid compartment of the local bookshop which ought to be called Self-Pity but instead is mysteriously labelled Self-Help. Apart from the telephone directory and the A–Z, Val's *petite* library consists of works designed to console and inflate her ego: such titles as *Life Can Be A Real Bitch Even To The Best People*, *Look Yourself In The Mirror And Say Howdy*, and *Life Is A Conga: Join In The Shuffle!* Translating the dank imponderables of the human spirit into a one-bite intellectual snack for the brain-dead: this is what your informant relishes.

Now listen: were it by any chance the case that Oliver's radiant sexuality occasionally put aside the workaday, and were his heliotropic gaze to turn towards Stoke Newington's unlikely Ganymede, then, to enlist a vernacular which my accuser herself will be able to grasp, *I wouldn't have any trouble there, mate.* The need for some carnal deputy would simply not arise.

S t u a r t   This isn't anything to do with anything. It's not even a side-issue. OK, I bent Val's ear a couple of times, I thought she was a friend, I thought that's what friends were for. Suddenly it's a crime to talk about one's problems and Oliver is some delinquent homosexual who's always secretly been after me. Now I think a number of bad things about this ex-friend, but not that. The only thing to do with mud is ignore it, otherwise it sticks.

For God's sake let's get on with the story.

V a l　　I see. Oliver says that of course he isn't queer (what on earth could have given anyone that idea?), but that if he were, he wouldn't have any trouble getting his leg over his best friend. And Stuart, despite being probably the most boringly conventional person it's ever been my misfortune to get entangled with, isn't at all surprised let alone alarmed by my psychological insight. All he wishes to say is No Comment. Members of the jury, I rest my case. Or rather, I'll make it clearer. I think they're both in this together.

G i l l i a n　　Most divorce petitions granted to women since 1973 have been on the grounds of unreasonable behaviour by the husband. Examples of unreasonable behaviour are: violence, excessive drinking, excessive gambling or general financial irresponsibility and a refusal to have sex.

The word they use in legal language when you ask for a divorce is *pray*. The petitioner *prays* that the marriage be dissolved.

O l i v e r　　And another thing. She likes to pretend that Val is short for the *éclat*-lacking but perfectly reasonable *prénom* Valerie. She reportedly subscribes her halting inter-departmental memos and amatory communications thus. But you can't even trust her on this matter. Val – and this is a detail you might care to savour – is short for Valda.

Stuart   Now this is what I call subtle, this is what I call dropping a delicate hint. What do I find casually lying on the table when I come home to my own house? One of those How-to books. Only this one is called *How to* ... *Survive Divorce*. It is subtitled *A Handbook for Singles and Couples.* Is that what I'll be? Is that what they're planning to make me into? A 'single'?

Did you know that since 1973 the principal reason for men divorcing women in English courts of law was because of the adultery of the wife? What does that tell you about women, I ask myself. Whereas the contrary isn't the case. Adultery by the man is not a principal reason for women seeking divorce. Rather the opposite. Getting pissed and refusing to have sex seems to be one of the grounds on which women frequently get rid of their partners.

There was one sentence in the book that I liked. Do you know how much solicitors cost? I didn't either. In the provinces it's anything upwards of £40 an hour (plus VAT). In London it's from £60 to £70 an hour (plus VAT) while posh firms charge £150 an hour or more (plus VAT). So the chap who wrote this book concludes: 'Clearly, with such charges involved, it may be cheaper to replace many minor items (a table, a chair, a set of glasses or whatever) than to face a legal bill for the fight.' Yes, that sounds very sensible. Of course I could just break this glass I'm holding in my hand, plus the other five over there on the sideboard, that way we wouldn't have any trouble over the division of the spoils. I've never liked them much anyway. They came from my wife's snooty mother.

If I just said No I won't, I haven't done anything wrong, I won't give you a divorce, you can't prove anything against me and in any case I shouldn't think 'violence' covers head-butting your wife's lover, that can't be grounds I wouldn't have thought, if I just said No and stuck my heels in, do you know what she'd have to do? She'd have to move out and wouldn't be able to get a divorce for five years.

Do you think that would fuck them up?

I mean, look at these glasses. You may be able to drink Pernod out of them, but not whisky. It would indeed be cheaper to replace such minor items rather than face a legal bill for the fight. She can have them – all except this one, whoops, it just slipped off the arm of my chair, didn't it? Just slipped off, jumped six feet through the air and smashed in the fireplace. You'll be a witness to that, won't you?

Or perhaps it wouldn't make any difference.

13: What I Think

Stuart I loved her. My love made her more loveable. He saw that. He'd fucked up his own life, so he stole mine. The premises were totally destroyed by a ZEPPELIN RAID.

Gillian I loved Stuart. Now I love Oliver. Everyone got hurt. Of course I feel guilty. What would you have done?

Oliver Oh God, poor old Ollie, up to his mucous membrane in a tub of *merde*, how crepuscular, how inspissated, how uncheerful ... No, actually, that's not what I think. What I think is this. I love Gillian, she loves me. That's the starting-point, everything follows from that. *I fell* *in love.* And love operates on market forces, a point I tried to get across to Stuart, though probably not very well, and in any case I could hardly expect him to see it objectively. One person's happiness is often built upon another person's unhappiness, that's the way of the world. It's tough, and I'm sorry as hell it had to be Stuart. I've probably lost a friend, my oldest friend. But I had no choice, not really. No-one ever does, not without being a completely different person. Blame whoever invented the universe if you want to blame someone, but don't blame me.

Another thing I think: why is everyone always on the side of the fucking tortoise? Let's hear it for the hare for a change.

And yes, I do know I've just said *crepuscular* again.

14: Now There's One Cigarette in the Ashtray

Stuart   I'm sorry. I really am. I know I don't come out of this next bit particularly well.

He came to mine. Why shouldn't I go to his?

No, that's not good enough.

Why did I do it? Was I trying to hang on, or trying to let go? Neither, both?

Hanging on: because I thought she might change her mind if she saw me?

Letting go: like not asking for the blindfold at execution; like turning your head so that you can watch the guillotine blade fall?

And that business with the cigarettes. Just chance, I know, just an accident. But that made it all worse, because the whole thing has been one ghastly accident, like a swerving lorry that

smashes across the motorway barrier and pulps your car. And
I was just sitting there, and I put my cigarette into one of
the little grooves in the ashtray, and then I noticed there
was another cigarette in one of the other grooves already. I
was so upset I must have lit another after putting down the
previous one. And *then* I noticed that there was a stub in the
ashtray as well. Three cigarettes in the ashtray – two of them
burning and one stubbed out. How could anyone stand that?
Can you imagine the pain I felt? No, of course not. You can't
feel someone else's pain, that's the problem. That's always the
problem, the whole world's problem. If only we could learn to
feel someone else's pain . . .

I'm sorry, I truly am. How can I apologise?

I'll have to think of a way.

G i l l i a n   It's Stuart's face I'll never forget. He looked
like a clown, a turnip head, a Hallowe'en mask. Yes, that's
right, one of those pumpkins you get at Hallowe'en with an
artificial smile cut into it, and some false, flickering, ghostly
light beaming out through the eyes. That's what Stuart looked
like. I was the only person to see him, I think, and the sight will
be with me forever. I screamed, Stuart disappeared, everyone
looked round, there was nothing but an empty stage.

I stayed with Maman the night before the wedding. It
was Oliver's idea. When he made the suggestion I assumed
he thought I might need a bit of help getting through. But
it wasn't really that at all. It was something about doing the
whole thing properly. He's quite old-fashioned in some ways,
Oliver. I was to be the child leaving the parents' house for that

holy trip to the church. Except that I was scarcely the virgin bride in white clutching the arm of her father.

I got to Maman at 7.00 in the evening the night before my second wedding day. We were both being consciously careful. She settled me down with a cup of coffee and made me put my feet up as if I were already pregnant. Then she picked up my case and went off to unpack it, which made me feel even more as if I'd just come into hospital. I sat there thinking, I hope she doesn't give me any advice, I don't think I could stand it. What's done is done, and what's about to be done can't be changed now. So, let's just be quiet, and watch some rubbish on television, and not talk about anything important.

But – mothers and daughters, mothers and daughters. Approximately ninety seconds later she was back in the room holding up my suit. There was a smile on her face as if I'd suddenly gone senile and needed treating with pitying affection.

'Darling, you packed the wrong clothes.'

I looked up. 'No, Maman.'

'But darling, this *is* the suit I bought you?'

'Yes.' Yes, you know it is. Why do parents go on like prosecuting lawyers, checking the most obvious facts?

'You are proposing to wear *this* tomorrow?'

'Yes, Maman.'

Whereupon the deluge. She started off in French, which is what she does when she's built up a head of steam and needs to let it off. Then she calmed down a little and switched back to English. Her basic line was that I'd clearly taken leave of my senses. Only a seriously disturbed person would dream of getting married twice in the same dress. It offended against good taste, good manners, good dress sense, the Church, everyone present at both ceremonies (though mainly her), fate, luck, world history, and a few other things and people.

'Oliver wanted me to wear it.'

'May I ask why?'

'He said he fell in love with me when I was wearing it.'

Outburst number two. Scandalous, ought to be ashamed, etc. Asking for trouble, etc. Can get married without your mother if that's what you're planning to get married in, etc. It lasted an hour or so, and I ended up handing over the key to my flat. She went off with the suit over her outstretched arm as if it had a dose of radiation.

She returned with a couple of substitutes, which I looked at with indifference.

'You choose, Maman.' I didn't want to fight. Tomorrow wasn't going to be easy, I just hoped one person would be satisfied. But no, it wasn't as simple as that. She wanted me to try on both alternatives. In order to be forgiven my enormous *faux pas*, I was expected to behave like a model. It was ridiculous. I tried them both on.

'Now you choose, Maman.' But that still wasn't good enough. *I* must choose, *I* must have opinions. I didn't have an opinion. I didn't have a second choice, I really didn't. It's like saying, Look, Gill, I'm afraid you can't marry Oliver tomorrow, that's out, so who would you like to marry instead? This one or that one?

When I told her this she didn't appreciate the comparison. She thought it in bad taste. Oh well. When I married Stuart I was encouraged only to think of myself. This is *your* day, Gillian, people said. It's your big day. Now I'm marrying Oliver and suddenly it's everyone else's day. Oliver insists on a church wedding which I don't want. Maman insists on a dress which I don't want.

I woke up still being niggled at by dreams. I was writing my name in the sand except it wasn't my name; Oliver started rubbing it out with his foot and Stuart burst into tears. Maman was standing there on the beach, wearing my green wedding suit, looking neither approving nor disapproving. Just waiting. Waiting. If we wait long enough anything and everything will go wrong and you'll be proved right, Maman. But where's the virtue in that?

When we got to the church Oliver was very jumpy. At least we didn't have to process down the aisle: there were only ten of us, and the vicar decided just to gather us at the altar. But the moment we started assembling I could see there was something up.

'I'm sorry,' I said to Oliver. 'She just wouldn't listen to reason.'

He didn't seem to understand. He kept looking over my shoulder towards the church door.

'The dress,' I said, 'I'm sorry about the dress.' It was bright yellow, an optimistic colour as Maman put it, and you would hardly have expected Oliver not to notice the change.

'You look like a jewel,' he said, though his eyes weren't on me.

I wore the wrong colours to both my weddings. I should have been wearing silly optimistic yellow at my first wedding, and cautious pale green at my second.

'And all my worldly goods I with thee share.' That's what I promised. We'd argued about it beforehand. The usual argument. Oliver wanted to have 'With all my worldly goods I thee endow.' He said it was what he felt, that everything he had was mine, that the language embodied a state of soul, that *share* was mean-spirited and *endow* poetic. I said this was the trouble. If you're making a vow it ought to mean something precise. If he endowed me with his worldly goods and I endowed him with mine, then what it meant was that we swapped what we owned, and swapping my mortgaged flat for his rented room didn't seem to me to be what marriage vows were about and besides, to be frank, if we swapped goods, I'd be the loser. He said that was ungenerous as well as literal minded, and of course we were going to share everything with each other anyway, but couldn't we still say endow. What, he argued, could more accurately define the difference between my two husbands than the words *share* and *endow*. Stuart would want to do a deal, whereas he, Oliver, wanted entire surrender. I said if he remembered Stuart and I had got married in a register office and didn't say either *endow* or *share*.

So Oliver went to the vicar and asked if a compromise were possible: if he could say endow and I could say share. The vicar said that wasn't on.

'And all my worldly goods I with thee *share*.' Oliver emphasised the verb, wanting people to know he didn't approve of the wording. The trouble was, it sounded as if he was complaining about having to give me anything. I told him this as we stood outside the church while Maman took photographs.

'All my worldly goods I thee do rent,' he replied. He seemed more relaxed now. 'All my worldly goods I thee do lend. All my worldly goods except for those I really want. All my worldly goods but I need a receipt . . .' and so on.

Once Oliver gets going like this it's best just to let him run on and on. Have you seen those new dog leads? The ones on a big reel which simply unwind for hundreds of feet if the dog suddenly takes off, and then wind back when the dog waits for you? That's what I think of when Ollie goes off on a riff like that. He's like a big dog. But he'll wait at the corner for you to catch up and give him a pat.

'And all my restaurant bills I with thee *share*.' We drove a couple of miles to a nice place which Ollie had chosen. We had a long table at the back. The manager had put lots of red roses in front of my place which I thought was very kind of him even if Ollie declared in a stage whisper that red roses were a bit naff. We sat down and had a glass of champagne and got through all that giggly talk about who'd been stuck in a traffic jam on the way, and how the vicar had seemed really interested even though he'd scarcely met me or Oliver before, and how we hadn't fluffed our lines, and how happy I looked. 'Any advance on *happy*?' said Ollie and he was off again. 'Do I hear radiant? Yes, I have radiant here on my left. Now, any advance on radiant? Beautiful? Do I have beautiful? thank you, sir. Now do I hear magnificent anywhere? Spectacular? Sensational? It's with beautiful on my right at the moment . . . Beautiful . . . beautiful . . . I have spectacular in front of me. Spectacular with me . . . are you all done at spectacular? Sold to the auctioneer, bought in by Ollie . . .' then he banged down a pepper-grinder like a gavel and kissed me to applause.

The first course came, and I felt Oliver wasn't hearing something I was saying, so I followed his glance, and there, sitting at a table by himself, not even looking at us, quietly reading a book, was Stuart.

Then it all started to go wrong, and I've just tried to wipe the rest from my memory, what we ate and what was said and how we all pretended nothing was really happening. But I can't wipe out the end of it, Stuart's face suddenly appearing like that over the top of the tablecloth and staring at me with a horrible grin and a ghostly light in his eyes. A Hallowe'en pumpkin come to life. I screamed. Not that it was frightening, really. It was just so truly sad I couldn't bear it.

O l i v e r Bastard. You fat little bank-wank turd-eating bastard. After all I've done for you over years and years. Who made you into a vaguely acceptable human being in the first place? Who got arm-ache sandpapering your rough patches? Who introduced you to girls, taught you how to hold a knife and fork, was your bloody *friend*? And what do I get in return? You fuck up my wedding, you fuck up the best day of my life. Cheap, vulgar, selfish revenge, that's all it was, though no doubt in your earth-closet of a soul you transmuted the motive into something vaguely noble, even judicial. Well, let me just tell you this, my steatopygous ex-mucker: if you come nosing around again you will be my ex-mucker in more than one sense. I'll have you eating broken glass for a week, don't let there be any ambiguity about that. Don't you misread Oliver for a moment. There is violence in this supposedly tender heart of mine.

I should have had you arrested the moment I spotted you. Got you locked up on some holding charge, like loitering with intent or despoiling the landscape or being a whining bore. Take this man into custody, officer, he's just not entertaining any more, he's simply stopped being *fun*. God I jest, it's always been my weakness, but if I didn't jest I'd have to come round and cut off your tufted ears and shove them down your throat and make you eat your antique spectacles for pudding.

The day had all been going so well until I saw you across the road trying to appear inconspicuous by stamping the pathway metronomically as if on sentry duty, smoking like some Arnold Bennett chimney and casting fetid glances at the church. It was apparent that some item of duncical knavery was afoot, so adjusting my white carnation with its faint blush of green I cut across the carcinogenic thoroughfare and accosted you.

'I'm coming to the wedding,' you said. I corrected this unlikely intention.

'You came to mine,' continued the whinge, 'so I'm coming to yours.'

I explained the divergence of etiquette that such a plan entailed, namely that in the moderately evolved society known as the United Kingdom of Great Britain and Northern Ireland one did not, on the whole, permit oneself to attend formal ceremonies to which one had not been invited. When you queried this arcane piece of protocol I urged you, in the nicest possible way, to bugger off instanter and preferably throw yourself beneath a double-decker in the process.

I can't say I put entire confidence in your apparent departure, and kept a weather eye on the church door as we stood there waiting for curtain-up from the vic. At any moment I thought the oaken portal might be thrust aside to reveal your unwelcome visage. Even once the conjoining was under way, I half expected that when we came to the bit about anyone present giving a shout if there was any let or hindrance or just impediment to my being allowed to unleash corporeal fury upon the fair Gill, you might pop up from some umbrageous segment of the kirk and register a quailing objection. But you didn't, and we romped playfully through the vows. I even had time to give an ironic accent to that crappy bit of the service in which you promise to 'share' your worldly goods with your partner. For centuries everyone has always 'endowed' his partner with his worldly goods – here, have the lot, what's mine is yours – and that, it seems to me, conveys the wholeheartedness central to the spirit of matrimony, encapsulates the quiddity of the biz. But not any more. The lawyers and the accountants have got at everything. I was a touch *bouleversé* when Gillian insisted upon *share*, and found our discussion of it all a trifle demeaning, as if I were planning to hot-foot it from the temple and immediately put my half of Gillian's flat on the market. Graciously I acceded to her whim in the matter. There is a zephyr of Mme Dragon about my bride, as you may have remarked.

In truth, it was part of a mildly grubby trade-off. I wanted a church wedding, whereas Gill saw even less point this time round than before. So I got to choose the theatre, and she was allowed to launder the script. She also, I can avow, squared the padre. Not every house of worship, desperate for custom though you might expect them to be nowadays, welcomes the nuptials of a fallen woman like Gillian. I myself did the rounds of a couple of likely basilicas and received a distinctly dusty answer. So Gillian went off and talked one of the recalcitrant sky-pilots down. Such an internuncio, that girl. Compare the way she persuaded Stuart to act the officer and gentleman despite historic evidence to the contrary. At first he behaved like a proper little caveperson whenever the D-word was mentioned; but Gillian coaxed him into concord. This is not a passage of world history I care to recall in much detail, incidentally. Gillian still seeing her First Husband overmuch. Gillian retaining her studio in FH's house even after she had left FH. Oliver banned from visiting the studio. Oliver, in fact, obliged *pro tem* to opt for quietism. Not so much a back seat as stuffed in the boot with only the spare tyre and an outdated road atlas for company.

But that time ended. Reversibility – lustrous watchword of my wife's profession – was effected in the domestic sphere. Gillian and Oliver became a single taxable unit and the spectre of time-share in Marbella was finally, utterly banished. The hawthorn tree beside the lych-gate was chivvied by the wind into casting its gentle confetti – none of that stuff from a box, *please* – and *la belle-mère* did the full Cartier-Bresson once I'd persuaded her that according to the photographic pioneers the instrument did on the whole work better with the lens-cap removed. Then we decamped in high humour to Al Giardinetto, and I promised Gillian not to call the manager Al, because frankly nowadays that joke was beginning to amuse only me.

The *prosecco* was lolling in the ice-buckets. This was to be a memorable meal, you understand, not a credit-card piss-up – would you order French champagne in an Italian restaurant? We loitered conversationally over the pastor's eccentricities and the vagaries – *vagari*, Latin, to wander – of the one-way system leading to Al's. Then the first course of *spaghetti neri alle vongole* arrived, and we hurdled with a mere jest the objection that Ollie's choice had a more funereal than nuptial aspect to it – 'Maman,' I said (for I had decreed this solution to the vocative problem), 'Maman, do not forget that at Breton weddings they used to drape the church in black.' In any case, as soon as the fork transported this *primo piatto* to the mouth all discord faded. I began to suck in happiness like a long, flexible, infrangible strand of pasta. And then I spotted the little bastard.

Let me set the scene. There were ten of us (who? oh, just a few hand-picked *amici* and *cognoscenti*) at the back of the restaurant, at a long table in a slight alcove – a touch Last Supper after Veronese – while below the salt a raggle-taggle of lunchers did their best to feign polite lack of interest in the jocund wedding party. (Oh, how English. *Don't* intrude on someone else's joy, don't toast them across the restaurant, just pretend *nobody's* got married unless they make too much noise and then you can *complain*. . . .) So I glanced around the discreetly downcast faces and what, brazenly opposite us, did I spy? The tactful First Husband, sitting all alone, pretending to read a book. A droll gambit for a start. Stuart reading a *book*? He'd have been much better camouflaged standing on his chair and waving at us.

I rose lightly from my place, despite a restraining bridal hand, went across to my new wife's ex, and amiably instructed him to hop it. He wouldn't look me in the face. He kept his eyes on his predictable lasagne which he'd been ineffectually torturing with a fork.

'It's a public place,' he replied feebly.

'That's why I'm asking you to vacate it,' I replied. 'If it were a private place I wouldn't do you the courtesy of language. You'd be on the pavement in several portions by now. You'd be on a skip with the trash.'

Perhaps I was being a trifle noisy, because Dino the manager came across at this point. 'Al,' I said, slipping back into my old joshing ways, 'we have an eyesore here. There is an Accident Black Spot in your trattoria. Kindly remove.'

Do you know, he wouldn't? He refused to kick Stuart out. Even began defending him at one point. Well, rather than disturb the peace any further I returned to my table where the sombre spaghetti tasted like ash in my mouth. I explained the technicality of British restaurant law whereby a dozen happy high-rolling customers are unable to enjoy themselves in peace (talk about siding with the underdog!) and we all resolved to concentrate on the immediate felicity.

'Ah,' I said, turning to Gill, 'I didn't know your second name was Felicity,' and everyone laughed, though it felt to Ollie as if he was labouring uphill in the wrong gear. And despite the resplendent *pesce spada al salmoriglio*, one's attention did keep on returning to the wretched Stuart twitching a podgy finger across the page (definitely not Kafka!) and trying to stop his lasagne-flecked lips from moving as he read. Why is the tongue inescapably drawn to any dental pothole, why does it evade command as it seeks out that patch of roughness and rubs against it like a cow on a post? Stuart was our patch of roughness, our sudden cavity. How could one be truly blithe for all one's surface glee?

I was advised to ignore him. Occupants of other tables began to leave, but this only made my wife's first husband more prominent. A twister of cigarette effluent rose above his table. Smoke-signals from a discarded brave signalling to his lost squaw. I've given up the weed myself. It's a stupid habit, encouraging self-indulgence. But that's just what Stuart needs and wants nowadays – self-indulgence. Eventually there remained in the restaurant only the ten of us (each seated before a flamboyant *dolce*), a late-lingering couple in the window doubtless plotting some itchy passage of *banlieusard* adultery, and Stu. As I got up I noticed him glance nervously at our table and light another cigarette.

I made him sweat a bit by taking a voluminous pee in the crepuscular *gabinetto*, then sauntered back past his table. I had intended merely to glance condescendingly at him, but as I approached he took a pulmon-shuddering drag on his cigarette, looked up quaveringly at me, gazed down at the ashtray, started to lay his fag in one of the notches, eyed me afresh and burst into tears. He just sat there gushing and hissing like a punctured radiator.

'Oh, for Christ's sake, Stu,' I said, trying not to let my irritation show. Then he started mumbling something about cigarettes. Cigarettes this, cigarettes that. I looked down at his ashtray and saw that the hopeless bugger had got *two* burning at the same time. That showed how pissed he was, and also what a desperately *unstylish* smoker he was turning out to be. I mean, a basic element of nicotine panache is available to even the hickest addict if he so seeks.

I reached down and stubbed out one of these two cigarettes he'd got burning – just for something to do, I suppose. Whereupon he looked up wildly and burst into giggles. Then he stopped just as suddenly and started blubbing. A lachrymose Stuart is not a sight I would wish to impose on you. Next he began bawling like a kid that's lost a whole muff of teddies. So I summoned Dino and said What about it now? But Dino appeared to have stiffened against my cause, and came on all dismayingly Latin, as if public despair was part of the attraction of his trattoria and customers actually came there to witness it, as if Stuart was his *star turn*. He actually began comforting the tormented banker, whereupon I merely dropped an order for twelve double grappas *if* he'd got time to break off from his voluntary nursing work, and glided back to our table. And guess what? I was met by a complete frost. Anyone would have thought that *I'd* made him cry. Anyone would have thought that *I* was the one who was wrecking the whole wedding party.

'Bring those bloody grappas, Dino,' I shouted, whereupon half the party including the wretched bride and my bloody mother-in-law informed me that they didn't like grappa. 'What's that got to do with it?' I shouted.

By now things were getting right out of hand. The restaurant staff were clustered round Stuart as if *he*'d first discovered the place rather than me, the nuptial party was throttling back on celebration, the adultery table was candidly staring, the grappas were being costively withheld, and old Ollie was frankly feeling that he was being treated like a three-day-old fish-head. Still, the ingenuity was not yet defunct, and I bullied a waiter into bringing me their largest tablecloth. Two hatstands, resited under protest, a few used carafes as weights, a couple of neat knife-wounds in the cloth, and there we had it: an improvised screen. Gone were the intrusive lovers, gone was the burbling Stuart, and here came the grappas! A tactical triumph for Ollie, who then turned up the anecdotal charm in an attempt to bump-start the party again.

It almost worked. Some of the frost began to melt. Every-one decided they'd better have a final push towards enjoying themselves. I was in the middle of one of my lengthier and droller oral tales when there was a distant sound of a scraping chair. Oh good, I thought, he's finally buggering off. But a mere few seconds later, as I was building to one of my anecdotal crescendi, Gillian screamed. She screamed, then she burst into tears. She looked as if she'd seen a ghost. She was staring at the top of the screen I'd rigged up. What was she looking at? There was only the stippled ceiling beyond. Her tears seemed unstoppable, her ducts pulsed like a severed artery.

No-one wanted to hear the end of my story.

Gillian   A clown. A turnip head. A Hallowe'en mask . . .

15: Tidying Up

Stuart   I'm leaving. That's my lot. There's nothing for me here.

I can't bear three things.

I can't bear that my marriage failed. No, let's get it straight. I can't bear that *I* failed. I suddenly started noticing the way people talk about these things. They say, 'The marriage failed,' they say, 'The marriage broke down.' Oh, it was *the marriage*'s fault, was it? Listen, there's no such thing as 'the marriage', I've decided. There's only you and her. So it's either her fault or your fault. And while at the time I thought it was her fault, now I feel it's mine. I failed her. I failed me. I didn't make her so happy that it was impossible for her to leave. That's what I didn't do. So I failed, and I feel shame about it. Compared to this I don't give a stuff whether or not anyone thinks my prick doesn't work.

I can't bear what happened at the wedding. Her scream still echoes in my brain. I didn't want to spoil things. I just wanted to be there, to watch unseen. It all went wrong. How can I apologise? Only by going away.

I can't bear that they say they want to be my friends. If they don't mean it, it's hypocritical. If they do mean it, it's worse. How can they say a thing like that after all that's happened? I am pardoned for my sins, the colossal impertinence of having for a brief period come between Romeo and Juliet has been forgiven. Well, piss off to both of you. I'm not going to be forgiven like that, and *neither are you*, do you hear? Even if I can't bear it.

So I'm going away.

The only person I'll miss, funnily enough, is Mme Wyatt. She's always been very straight with me from the beginning. I rang her last night to say I was going away and to apologise for how I had behaved at the wedding.

'Don't think about it, Stuart,' she said. 'You may even have helped.'

'What do you mean?'

'Maybe if you start off with a disaster, you aren't tempted to look back and pretend that things were once perfect.'

'You're a philosopher, Mme Wyatt, you know that?'

She laughed in a way I hadn't ever heard her laugh before.

'No, really,' I said, 'you're a wise woman.'

And that, for some reason, made her laugh even more. I suddenly realised she must have been quite a flirt in her younger days.

'Keep in touch, Stuart,' she said.

That was very nice of her, wasn't it? I might just do that.

O l i v e r   Impossible not to clock, *de temps en temps*, the fact that life has its ironic side, isn't it? Here is Stuart the joyful banker (*I Banchieri Giocosi* – why are there so few operas about the trade, I wonder, I wonder), the diminutive yet dogged bulwark of capitalism, the scurrying caresser of market forces, the Mountjoy of the take-over, the legman of buy-in and sell-off. And here am I, credulous liberal who votes with pin and blindfold, tender ringmaster of the arts of peace, one who instinctively supports the weak against the strong, the whale against the all-Nippon fishing fleet, the dank seal-cub against the culling brute in the lumberjack shirt, the rain forest against the under-arm deodorant. And yet, when the purveyors of these rival philosophies direct their attention to matters of love, one of them suddenly believes in protectionism and the Monopolies Commission, while the other asserts the natural wisdom of the free market. Guess which turns out to be which?

And it's also about bonking, too, about rumpy pumpy, about that little prod of extendable tissue which causes so much anxiety. The heart's afflatus, as hymned by minstrels high and low, also leads to fucking, we shouldn't forget that. I must resist the triumphalist tone here (a little anyway), but we shall not fail cautiously to note that when the free marketeer becomes protectionist, perhaps it's because he realises that his *goods don't measure up*. That sometimes merely going *Sh-chug-a-chug* like a shaken box of breakfast cereal does not make the *inamorata* thrum until the sun goes down. That there are times when what is called for is summer lightning across a sub-Saharan sky. Who would opt for the model aeroplane with plastic propellor and wind-up rubber band when there are still shooting stars up there in the heavens? Is not the human race marked out from the lower beasts by the fact that it knows how to *aspire*?

But if one of necessity wields a touch of the seal-clubber when it comes to love, if the Japanese whaler within one must be sent forth across the Southern waters to do his business, this does not entail a continuing brutishness when one returns to port. Poor Stuart – I offer him still the palm of friendship. In fact, I telephoned him. There I was, with the scar from our little *contretemps* still upon my cheek (but that was fine: I was Ollie the Jaunty Duellist rather than Oliver Russell the Semi-Employed Crime Victim), attempting to wheedle him back towards normality.

'Hi, it's Oliver.'

There was a pause whose medium length made it difficult to interpret, followed by a less ambiguous utterance. 'Fuck off, Oliver.'

'Look . . .'

'Fuck off.'

'I can imagine . . .'

'FUCK OFF FUCK OFF FUCK OFF.'

Anyone would have thought that I was ringing to apologise to *him*, that *I* was the one who'd come pestering *his* nuptials. The Ancient Mariner had nothing on Stu, turning up at the church then dogging us to the restaurant. I really should have had him arrested, you know. Officer, bespy thou that antique salt yonder? He's been whingeing on to one and all about downing a seagull. Move him on, would you please, or preferably fix him up with a night in Newgate at Her Majesty's Pleasure.

But I didn't, I was reasonable, and this is the thanks I get. A drip-drip of Fuckoffs like a dosage of Earex. It seemed especially coarse, given that the instrument through which these repeated incitements to departure were conveyed was none other than the matt-black leather-encrusted portable through which I had declared myself to his wife. Had my friend stayed on the line long enough I might have shared this deft irony with him.

Of course, I did not compose Stuart's number – *her* number! all I did was press that sacred ever-remembering 1 upon the dial! – entirely on my own initiative. Sometimes magnanimity requires an *accoucheuse*. Gillian suggested I call.

Don't get the wrong idea about Gillian, by the way. Not that I've any notion of the colour transparency you hold up to the light when dreaming of her. It's just that she's stronger than me. I've always known it.

And I like it. Bind me with silken cords, *please*.

G i l l i a n   Oliver said that Stuart didn't want to talk to him. I tried calling him too. He answered the phone. I said, 'It's Gillian.' There was a sigh, and he put the phone down on me. I can't blame him, can I?

Stuart bought out my share of the house. The division of money and possessions was fair. Do you know what he did, Stuart? It was one of those really surprising things. When we agreed to divorce – when he agreed to let me divorce, to be more accurate – I said something about the way I hated the idea of having lawyers come in and decide who gets what, how it had been painful enough already, but then the lawyers supposedly made it worse by insisting that you fight for every penny. And do you know what Stuart's reaction was? He said, 'Why don't we ask Mme Wyatt to decide?'

'Maman?'

'I'd trust her to be fairer than any lawyer I've met.'

Isn't that rather extraordinary? So she did, and the lawyers were told what we'd agreed. Then the court approved.

Another thing. It wasn't anything to do with sex, the break-up. Whatever anyone might imagine. I'm not going into detail, so I'll just say this. If someone thinks he or she hasn't got love-making completely mastered, then he or she is likely to try harder, isn't he or she? And if on the other hand he or she believes he or she has got the whole thing taped, then he or she might become lazy, even complacent. And so to the person with them, the difference might not seem very great. Especially if what's really important is who they are.

After I moved out, Stuart let me keep on the studio. He wouldn't accept rent either. Oliver didn't like it. He said Stuart might attack me. Well, of course he didn't.

When we were dividing the spoils, Stuart insisted that I keep the glasses Maman gave us. Or what remained of them. There used to be six, now there are only three. It's funny, I don't remember breaking any of them.

M m e W y a t t   I regret the incident with the wedding dress. I had no intention to upset Gillian, but really her idea was absurd. More than absurd, the idea of an imbecile. To marry twice in the same dress – who heard of it? So sometimes it is necessary for a mother to behave like a mother.

The wedding was a *disaster*. It is impossible to exaggerate how much everything went wrong. I could not avoid noticing that the champagne did not come from Champagne. We began with some black food that would have been more appropriate for a funeral. There was that difficulty with Stuart. All a disaster. And finally Oliver insists on ordering for us some Italian *digestif* of the sort which you would perhaps rub on the chest of a sick child. But put it inside oneself? Never. All a disaster, as I say.

V a l   I give it a year. No, seriously. I'll put money on it. What d'you fancy? A tenner, fifty, a hundred? I give it a year.

Listen, if Stuart, who's all cut out to be a husband, lasts as short a time as he did with that prim ballcrusher, what chance for Oliver, who's got no money, no prospects and is basically queer? How long will the marriage last once he starts calling her Stuart in bed?

And another thing . . .

O l i v e r   &   S t u a r t   Out.
Get that bitch out of here.
Go on.
Out.
Out.
OUT.

Val   They can't do this to me. *You* can't let them do this to me. I've got just as much right . . .

Oliver & Stuart   OUT. It's her or us. Out, you bitch. OUT. Her or us.

Val   You know this is against all the rules?
    I mean, you realise what you're doing here? You know what the consequences of this are likely to be? Have you thought about them? This is player power. Hey *you* – aren't you meant to be the manager, aren't you meant to *own* the whole fucking team?

Oliver   Have you got a scarf, Stu?

Val   Can't you see what's going on? This is a direct challenge to your authority. Help me. Please. If you help me, I'll tell you about their cocks.

Oliver   I'll hold her, you gag her.

Stuart   Right.

V a l   You're pathetic, you know that? You two.
Pa the tic.
  Stuart . . .
  Ol . . . .

O l i v e r   Woof. That was sport. Valda the Vanquished.
Woof, woof.
  Stuart, look . . .

S t u a r t   NO.

O l i v e r   It was just like old times, wasn't it, that?
  Just like old times. Remember? *Jules et Jim?*

S t u a r t   Fuck off, Oliver.

O l i v e r   When I get your scarf back, shall I send it on?

S t u a r t   Fuck off, Oliver.
  If you open your mouth again, I'll . . .
  Go on, fuck off.

O l i v e r   I've been reading Shostakovich's memoirs. The foregoing histrionics of Valda reminded me of its opening page, on which the composer promises that he will try to tell only the truth. He has lived through many important events and known many outstanding people. He will try to give an honest account of them and not falsify or colour anything: his will be the testimony of an eye-witness. Good. Fair enough. Whereupon this underrated ironist continues, and I quote: 'Of course, we do have the saying, "He lies like an eye-witness." '

That just about sums up Val. She lies like an eye-witness.

Another footnote. Or rather, something Stuart might have wished to discuss had he been in a mood to spare me the time of day. Shostakovich on his opera *Lady Macbeth*: 'It's also about how love could have been if the world weren't full of vile things. It's the vileness that ruins love. And the laws, and properties, and financial worries, and the police state. If conditions had been different, love would have been different.' Of course. Circumstances alter love. And what about extreme circumstances, those of the Stalinist Terror? Shostakovich goes on: 'Everyone seemed worried about what would happen to love. I suppose it will always be like that, it always seems that love's last days are here.'

Imagine that: the death of love. It could happen. I wanted to say to Stuart, you know that PhD I gave you about market forces and love, well I wasn't sure how much I meant it, just a riff, really. Now I realise I was on to something. 'If conditions had been different, love would have been different.' It's true, so true. And how little we reflect upon it. The death of love: it's possible, it's thinkable, I can't bear it. 'Officer Cadet Russell, why do you wish to join the Regiment?' 'I want to make the world safe for love. And I mean it, sir, I mean it!'

Mrs Dyer   I enjoyed having that young man here. Of
course, he told terrible fibs, and I still haven't had the last
two weeks' rent he promised to send on.

He was probably a bit round the bend, if you ask me.
I used to hear him talking to himself in his room. And he
did tell these fibs. I don't think he was really writing for the
films. and he never parked his car in the street. Do you think
he had the AIDS after all? They say it makes people go round
the bend. That could be the explanation. Still, he was a nice
young man.

When he left, he asked if he could cut something off that
tree outside. For a keepsake, he said. He went off with a bit
of monkey-puzzle in his hand.

Gillian   Stuart is going away. I'm sure that's a wise
decision. Sometimes I think we should do the same. Oliver's
always talking about the fresh start he's on the point of making
but we're still both living in the same city, doing the same jobs.
Maybe we should just *go*.

Oliver   The test was negative, of course. I knew it
would be. You weren't actually *worrying* on my behalf, were
you? *Mes excuses*. I'm really touched. Had I realised I'd have
told you as soon as I knew.

M m e   W y a t t   You ask me what I think of them, Stuart
and Oliver, whom I prefer? But I am not Gillian, and that is all
that counts. She said to me, 'I suppose I knew what it was to be
loved. I didn't know what it was like to be adored.' I replied,
'Then why pull such a long face?' As you English say, if you
pull a face, the wind might change.

I suppose also, it never happens quite as you expect. I
have the same prejudices as any mother. When I first met
Stuart, and then afterwards when they married, I was thinking,
Don't you dare to harm my daughter. Stuart would always sit
in front of me as if he was being examined by a doctor or a
schoolmaster or somebody. His shoes were always very well
polished, I remember, and when he thought I was not noticing
he would cast an eye down on them to see that they had not
got scuffed. He was so eager to please, for me to like him. I
found this touching, but of course I resisted it a little. Yes,
you love her now, I can see that, yes you are very polite to
me and polish your shoes, but if you do not mind I will wait
a few years. When Chou En-lai was asked what he thought the
effect of the French Revolution had been on world history, he
replied, 'It is too early to tell.' Well, that is what I thought with
Stuart. I saw him as an honest young man, perhaps a little dull,
who earned enough money to look after Gillian, and that was
a good start. But if I was examining him as he thought, then I
would have come to this judgment: it is too early to tell, come
back in a few years. I am waiting, I am watching. And I never
once asked myself the question the other way round: what if
my daughter does harm to Stuart? So I am not such a wise
woman, you see. I am like those fortresses who have all their
guns pointing to where they think the enemy is coming from,

and are undefended when he arrives by the back door.

And then we have Oliver instead of Stuart, and what do I think about that? Oliver who does not think that polishing his shoes is the best way to persuade me to like him. On the contrary, Oliver behaves as if it was impossible for me not to like him. He behaves as if we have always known one another. He gives me advice about which sort of English fish are best to replace in the *bouillabaisse* the Mediterranean fish I cannot obtain. (He does not ask me first if I like *bouillabaisse*.) He flirts with me, in a certain way, I think. And he does not for a moment allow himself to imagine that I could disapprove of him for having broken up my daughter's marriage. He wants – how can I put this? – he wants me to have a part of his happiness. It is strange, and rather touching.

You know what he said to me the other day? 'Maman,' he said – he has called me that instead of Mme Wyatt ever since he broke up my daughter's marriage, which I find perhaps a little peculiar – 'Maman, why don't we find you a husband?'

Gillian looked at him as if in the circumstances it was probably the worst thing he could have said, and maybe it was but I didn't mind. He said it too in a flirting way, as if he would have suggested himself for the role had he seen me before he had seen my daughter. What a cheek? Yes, but I could hardly dislike him for it.

'I do not think I will marry again,' was all I said, though.

'Un oeuf is enough?' he replied, and started giggling at his own joke. It wasn't even a good joke. Gillian joined in, and laughed more than I knew she could laugh. They forgot I was there, which was a good idea at the moment.

You see, I do not think I will marry again. Oh, I do

not say that I will not fall in love again, but that is another business. Everyone is vulnerable to that, whatever they say, until the day one dies. No, but marriage ... I will tell you the conclusion I came to, after all those years with Gordon, years which despite what you might think were mostly happy; as happy as anybody else, I would say. And my conclusion was this: that as you go on living with someone, you slowly lose the power to make them happy, while your capacity to hurt them remains undiminished. And vice versa, of course.

Not an optimistic view? But one only has a duty to be optimistic in the eyes of others, not for oneself. Ah, you will say – Oliver would certainly say it – that was just with Gordon, he just ground you down, it was not a fair trial, give it another go, love. Well, it is not just from living with Gordon that I decided this: I have eyes for other marriages. And I tell you this in all honesty. There are certain truths which you can live with if they have been demonstrated to you only once. That way they do not oppress you, there is room for an interrogation mark beside them. But if such a truth is demonstrated twice, it will oppress and suffocate. I could not bear for this to be true, twice true. And so I keep my distance from that truth, and from marriage. Un oeuf is enough. And what do you also say? You cannot make an omelette without breaking eggs. So, no omelette for me.

16: *De Consolatione Pecuniae*

S t u a r t   If you ask me — and I have now had time to think about this — love — or what people call love — is just a system for getting people to call you Darling after sex.

I hit a bad time after that Business. I didn't Go to Pieces. I didn't Have a Breakdown. I'm not the sort of person for things like that. I know that I'm probably going to go on, with roughly the same job, and certainly the same personality, and definitely the same name (I'm the one who sticks by his name, remember?) until . . . well, until I give up my job, and old age starts to eat away at my personality, and death finally takes away my name. But the Business changed me. Oh, it didn't Mature Me, it didn't Make Me Grow Up. But it did change me.

You remember about my parents, how I always had the

feeling that I was disappointing them? I thought that was just between parents and children, and if you were lucky you didn't even get it there. Now I think it's general. It's just a question of who does it to whom. For instance, when the Business happened, and we were all of us going through it – I can see that now, it wasn't just me going through it – I used to think that I was disappointing Gillian. I thought, here we go again: I failed my parents in some way they never quite explained to me, and now I'm failing my wife in some new but equally unfathomable way. Then, a bit later, I began to realise that it wasn't *me* who'd disappointed *her*, it was *they* who'd disappointed *me*. My wife let me down, my best friend let me down, it was only my character and my bloody tendency to feel guilt that made me not see this before. *They* let *me* down. And so I formulated a principle. I don't know if you follow rugby, but some years ago there was a famous saying in the game: Get your retaliation in first. And now the way I live my life is according to this principle: Get your disappointment in first. Disappoint them before they disappoint you.

Work helped a lot. At first it was just somewhere to go, something I could still respect. It had its own system, it could go on forever without me; but it let me sit at a screen and deal with it. I was grateful to work, to money, for doing that. I would get miserable, and I would get drunk, of course, and I would get angry, but as soon as I sat down in front of money I felt calmer. And I always paid it respect. I never got drunk the night before coming in to work. I always wore a clean shirt. If I binged it was only on Fridays and Saturdays. For a while it was every Friday and Saturday. But come Monday I was sitting there in a clean shirt with a clear head, talking to money.

And since this was what I did best in my life, I got better at it. Or I got to know more. I was never going to be a high flier, but I am a medium flier. I was never going to take a punt on some high-risk offshore megabuck Saudi whatsit. I was the fellow advising against all this. I was the chap who said not so fast, have we got everything covered, remember what happened to the Second City Bank of Cornbelt. I'm good at saying things like that. We can't all be barrow-boys in sharp suits who coin it when times are good and get burnt out at twenty-five. So when the Bank opened more branches in the States, they sent me along to Washington as a sensible middle-ranking person. That's where I am now.

And money helped too. I showed respect to money, and money paid me back, money helped me. I remember the first time money helped. It wasn't long before my ex-wife and my ex-best-friend inflicted the final, terminal disappointment on me of marrying one another. That was a bad time as you can imagine. It wasn't a period when I could put much trust in people, not over the simplest things. How did I know someone wasn't just waiting for me to become attached to them so that they could stab me with disappointment?

One day, one afternoon to be precise, I decided I was bloody well going to have sex. Apart from everything else she'd done to me, Gillian had put me off sex. I didn't *want* sex, you understand, when I decided to have it. The point was, I was fighting back against what they'd done to me. So I thought, how shall I go about this? And then I remembered that to the outside world I probably looked like a businessman in a suit, and so decided to behave as such people are supposed to behave. It was a Saturday afternoon, and I packed a case, took a cab to a hotel in Bayswater, checked in, went out and bought a magazine of the sort businessmen might buy, and went back to the hotel.

I scanned the ads and eventually settled on an organisation which offered Sophisticated Girls for both Relaxing Massage or Escort Duties, at Your Hotel, Credit Cards Accepted. I paused over the credit card thing. Was this a good idea? I hadn't anticipated it as a possibility – indeed, I'd come equipped with lots of cash. Perhaps they just wanted your credit-card number in order to blackmail you? But I must be one of the few unblackmailable people around now. I don't have any family to hide anything from. And what if the Bank found out? They'd probably only object if I used a credit card they disapproved of, one with an interest rate that cast doubt on my professional competence.

Then, as I made the call, I had a sudden panic. What if they sent a girl who looked like Gillian? That really would have been a kick in the guts. So when they asked if I had any particular sort of escort in mind, I asked if they had an Oriental girl. So they sent Linda. Or they sent a girl who called herself Linda. She cost £100. That was her price, that was what money bought. I'm not going to go into details because I'm not the sort of person who goes into details about that kind of thing, but it was worth every penny. She was very good at what she did. I didn't want sex, as I said, I just decided to have it; but very soon I wanted it as well and was glad I wanted it. After she left I looked at the credit-card slip to see what she'd written in the box headed Quantity and Description. She'd put 'Goods'. Just that. 'Goods'.

Sometimes they put jokey things like 'Servicing Equipment', and sometimes they put nothing, or whatever you ask them to; but I'll always remember that Linda put 'Goods'. It was a transaction, a piece of business, so why not? Since then there've been lots more girls like Linda, some of them also called Linda. There seems to be a certain level of name the girls assume: I've met a lot of Lindas and Kims and Kellys and Lorraines and Linzis. I haven't met many Charlottes and Emmas in this line of work, I can tell you. And another plus for the profession is this: when the girls decide on their names they rarely think that the businessman in the grey suit with the eager credit card wants them to be called Gillian. At least, not Gillian in full. I don't think I could handle that. There was a girl once – in Manchester, I think – who said her name was Gill.

'How do you spell it?' I said. I was pulling my credit card out of my wallet and just froze.

'What d'you mean?' She looked a bit miffed, as if I was giving her some sort of IQ test before engaging her.

'Just how do you spell it – with a J or with a G?'

'J of course.'

Of course.

I like it in America. It suits me being foreign in America. Foreign but English-speaking, that is. And English, too. Americans are very friendly, as we've all been told a million times, and the ones I know are nice to me, but if they look like getting too close and I back off, then they just put it down to my being English. They think I'm just a bit reserved, a bit tight-assed, and that's OK by me. I back off – I get my disappointment in first.

And the girls are good too. The professional ones, I mean.

The Shelleys and the Marlenes. Not a Charlotte or an Emma on this side of the water either. Not in this business. Not a Gillian either. Not in the full form, and with a G, anyway.

Look, you may not like me much now. Perhaps you never did. But that's OK. I'm not in the business of being liked any more. I don't mean I'm planning to be some ferocious mega-tycoon who's always shitty – I'm never deliberately nasty to people, that's not part of my make-up. It's just that it matters far less to me whether or not people like me. I used to do quite a lot to please them, to get approval. Nowadays I find I don't care so much one way or the other. As a small example, I've gone back to glasses. I only started wearing contact lenses because I thought Gillian would like me more that way.

One of the first things people tell you about money is that it's an illusion. It's notional. If you give someone a dollar bill it's not 'worth' a dollar – it's 'worth' a small piece of paper and a small amount of printer's ink – but everyone agrees, everyone subscribes to the illusion that it's worth a dollar, and therefore it is. All the money in the world only means what it does because people subscribe to the same illusion about it. Why gold, why platinum? Because everyone agrees to place this value upon them. And so on.

You can probably see where I'm leading. The other world illusion, the other thing that exists simply because everyone agrees to place a certain value on it, is love. Now you may call me a jaundiced observer, but that's my conclusion. And I've just been pretty close up to it. I've had my nose rubbed in love, thank you very much. I've put my nose as close against love as I put my nose to the screen when I'm talking it over with money. And it seems to me there are parallels to be drawn.

Love is only what people agree exists, what they agree to put a notional value on. Nowadays it's prized as a commodity by almost everyone. Only not by me. If you ask me, I think love is trading artificially high. One of these days the bottom is going to fall out of love.

Oliver used to carry around with him a book called *The Consolations of Philosophy*. 'So, *so* consoling,' he used to coo pretentiously, and give the cover a patronising tap. I never saw him reading it. Perhaps he just liked the title. But I'm the one with the title of today's book, the up-to-date version. It's called 'The Consolations of Money'. And believe me, they work, those consolations.

People find me more interesting now I've got more money. I don't know if I am – I'm probably not – but they find me so. That's a consolation. I like buying things and owning things and throwing them away if I don't like them. I bought a toaster the other day and after a week I didn't like the way it looked so I chucked it out. That's a consolation. I like employing people to do things for me that I don't feel like doing myself – washing the car, cleaning the apartment, doing the shopping. That's a consolation. While I have a lot less money than some of the people I deal with, I have a lot more money than many of the people I deal with. That's a consolation. And if I go on earning at the rate I seem to be doing at the moment and invest wisely, then I shall be able to live comfortably from the time I retire until the time I die. Money, it seems to me, is a good deal more consoling than philosophy when it comes to worrying about that stretch of one's life.

I'm a materialist. What else is there to be, if you're not

a Buddhist monk? The two great creeds that have ruled the world this century – capitalism and communism – are both materialist; one's just better at it than the other, as recent events have proved. Man likes consumer goods, always has, always will. We may as well get used to it. And the love of money isn't the root of all evil, it's just the starting-point of most people's happiness, most people's consolation. It's much more *reliable* than love.

What you see is what you get. What you get is what you pay for. That's the rule in the world of Kim and Kelly and Shelley and Marlene. I don't mean that there aren't cheats. Of course there are, just as there are girls with diseases and girls who turn out to be boys; it's like any other business, there are frauds and bad buys. But go to the right people, pay the right price, and you get what you want. Reliably, professionally. I like the way they have their little codes when they arrive. How can I be of assistance? What do you have in mind? Is there anything special you'd like? No doubt with other customers this leads to prolonged bargaining before the metallic crunch of the credit-card machine they carry in their bag along with contraceptives. But my bargaining is always simple. When they ask me if there's anything special I want, I never bother them with schoolgirl outfits and whips or whatever. I just say that I want them to call me Darling afterwards. Just once, that's all. Nothing more.

I'm not friendless. Don't misjudge me. I go to work, and I work hard, and I earn my money. I live in a nice apartment not too far from Dupont Circle. I have friends, both male and female, with whom I spend time; I get as close to them as I want to, but no closer. Get your disappointment in first. And yes, I've had girlfriends over here. I've been to bed with some of them, and some of them have called me Darling, before, afterwards, during. I like that, of course, but I don't trust it. The only Darling I can trust is a Darling I've paid for.

You see, I don't think of myself as jaundiced or cynical or disillusioned or whatever. I just think of myself as seeing things more clearly now than I did before. Love and money are two great holograms that glitter before us, turning and twisting like real 3-D things. Then you reach out and your hand goes straight through them. I always knew that money was an illusion, but I also knew that even so it had limited powers, and wonderful powers they are. I didn't know love was the same. I didn't know you could put your hand straight through it. Now I do, and I'm wiser.

So you see, in a way I've come round to Oliver's point of view, to what he was insultingly trying to explain to me when we were both drunk and I ended up nutting him. Love operates according to market forces, he said, as a justification for stealing my wife. Now, a bit older and a bit wiser, I'm beginning to agree: love does have many of the same properties as money.

None of this means that I've forgiven the two of them for the Business. It isn't over either, for that matter. It isn't finished yet. I don't know what's to be done, how or when . . . I've got to get it out of my system . . . How?

As I see it, there are two systems. Pay Now, or Pay Later. Pay Now works as I've just described – and works very efficiently, provided you take the normal economic precautions. Pay Later is called love. It doesn't surprise me that on the whole people seem to choose Pay Later. We all like hire purchase. But we rarely read the small print when we make the deal. We never think of the interest rates . . . we never calculate the final cost . . . Give me Pay Now.

Sometimes people say to me, when I explain how I feel about things, Yes, I can see your point of view. It must make things simpler. But the thing about buying sex (we are, of course, usually drunk by the time such levelling takes place), the thing about buying sex — they say authoritatively, never having bought it in their lives — is that whores don't kiss. They say this a little sadly, and thinking fondly of their wives who do kiss (but who? *who else?* I want to ask). I nod, and don't bother to disillusion them. People have such sentimental ideas about hookers. People think they just simulate the act of love, then retire behind a screen of modesty, saving their hearts and their lips for their beloved. Well, some of that may be true. But whores don't kiss? Of course they do. You just have to pay them enough. Think about where else they'll agree to put their lips in exchange for money.

I don't want your pity. I'm wiser than I used to be, and you can't patronise me so easily now. You may not like me (perhaps you never did). But as I say, I'm no longer in the business of being liked.

Money can't buy you love? Oh yes it can. And as I say, love is just a system for getting someone to call you Darling after sex.

17: *Sont fous, les Anglais*

G o r d o n   Gordon's the name. No, no reason why you should. Gordon *Wyatt*. That ring a bell?

I shouldn't be talking to you, I'm sure it's against the rules. After all, you know what you think about me, don't you? Filthy old lecher, seducer of schoolgirls, abandoner of wife and child ... A chap can't expect to get much of a hearing with those labels attached.

Points to make *re* the case of Gordon Wyatt, long ago court-martialled and sent to the salt-mines:

1) She was bags of fun when we met, Marie-Christine. Married her, brought her back to England. She had an affair after we'd been married a year or so. Thought I didn't twig. Course I twigged. Gives a chap a bit of a

jolt, but I got over it. Suspected she had another fling after Gillian was born, not altogether sure. I could have handled that. What I couldn't handle was the way she stopped being fun. Got all sort of middle-aged before her time, had *ideas* about things. Awful. Didn't suit her at all. Kept on being *right*, if you know what I mean.

2) Access to daughter refused by the court on grounds of applicant's delinquency in respect of young women (did they think I'd try and seduce my own daughter, for God's sake?). Subsequent private requests for access always peremptorily denied by Madame. Decision time: do you go on trying to see your child knowing that everything is against you (contempt of court, gentlemen of the law, bailiffs, etc.) and torturing yourself with hope, or do you make a clean break? Ditto, what about the said child: best for her to think there's a Possible Someone out there, or a Definite No-one? Not easy.

3) Main thing to say is, I won't put up with this slander on my wife. My present wife. I didn't 'seduce' her, she didn't do a Lolita act on me. We met (out of school as it happens), and bang, that was that. Nothing to be done. Been in love ever since, never a cross word, two smashing kids. Course it was hard to get a job teaching anywhere else. Made ends meet for a while with some translation work, still do a little. But Christine's become the bread-winner. I'm what they call a 'house-husband' I suppose. Taken to it like a duck to water as well, which would have surprised Madame. To be quite honest, I don't know what women are complaining about. I love being 'stuck at

home', as they say.

Ah, there's the door. Look, I did promise I wouldn't ever go on the record about all this. Christine doesn't really like it. The past is another country and all that. So, mum's the word, if you don't mind. Much obliged. Cheerio, then.

Oliver　　I drive this antique Peugeot 403. Bought it off a peasant who probably fancied himself in a Toyota Land Cruiser. It's a sort of greeny-grey – they don't make colours like that any more, not for cars – and all rounded at the corners. Tiny radiator grille like a gaoler's spyhole. Very retro. Has been known to break down usefully on occasion, as well.

Every morning I climb behind the wheel to the creak of ancient leather and drive up to Toulouse. I motor carefully through the village because of Monsieur Lagisquet's dog. I don't know what brand it is, but its immediate characteristics are medium size, conker-brownness and a raging affability. Its less immediate characteristic was explained to us by Monsieur Lagisquet the first time Gill and I were walking through the village and this four-legged tongue hurled itself upon us. 'Il est sourd,' said the owner, 'il n'entend pas.' A deaf dog. God how sad. Mega-sad. Imagine not being able to hear its master's fluted whistle any more.

So I motor carefully, nodding to the locals like minor British royalty. Past the dusty rhombus which is half village square and half café forecourt, where a couple of senior citizens sip their morning beverage from fat cups bearing the slogan of Choky. Past the racks of Totalgaz outside the *alimentation* and the faded ads painted on the side wall for BRILLIANTINE PARFUMÉE and SUZE. The names, the names! Then past the disused *lavoir* next to the little bridge – *où sont les blanchisseuses d'antan?* – and swing on to the main road by the Cave Coopérative. Like most villages around here, ours has two castles: the old *château fort*, whose walls once ran with blood, and this new one in shiny stainless steel, where the red juice comes from the crushed grape rather than the crushed prisoner. The arts of war and the arts of peace! Architects should make more of the comparison, I feel: the glinting silos of the Cave Coopérative should be topped with satirical pepperpot towers, and trompe-l'oeil arrow-slits might embellish the lustrous verticals.

This is the life, I tend to reflect as I romp through the vineyards. A little Cinsault, a peppering of Mourvèdre, a jolt of Malbec and a stiffy of Tempranillo: mix them up and make them nice, pop goes the weasel. We're VDQS at the moment, but hoping for promotion.

See that little tower over there – the round stone job? A humble store-shed, yet built to resist the lapping of time as well as the boll-weevil. Impressive? Nasalise that air, cop that hanging hawk in the sky. Isn't this the life? Excuse me a mo while I give a royal wave to yonder blue-bibbed workman breast-feeding his shovel. And I was the one who used to be so gloomy about things. I used to say that life was like invading Russia: a flying start, a grim slowing down, a fearful scuffle with General January, then blood on the snow. But now I don't see things like that. There's no reason why the route shouldn't be a sunny back road through a vineyard, is there? Everything's so much more cheerful down here. Maybe it's just as simple as the sun. Do you remember when they discovered the connection between depression and the level of domestic illumination? Bump up your wattage and save on psychiatrist's bills! Why shouldn't it work for the great outdoors as well? The argument from climate certainly applies to Jolly Ollie nowadays.

It's an hour or so up the A61 to Toulouse, with early morning mist steaming off the meadows and lapping round the farmhouses like dry ice. Then I slew the 403 to a stop in the School's courtyard and scatter *bons mots* like sunflower seed among the waiting pupils. They're so well-dressed and . . . well, *pretty*. Boys and girls alike. And they want to learn English! Isn't it amazing? I know the pedagogue is meant to enthuse his charges by an infectious zest for learning and all that, but the principle doesn't apply when faced with a row of damp corn-sacks on a rainy Tuesday off the Edgware Road. Here it's the other way round: they make me want to teach!

And I do, all day. Then a leisurely *coup de rouge* perhaps, with a pupil who has a little trouble getting her mind round the various kinds of past tense (don't we all?), and a sauntering return through the vineyards. From a couple of kilometres away you catch the steel flash of the Cave Coopérative in the clear low sun. I pass my favourite road sign: ROUTE INONDABLE. Such Gallic economy. In England it would be DANGER ROAD LIABLE TO FLOODING. Here, just ROUTE INONDABLE. Then carefully through the village, and into the welcoming arms of wife and child. How she hugs me, the iridescent bambino, little Sal. She clings to me like a wet shower-curtain. Isn't this the life?

Gillian   Now listen to me. To *me*.

I think I had better start with a description of the village in which we live. It's south-east of Toulouse, in the department of the Aude, on the edge of the Minervois, near the Canal du Midi. The village is surrounded by vineyards, although this wasn't always the case. If you drive around here nowadays, you might think this is how it has always been, because most of it looks so old, but that isn't true. Everything changed with the arrival of the railway. Previously, areas like this had to be largely self-sufficient, from an agricultural point of view. So there were sheep for wool, and cattle for milk, goats perhaps, and vegetables and fruit, and – I don't know, probably sunflowers for oil and chick-peas and so on. But the railway changed the economic profile of the region, as it did everywhere, flattened it out. People stopped farming sheep because the wool that came on the railway was cheaper than the wool they could make. Mixed agriculture died out. There's an occasional goat in a back garden, of course, but that's about it. Nowadays the whole region makes wine. So what happens when some other region makes better, cheaper wine than ours, when our slopes and our vines have been exploited to the best of their ability and yet simply can't compete? We won't starve, of course, we'll be put on the Euro-dole by the economists. We'll be paid to produce wine that nobody wants, to make it and then turn it into vinegar or simply pour it away. And that will be a second impoverishment, do you see? That will be sad.

Those little stone towers in the fields are a reminder of what it was like. People think they're just store-sheds, but they used to have sails on them: they were windmills, they used to grind the corn from the very fields in which they sat. Now they've been amputated, they've lost their butterfly wings. And you saw the 'castle' on your way through the village? Everyone calls it 'the castle' nowadays, and Oliver makes up stories of derring-do and boiling oil. Of course the area has been fought over, at the time of the Cathar rebellion mainly; and I think the English came this way a century or two later. But this is a small village in the middle of a plain entirely lacking in strategic importance. So it never needed a castle. That squat tower is just the old grain store, nothing more.

The only bit of the village which attracts visitors is the medieval frieze on the west end of the church. It runs all the way along the outside wall, doing a curve over the door in the middle. There are about thirty-six carved stone heads, alternating in design. Half of them are angels' heads, the other half skulls with a neat pair of crossed bones beneath. Paradise, hell, paradise, hell, paradise, hell, they go. Or perhaps it's resurrection and death, resurrection and death, resurrection and death, clatter, clatter like the railway that passes. Except that we don't believe in hell and resurrection any more. And to me the angels don't look like angels, but like small children. No, like *a* small child, my daughter, Sophie Anne Louise. We gave her three names, all of which exist in English as well as French, so she can change her name just by changing her accent. But those heads, now rubbed flatter with time, they remind me of my daughter. And they say to me now, life, death, life, death, life, death.

What is it about this place? I never thought so much about time and death in London. Here everything is calm and beautiful and quiet, and my life has been worked out for better or for worse, and I find myself thinking of time and death. Is it Sophie's doing?

The fountain, for instance. It's just a normal, slightly grandiose public fountain, put up in the reign of Charles X. An obelisk made from the pink marble they still quarry on the other side of the mountain. There are four Pan heads at the base with pea-shooters coming out of their mouths. Except that the water doesn't flow from these spouts any more. It must have been wonderful when they put it up in 1825 and drew the first fresh water from the dusty distant hills. But nowadays the villagers prefer the bottled variety, and the fountain is dry. Instead, it now doubles as a war memorial. On one sloping side, a list of the twenty-six men this small village lost in the First World War. On the opposite side, three lost in the Second World War, then underneath one *mort en Indochine*. On a third side you can make out the original inscription of 1825 cut into the pink marble:

MORTELS, SONGEZ BIEN
LE TEMS PROMPT A S'ENFUIR
PASSE COMME CETTE EAU
POUR NE PLUS REVENIR

Water is like life, it says. Only the water doesn't flow here any more.

I watch the old women. For housework they wear button-through print over-dresses; not exactly overalls, smarter than that. They come out every morning and sweep the pavement outside their houses. Then they sweep the roadway. They do, they brush the dust off the first few feet of the tarmac with their old brooms. Later in the day, when the heat dies down, they are back out on the pavement again, this time sitting on little upright rush-seated chairs. They sit there until after dark, knitting, chatting, feeling the heat of the day disappear, and you realise now why they swept the road. Because it's part of their front yard, where they like to sit.

New money from Montpellier comes in this direction at weekends, but not to our village. We aren't picturesque enough for them: they take their jeeps elsewhere and light their hibachis where there is a hill view. Here they find it flat and dull, and there is no Video d'Oc to supply their wants. We have two bars, a hotel-restaurant just opposite where we live, a boulangerie which has started making *pain noir* and *pain complet* since the *épicerie* began to stock bread as well, and a hardware shop which sells light bulbs and rat poison. Last year most of the country celebrated the Bicentennial of the French Revolution. In our village the only display was outside M. Garruet's hardware store: he'd ordered six plastic brooms, two red, two white and two blue, and stuck them in a display pot outside his shop. The bristles were the same colour as the handles: they looked very jolly. Then someone bought both the red ones – a passing communist, one old woman said – and that rather put paid to the display. That was the end of the Bicentennial for us, though we heard the fireworks from other villages.

Every Wednesday morning at 9.00 the fish-van comes up from the coast and stops in the village square. We buy *dorade* and something called a *passard* which I've never been able to find the translation for. The square is a sort of wonky oblong and has a little central alley of brutally pollarded limes beneath which the old men play *boules*; the women sometimes bring their rush-seated chairs to watch this activity from which they are always excluded. The men play in the evenings under floodlight; beyond their heads you can see the black tips of a distant row of conifers. Everyone knows what that means in a French village: the graveyard.

The *mairie* and the PTT are side by side, two halves of the same building. The first few times I went to buy a stamp I found myself in the *mairie* by mistake.

You're not interested in this, are you? Not really. I'm boring you, I can tell. You want to hear about other things. Very well.

S t u a r t   Shall I tell you something I always slightly resented? This is probably going to sound incredibly petty, but it's true.

At the weekends she used to have a lie-in. I'd be the first to get up. We always had a grapefruit, or at least, one of the mornings we did, either Saturday or Sunday. I'd be the one to decide. If I went down and felt like a grapefruit on Saturday, I'd take it out of the fridge, cut it in half and put each half in a bowl. Otherwise we'd have it on the Sunday. Now, when I'd eaten my half, I'd look at Gillian's sitting in its bowl. I'd think, that's hers, she's going to eat that when she wakes up. And I'd carefully take out all the pips from her half, so she wouldn't have to do it herself. Sometimes there were quite a lot.

Do you know, in all the time we were together, she never noticed this. Or if she did notice, she never mentioned it. No, that wouldn't have been like her. She simply can't have noticed. I kept expecting her to cotton on, and each weekend I was just a tiny bit disappointed. I used to think, Perhaps she believes some new strain of seedless grapefruit has been invented. How does she think grapefruit reproduce?

Maybe she's discovered the existence of pips by now. Which of them cuts the grapefruit? I can't imagine Oliver . . . oh shit.

It's not over. I don't know how it's not over, but it isn't yet. Something's got to be done, something's got to be seen. I've gone away, they've gone away, but it's not over.

O l i v e r   She's stronger than me, you know. Woof! Woof, woof! And I like it. Bind me with silken cords, *please*.

Oh, I see I've said that before. No need to scowl so. The scowl and the sigh – they're so un-life-enhancing, I find. Gillie does a little sigh sometimes when I'm being *troppo* entertaining. It can be a strain, you know, sensing the expectation out there in the hushed blackness. People are either performers or audience, aren't they? And sometimes I do wish the audience would try it out on stage just for once.

I'll tell you something you haven't heard before. *Pravda* is Russian for truth. No, I guessed you knew that. What I'm going to tell you is this: there is no rhyme for *pravda* in Russian. Ponder and weigh this insufficiency. Doesn't that just echo down the canyons of your mind?

Gillian   We came here because Oliver got a job at the school in Toulouse.

We came here because I heard there was a chance of work from the Musée des Augustins. There are also some private clients, and I was given a couple of introductions.

We came here because London is no longer a place to bring up children, and we want Sophie to be bilingual like Maman.

We came here because of the weather and the quality of life.

We came here because Stuart started sending me flowers. Can you imagine that? Can you imagine?

We talked it over beforehand. We talked about all these things except for the last one. How could Stuart do that? I couldn't work out whether it was genuine – saying he was sorry – or some kind of sick revenge. Either way I couldn't handle it.

Oliver   It was Gill's decision. Well, of course we brown-nosed democracy, went through the hallowed process of con-sultation, but when *les frites* are down a marriage always consists of one moderate and one militant, don't you find? From which statement you are not to truffle out some routine whine of the orchidectomised male. Rather, let us agree upon the following generality: that those who have inflicted marriage upon themselves assume such rival guises alternately. When I wooed her I was the single-issue hard-liner, she the quailing middle-of-the-roader. But when it came to exchanging the hot pong of stagnant London bus for the genteel waft of *herbes de Provence*, then it was Gillian's migratory pulse which resounded like the mighty dented gong of J. Arthur Rank. My own heart-flutter of expatriation could only be detected with auscultatory assistance.

Look, she found me the job. Discovered the mildewed quarterly in which might be discovered the whereabouts of honest employ à *l'étranger*. I was feasting upon London, given that the steatopygous one had taken his chubbiness off to another continent. But I could catch the anticipatory rustle of Gill's wings; I could sense her sitting on the telephone wire at dusk, dreaming of the south. And if, as I once ventured to Stu-baby, money may be compared to love, then marriage is the bill. I jest. I half-jest, anyway.

Gillian Of course Oliver, like most men, is fundamentally lazy. They make one big decision and think they they can spend the next few years sunning themselves like a lion on a hilltop. My father ran off with his schoolgirl and that was probably the last decision he took in the whole of his life. Now Oliver's a bit the same. He makes a lot of noise but he doesn't get much done. Don't misunderstand me: I love Oliver. But I do know him.

It simply wasn't realistic for us to go on in the same old way, except with Oliver slotted into my life in the exact position that Stuart had occupied. Even when I got pregnant it didn't seem to concentrate Oliver's thoughts. I tried to explain these things to him, and he just said, in a rather pained way, 'But I'm happy, Gill, I'm so happy.' I loved him of course, for that, and we kissed, and he stroked my tummy which was still as flat as a pancake, and made some silly joke about the tadpole, and everything was fine for the rest of the evening. That's the thing about Oliver: he's very good at making things fine for the rest of the evening. But there is always the next morning. And on that next morning, I thought, I'm very glad he's happy, I'm happy too, and this ought to be enough, but it isn't, is it? You have to be happy and practical, that's the truth.

Now, I don't want my husband to rule the world – if I'd wanted that, I wouldn't have married the two I did – but equally I don't want him to bumble along without thought of the future. In all the time I'd known him, Oliver's career, if that isn't too grand a word for it, had made only a single movement, and that was downwards. He was sacked by the Shakespeare School and moved to Mr Tim's. And anyone could see he was better than that. He needed pointing in the right direction, especially with me being pregnant. I didn't want . . . Look, I know I've said this before, I said it about Stuart, but it's true, and I'm not ashamed of it. I didn't want Oliver to be disappointed.

I expect he's mentioned Monsieur Lagisquet's dog. There are two things he tells everyone about, the castle in the village, which with every retelling becomes a more and more important Crusader fortress or Cathar stronghold, and the dog. He's a very friendly, russet-brown, shiny-coated dog called Poulidor, but he's now got so old that he's gone stone deaf. Both Oliver and I find this terribly sad, but not for the same reason. Oliver finds it sad because Poulidor can no longer hear his master's friendly whistle as they walk across the fields, and he's cut off in a world of silence. Whereas I find it sad because I know he's going to be run over one day. He just comes bursting out of Monsieur Lagisquet's house all panting and hopeful, as if once he gets outside he'll rediscover his hearing. Drivers don't imagine dogs being deaf when they see them. I keep thinking about some young man, going a bit too fast through the village, seeing Poulidor lolloping along, and this impatient driver hooting, hooting again at the stupid dog, then swerving just too late. I see it all. And I told Monsieur Lagisquet he ought to tie the dog up, or put him on a long rope. He said he'd tried once and Poulidor had just moped all the time and wouldn't eat, so he untied him. He said he wanted the dog to be happy. I said you can be happy but you have to be practical as well. And now the dog is going to get run over some time. I just know it.

Do you see what I mean?

Stuart   I had a lot of plans. One of the first ones was to pay a girl at that tacky school Oliver was reduced to teaching at to denounce him. Say he'd made advances to her. It would probably have been true anyway – if not that girl, it would have been true of another. Perhaps he'd have got the sack. Perhaps the police would have come in this time. But in any event Gill would have known the sort of man she'd left me for. It would always rankle, and she'd never have felt safe again. That was a good plan.

When I got to the States I had another plan. I was going to pretend to have killed myself. I wanted to hurt them a lot, you see. I wasn't sure how I was going to do it. One idea was to write under another name to the old boys' magazine, the *Edwardian*, and have them put in an obituary notice, and then make sure it got sent on to Oliver. I also thought about getting some intermediary to pass on the news on a visit to London, casually somehow. 'Sad about Stuart topping himself, wasn't it? No, he never got over the break-up. Oh, you didn't know . . . ?' Who would do it? Someone. Someone I'd pay.

I thought about that idea rather too much. It made me gloomy. It got a bit tempting, if you know what I mean. To do it really. To make it all true, and punish them. So I stopped.

But it's not over. Oh, my marriage is over, I know that. But *it's* not over, not until I feel it is. It's not over till it stops hurting. There's a long way to go. And I can't get over the feeling that it wasn't *fair*, what happened. I ought to be able to get over that, oughtn't I?

Mme Wyatt and I write to one another. Guess what? She's having an affair. Good for you, Mme Wyatt.

O l i v e r   This is probably not the right thing to say, but then I never made a career out of saying the right thing. There are times when I miss Stuart. Yeah, yeah, you don't have to tell me. I know what I did. I have chewed guilt like an old Boer trekker with biltong between his teeth. And what makes it worse is that sometimes I think Stuart was the person who understood me best. I hope he's all right. I hope he's got a nice cuddly inamorata. I see them barbecuing over mesquite wood while the cardinal birds swoop low over the lawn and the cicadas thrum like the assembled strings of the Chicago Symphony Orchestra. I wish him everything, that Stuart: health, hearth, happiness and herpes. I would wish him a hot tub if I didn't think he'd keep tropical fish in it. Oh Lordie, just the thought of him makes me chuckle.

Do you know if he's got a girl? I wonder if he's got some crepuscular secret, some sexual hidey-hole. What could it be? Porn? Flashing? Erotic phone calls? Filthy faxes? No, I hope he's making out. I hope life isn't making him poo-scared. I wish him . . . reversibility.

S t u a r t   I'd like to put the record straight in one respect. You've probably forgotten, but Oliver used to have this joke with me. Well, not so much with me as at my expense. About how I thought a Mantra was a make of car. I let him get away with it at the time, but what I wanted to say was, 'Actually, it's a Manta, Oliver, not a Mantra.' The Manta Ray, to be exact. Very powerful job, made by General Motors, based on the Corvette. I even toyed with buying one when I got over here. But it's hardly my image. And it would have been giving in to the past a bit too much, don't you agree?

Trust Oliver to get it wrong.

M m e W y a t t   Stuart writes. I send him news, what news there is. He can't let go. He says he is making a new life for himself, but I feel that he is unable to let go.

The one thing that might help him let go I cannot bring myself to tell him. About the baby. He does not know they have a child. It is terrible to be in possession of a piece of information which you think can hurt somebody. And because I did not tell him at once this made it harder to tell him later.

You see, there was an afternoon they came to see me, and my daughter was out of the room, and Stuart was sitting there waiting to be examined, with his shoes all shiny and his hair brushed back, and he said to me, 'We are going to have children, you know.' And then he suddenly looked embarrassed, and said, 'I mean, I do not mean now ... I do not mean she is ...' And then there was a noise from the kitchen and he looked even more embarrassed, and said, 'Gill does not know yet. I mean, we have not talked about it, but I am sure, I mean, oh dear ...' And he just ran out of words. I said, 'It is all right, it is our secret,' and he looked suddenly very relieved, and then I could see from his face that he could not wait for Gillian to come back into the room.

I kept remembering this when Oliver told me that Gillian was pregnant.

Sophie Anne Louise. It is a bit pretentious, do you not find? Maybe it is better in English. Sophie Anne Louise. No, it still sounds like one of Queen Victoria's grandchildren.

Gillian   Oliver is a good teacher, I wouldn't want you to think otherwise. There was a little *vin d'honneur* at the end of last term and the director made a point of telling me how good he was with the pupils and how they all appreciated him. Oliver pooh-poohed this afterwards. The line he takes is that teaching English 'Conversation et Civilisation' is a push-over, as you can say any weird thing that comes into your head and the pupils treat it as a priceless example of *le British sense of humour*. But he would say that. He's got a lot of bravado, Oliver, but he hasn't really got any self-confidence.

Sending your ex-wife flowers two years after you've broken up. What's that about?

When I was growing up, which seems to me a long time ago now, I had all the usual conversations. What did we want from a man, what were we looking for? Usually, with other girls, I'd just name film stars. But to myself I'd say that what I wanted was someone I could love, respect and fancy. I thought that was what one should be aiming for, if the thing were to last. And when I started with men it always seemed as difficult as getting three strawberries in a row on a fruit machine. You'd get one, and then you might get another, but by that time the first one had spun away. There was a button marked HOLD but it didn't seem to work properly.

Love, respect, fancy. I thought I'd got all three with Stuart. I thought I'd got all three with Oliver. But maybe three's not possible. Maybe the best you can get is two, and the HOLD button is always on the blink.

Mme Rives   He says he's Canadian. Quebecois he isn't. He wanted a room at the front. He didn't know how long he'd be staying. He told me again he was Canadian. So what? Money has no colour.

Gillian   There had to be rules. There had to be very firm rules, that's obvious, isn't it? You can't just 'be happy'; you have to manage happiness. That's one of the things I know now. We came here, we were starting again, and properly this time. A new country, new jobs, the baby. Oliver would make speeches about the New Found Golden Land, and so forth. One day when Sophie had taken more out of me than usual, I interrupted him.

'Look, Oliver, one of the rules is, no affairs.'

'*Che?*'

'No affairs, Oliver.'

Perhaps I said it the wrong way, I don't know, but he really flew off the handle. You can imagine the rhetoric. I don't remember it all, because I'm afraid that when I'm tired I have a sort of filtering system for Ollie. I just take out what I need to keep the conversation going.

'Oliver, all I'm saying ... Given the circumstances in which we met ... given that everyone thought we were having an affair and that's why Stuart and I broke up ... I just think, for our own sakes, we have to be careful.'

Now Oliver can be extremely sarcastic, as you may have noticed. He denies it, he says sarcasm is vulgar. 'Playful irony *au maximum*,' he claims. So maybe he was merely being playful and ironic when he pointed out to me that *if* he remembered correctly, the reason we didn't have an affair while I was married to Stuart was because *he'd* declined *my* very pressing offer (various anatomical references at this point, which I'll leave out), and so if anyone was to be suspected of having affairs it was *me*, etc. etc. Which I suppose was a fair point to make, except that mothers with small babies who also work don't on the whole have the energy to jump into bed with other people, and so on.

It was awful. It was a shouting match. I was just trying to be practical, trying to express something that I thought came out of my love for Oliver, and he got all jumpy and hostile.

These things don't immediately go away, either. And the heat down here makes it worse. We were scratchy with one another all the following week. And guess what? That stupid old tank he drives because he thinks it's stylish broke down three times. Three times! And the third time he mentioned the carburettor I must have looked a bit sceptical, because he turned on me.

'Say it, then.'

'What?'

'Go on, say it.'

'All right,' I said, knowing that I shouldn't. 'What's she called?'

He gave a sort of roar, as if he'd won by making me say it, and as I looked at him standing over me I knew – we both knew, I think – that he could easily hit me. If I'd gone on, he would have hit me.

He'd won, and we'd both lost. It hadn't even been a real quarrel either, not *about* something, it was just made out of some senseless need to quarrel. I hadn't succeeded in managing happiness.

Later I cried. And I thought: SWEDE'S TURNIP'S SWEET POTATO'S CAULI'S COX'S SPROUT'S. No-one ever told that chap, no-one corrected him. Or they did, and he never listened.

No, this isn't England. This is France, so I'll give you a different comparison. I was talking to Monsieur Lagisquet the other day. He's got a few hectares of vines outside the village, and he told me that in the old days they used to plant a rose-bush at the end of each row of vines. Apparently a rose shows signs of disease first, so the bushes act as an early-warning system. He said that locally this tradition had now died out, but they still do it in other parts of France.

I think people should plant rose-bushes in real life. We need some sort of early-warning system.

Oliver's different out here. Actually, I mean the opposite of that. Oliver's exactly the same as he's always been and always will be, it's just that he comes across differently. The French don't really read him. It never struck me before we moved down here, but Oliver is one of those people who makes more sense in a context. He seemed terribly exotic when I first met him; now he seems less colourful. It's not just the effect of time and familiarity, either. It's that here the only English person he's got to set him off is me, and that's not really enough. He needed someone like Stuart around. It's the same as colour theory. When you put two colours side by side, that affects the way you see each of them. It's exactly the same principle.

Stuart   I took three weeks' leave. I went to London. I thought I'd be able to handle it better than I did. I wasn't stupid, I didn't try going back to places I'd been with Gill. I just felt angry and sad at the same time. People say angry-sad is an improvement on sad-sad, but I'm not so sure. If you're sad-sad people are nice to you. But if you're angry-sad you just want to go to the middle of Trafalgar Square and scream at people. IT'S NOT MY FAULT. LOOK WHAT THEY DID TO ME. WHY DID THIS HAPPEN? IT ISN'T FAIR. People who are angry-sad aren't really working it through; they're the ones who go mad. I'm that person you see on the Underground talking to himself just a bit too loudly, the sort of person you keep out of the way of. Don't go too near him, he might be a jumper or a pusher. He might suddenly leap in front of the train — or he might knock you under it.

So I went to see Mme Wyatt. She gave me their address. I said I wanted to write because the last time we'd met they'd tried to be friends and I'd shoved them away. I'm not sure Mme Wyatt believed me. She's a good reader of people. So I changed the subject and asked her about her new lover.

'My old lover,' she replied.

'Oh,' I said, imagining some elderly gentleman with a rug over his lap. 'You didn't tell me how old he was.'

'No, I mean to say, my former lover.'

'I'm sorry.'

'Don't be. It was just . . . a passage. *Faut bien que le corps exulte.*'

'Yes.' You know, that's not a word I'd have thought of using. Does the body *exult* in English? The body has a jolly good time, I think, but I don't know if it exactly exults. Or perhaps that's just me.

When it was time to go Mme Wyatt said, 'Stuart, I think it's a bit early.'

'What is?' I thought she meant I hadn't stayed long enough.

'To get in touch. Give it time.'

'But they asked me . . .'

'No, not for them. For you.'

I thought it over, then bought a map. The nearest airport seemed to be Toulouse, but I didn't fly to Toulouse. I flew to Montpellier. I could be going somewhere else, you see. I did at first. I drove in the opposite direction. Then I thought, this is stupid, and I looked at the map again.

I drove through the village twice without stopping. The

first time I was nervous and so I was going a bit too fast. Some damn dog ran out and almost went under my wheels; I had to swerve. The second time I went more slowly and saw the hotel.

I came back after dark and asked for a room. There wasn't any difficulty. It looks a pleasant enough village, but it's not exactly a tourist trap.

I didn't want them to say, 'Oh, we have some English people in the village,' so I told Madame I was Canadian, and just to make sure I checked in under a false name.

I asked for a room at the front. I stand at the window. I watch.

G i l l i a n   I don't have premonitions, I'm not psychic. I'm not one of those people who say, 'I had this feeling in my bones.' But when I was told, I knew.

To be honest, I haven't thought much about Stuart since we moved down here. Sophie occupies most of my time. She changes so fast, she comes into a fresh focus all the time, I need every moment. Then there's Oliver, and my work as well.

I've only thought of Stuart at bad times. That sounds unfair, but it's true. For instance the first occasion you realise you can't, or at any rate you aren't going to, tell the man you've married everything. I had that with Oliver as I had it with Stuart. I don't mean lying, exactly, I just mean adjusting things, economising a bit with the truth. The second time round it comes as less of a surprise, though it does make you remember the first time.

I was standing by the fish-van on Wednesday morning. In

England everyone would form a queue. Here you just huddle near the van, and people know who's next, and if you're next but not in a hurry you just let someone else go first. *Suis pas pressée.* After you. Mme Rives was next to me and asked me if the English liked trout.

'Of course,' I said.

'I've got an Englishman at the moment. *Sont fous, les Anglais.*' She laughed as she said it, to let me know I wasn't included in the generalisation.

This particular Englishman had arrived three days ago and stayed in his room all the time. Except for once or twice, late at night, when he'd slipped out. He said he was a Canadian but he had an English passport, and the name on it was different from the one he had given when he arrived.

When I was told, I knew. I *knew*.

'Does he have a Canadian name?' I asked casually.

'What's a Canadian name? I can't tell the difference. He's called "Uges" or something. Is that Canadian?'

Uges. No, that's not particularly Canadian. It's the name of my first husband. I used to be Mme Stuart Uges, except that I never took his name. He thought I did, but I didn't really. I haven't taken Oliver's name either.

O l i v e r   I'm being good. I am aping the *fons et origo* of domestic virtue. If we had twins I'd call them Lares and Penates. Do I not phone whenever Toulousain tardiness threatens? Do I not rise nocturnally to trade in the besmirched swaddling of little Sal and make with the cleansing cotton wool? Am I not the proud tender of an incipient vegetable garden, and do not my scarlet runners strain even now to corkscrew their trembling way up my bamboo wigwams?

The fact is, Gill's a bit off sex at the moment. Like trying to ease a parking meter into an oyster shell. It happens, it happens. According to the mildewed myth handed down by *les blanchisseuses d'antan*, it is an established verity that the lactating *moglie* cannot get pregnant. At last I am now in a position to locate the swerving mercury-ball of truth which gives this myth its specific gravity (excuse the chemistry). The fact of the matter is that the lactating *moglie* not infrequently declines the impress of the ardent gene-pool she married: *niente* horizontal jogging. No wonder she doesn't get pregnant.

Which is a tad tough when little Sal was her idea in the first place. I was all for trundling along as we were.

Stuart   I told myself I didn't have a plan but I did. I pretended I was coming to London on the off-chance. That I was flying to Montpellier just for something to do. That I happened to be driving through the village and what a co-incidence . . .

I came here to confront them. I came here in order to stand in the middle of Trafalgar Square and bellow. I would know what to do when I got here. I would know what to say when I got here. IT WASN'T MY FAULT. LOOK WHAT YOU DID TO ME. WHY DID YOU DO IT TO ME? Or rather, I wouldn't confront *them*, I would confront *her*. It was her doing. Finally, she was the one who said yes.

I was going to wait until Oliver had set off for the crappy little school in Toulouse where he teaches. Mme Wyatt made it sound quite nice but I expect she was exaggerating loyally. I bet it's a dump. I was going to wait until he'd gone and then call on Gillian. I would have found the words, some words.

But I can't now. I looked out of the window and saw her. She seemed exactly the same, in a green shirt I remembered too well. She's had her hair cut short, which gave me a jolt, but there was something that gave me a much bigger jolt. She was holding a baby. Her baby. Their baby. Bloody Oliver's baby.

Why didn't you warn me, Mme Wyatt?

It's thrown me. It's reminded me of the future I never got to have. Of everything that was stolen. I'm not sure I can handle this.

Do you think they were fucking all the time? You never told me your opinion, did you? I used to think they were, then I calmed down about it and thought they weren't, now I think they were again. All the time. What a disgusting memory to get stuck with. I can't even look back on that little stretch of my life and call it happy. They've poisoned the only good bit of my past.

Oliver's lucky. People like me don't kill other people. I wouldn't know how to saw through the brakes of his car. I once got drunk and head-butted him, but it didn't give me a taste for that sort of thing.

I wish I could beat Oliver in argument. I wish we could have some debate and I'd prove to him what a shit he's been and how none of it was my fault and how Gill would have been happy with me. But it wouldn't work. Oliver would enjoy it too much for a start, and it would all turn out to be about him not me, and how *interesting*, how *complicated* he was. And I'd end up saying SHUT UP YOU'RE WRONG FUCK OFF and that wouldn't be very satisfactory either.

I comfort myself sometimes with the thought that Oliver is a failure. What's he done in the last ten years except steal someone's wife and give up smoking? He's clever, I've never denied that, but not clever enough to see that you have to be more than clever. It's not sufficient just to know things and be amusing. Oliver's life strategy has always gone a bit like this: he's pleased with being himself, and he reckons that if he hangs around long enough someone will come by and give him money just to carry on being himself. Like they do with those performance artists. Except that no-one's done this yet, and frankly the chances of someone happening on this little village and making him a proposition are pretty slim. So what do we have in the meantime? An expatriate Englishman in his middle thirties, scraping along in provincial France with a wife and baby. They're out of the London property market now, and believe me, once you're out you never get back in. (That's why I bought Gillian's share of the house. I'll have somewhere to come back to.) I can see Oliver in years to come, one of those old semi-hippy types who hang around bars bumming drinks off Englishmen and asking if there are still big red buses back in London, and have you finished with your copy of the *Daily Telegraph* by the way?

And I'll tell you something. Gillian isn't going to stand for it. Not year in, year out. Basically, she's a very practical, efficient person who likes to know what's happening and hates mess. Oliver is a mess. Perhaps she ought to go out to work and leave him at home with the kids. Except that he'd put the casserole in the pram and cook the baby by mistake. The fact of the matter is, she's much better suited to me than she is to Oliver.

Oh shit. *Shit*. I said I wouldn't ever think that again. Shit, I . . . look, give me a moment will you? No, it's all right. No, just leave me alone. I can tell exactly how long this moment lasts. Exactly how long. I'm practised enough, for God's sake.

Aaah. Fffff. Aaah. Fffff. Aah.

All right.

OK.

OK.

One of the good things about the States is that you can get anything you want at any time of the night or day. Quite a few times I'd be lonely and a bit drunk and I'd order Gill some flowers. International flowers by telephone. You just give them your credit-card number and they do the rest and the good thing is you don't have time to change your mind.

'Message, sir?'

'No message.'

'Ah-ha, secret surprise?'

Yes it's a secret surprise. Except that she'll know. And maybe she'll feel guilty. I wouldn't mind that. It's the least she could do for me.

As I say, I'm not in the business of being liked any more.

O l i v e r   I was out in the garden assisting one or two maladjusted scarlet runners. They grow with the necessary twist in them but they're as blind as kittens to begin with and set off in the wrong direction. So you take this delicate twirly stem and guide it gently round the cane and feel it take hold. Like watching the infant Sal grip the bamboo of my middle finger.

Isn't this the life?

Gill's been a bit grouchy the last few days. Post-partural, pre-menstrual, mid-lactatory, hard to tell the difference nowadays. The *tiercé* of the temperament, and Ollie loses. Ollie fails to entertain once more, Part Fifteen. Perhaps I should hie me to the *pharmacie* and seek out a febrifuge.

But you still find me fun, don't you? Just a little? Go on, admit it. Crack us a smile! Corners up!

Love and money: that was a mistaken analogy. As if Gill were some publicly listed company and I'd put in an offer for her. Listen, Gill runs the whole goddam market, always has. Women do. Sometimes not in the short term, but always in the long term.

Gillian   He's in the hotel across the street. He can see our house, our car, our life. When I'm outside in the morning with my broom, sweeping the pavement, I think I can see a shape at one of the hotel windows.

Now what I probably would have done in the old days is this. I'd have gone across to the hotel, asked for him, and suggested we talk things over in a sensible manner. But I can't do that. Not after the way I've hurt him.

So I must wait for him. Assuming he knows what it is he wants to do, or wants to say. And he's been there days now. What if he doesn't know what he wants?

If he doesn't know, then I have to give him something,

show him something. What? What can I give him?

M m e   R i v e s   Paul did the trout with almonds, his usual way. The Englishman said he liked it, which is the first comment he has made so far on the hotel, the room, the breakfast, the lunch or the dinner. Then he said something I didn't understand at first. His French isn't very good, he has a thick accent, so I asked him to repeat it.

'I eat this once with my wife. In the north. In the north of the France.'

'She is not with you, your wife? She remains in Canada?'

He did not reply. He just said that he wanted a *crème caramel* and afterwards coffee.

G i l l i a n   I've got an idea. It's scarcely a plan, not yet. But the main thing about it is that I can't, I mustn't tell Oliver. There are two reasons for this. The first is that I can't trust him to do the right thing unless it's *real*. If I ask him to do something, he'll mess it up, he'll turn it into a performance and it's got to be real. The second reason is that *I*'ve got to do it, arrange it, fix it. It's something *I* owe. Do you understand?

S t u a r t   I stand at the window. I watch and wait. I watch and wait.

Oliver   The courgettes are romping away at the moment. I grow a variety called *rond de Nice*. I doubt you have them in England, where you prefer those long bonky ones suitable only for seaside postcards. 'Just admiring your vegetable marrow, Mister Blenkinsop!' Har bloody har. *Rond de Nice* are, as their name implies, spherical. Pick them when larger than a golf ball yet smaller than a tennis ball, lightly steam, slice in half, a gout of butter, black pepper, then *wallow*.

Last night Gillian started quizzing me about one of the girls at the School. Talk about wide of the mark. Might as well accuse Pelléas of leg-over with Mélisande. (Though I suppose they must have done it, mustn't they?) Anyway, Gillian just started dog-and-boning it. Did I fancy Mlle Whatsername – Simone? Was I seeing her? Is that why the noble Peugeot had another fainting-fit last week? Eventually, seeking to defuse, I murmured, 'My dear, she's not *half* pretty enough' – an uncoded allusion, as you will appreciate, to one of Oscar's ripostes at his trial. Unwise, unwise! For Ollie, as for Oscar, wit merely landed him in the slammer. And by the end of the evening, Reading Gaol would have felt like the George V. What is it with Gill at the moment? Can *you* tell?

If there's one thing that bitches me off, it's being accused of venery when my palms haven't even broken sweat.

Gillian   It's unfair? What's fair? When did *fair* have much to do with the way we run our lives? There's no time to think about that. I just have to get on with it. Arrange things for Stuart. I owe him this.

Stuart   She comes out every morning after Oliver has left and sweeps the pavement. Then she does a bit of the road as well, like the other village women. What do they do it for? To help save on the municipal cleaning bill? Search me. She puts the baby in a high-chair just inside the doorway. I can't tell if it's a boy or a girl and I don't want to find out either. She puts it in the shade, where it can't lose sight of her and won't get dust in its face. Then she sweeps, and from time to time she looks over to the baby and I can see her lips opening as she says something. And she sweeps, then she goes inside again with her baby and her broom.

I can't bear it. That used to be my future.

Gillian   It might work. It might be what Stuart needs. And in any case it's the best I can come up with. It's horrible to think of him sitting in his room over the road and brooding.

I started last night, and I'll go on some more this evening. Tomorrow morning is the time to try it. I know that Stuart watches Oliver drive off – I've seen him at the window. And Oliver does get grouchy if he's had to get up in the night and change Sophie. I normally stay out of his way when it's been his turn, but not tomorrow.

With most people, it's like this: if they've done something they shouldn't, they get angry when they're accused of it. Guilt expresses itself as outrage. That's normal, isn't it? Well, Oliver's back to front. If you accuse him of doing something he shouldn't and he has done it, he's sort of half-amused, he almost congratulates you for finding him out. What really irritates him is to be accused of doing something he hasn't done. It's as if he thinks, God, I *could* have done that after all. As long as I'm being suspected of it, I might as well have done it, or at least tried to. So he's cross because he's missed his chance, partly.

This is why I chose Simone. One of those very serious-minded French girls with a slight frown on their foreheads all the time. The sort of girl who wouldn't see the point of Oliver. I remember at the *vin d'honneur* she was pointed out to me because apparently she'd once tried to correct Oliver's English in class. He wouldn't have liked that at all.

So I've settled on her. It seems to be working.

Just out of interest, do you think Oliver's been faithful to me since we were married? Sorry, that's neither here nor there.

There are various problems with what I'm doing. The first is, if it works, we'll probably have to leave the village. Well, that can be arranged. The second is, do I tell Oliver afterwards? Or ever? Would he understand what I've done, or would he merely distrust me the more? If he knew it was all planned he might never trust me again.

There's another risk as well. No, I'm sure I'll be able to get us back to where we were before. I can manage things, that's what I'm good at. And after it's over we'll be free of Stuart and Stuart will be free of us.

I don't think I'm going to sleep much tonight. But I'm not going to let Oliver off his turn changing Sophie.

I hate doing this, you know. But if I stopped to think more I might hate it so much that it wouldn't get done.

Stuart   I'm stuck. I'm completely stuck. Paralysed.
When their lights go out, which is normally between 11.45
and 11.58, I take a walk. But otherwise I stand at the window.
I watch. I watch, and I think, that used to be my future.

Gillian   I do have this fear. Is that the right word?
Perhaps I mean premonition. No, I don't. I mean fear. And
the fear is this: that what I'm showing Stuart turns out to be
real.

Oliver   You know what I think? I think they ought
to put up road-signs on the Highway of Life. CHUTE DE
PIERRES. CHAUSSÉE DEFORMÉE. ROUTE INONDABLE. Yes, that's
the one. ROUTE INONDABLE. DANGER: ROAD LIABLE TO
FLOODING. They should put that up at every corner.

Stuart   I go out walking. After Midnight.

          And as the skies turn gloomy
          Nightbirds whisper to me . . .

Gillian   When I was little, my father used to say,
'Don't pull a face, or the wind might change.' What if the
wind changes now?

Oliver   Jesus. Jesus.

OK, I'm sorry. I shouldn't have done it. It won't happen again. I'm not really like that.

Christ, on the other mitt I've got a bloody good idea to barrel on straight past Toulouse and never come back. Everything they say about women's true, isn't it? Sooner or later, it *all* turns out to be true.

She's been on my back for days. It was just like ... oh, fill in your own fucking opera reference for a change. I'm fed up doing all the work.

She's tired, I'm tired, all right? Who's been on junior bedpan duty every night this week? Who spends hours every day on the A61? The last thing I need to get home to is the Spanish Inquisition.

It went like this. La Gillian didn't exactly seem nipple-puckeringly pleased to see me when I returned last night. So I decamp to the garden and start burning some foliar detritus. Why am I doing this? Of course, she immediately concludes, in order to cover up the incriminating whiff of my presumed mistress's Chanel Numéro Soixante-Neuf. I ask you.

And so on. Most of the evening continued thus. Went to bed exhausted. Usual padlocks on the night-dress, not that I tried to pick them. Three a.m. latrine duty. Apparently the faecal pong gets even more eye-watering after the little thing's finally on solids. This part's a breeze, I am reliably informed. Rosewater and fresh primroses in comparison to later on.

Alarm-clock goes off with the gentleness of a cattle prod. Then it all starts up again. Over *breakfast*. I've never seen her like this before, winding me up as if she'd been doing it for years. Knowing just where to prick. The Acupuncture of

Quarrel. I looked at her face, that face I fell in love with on the day she married the wrong person. It was scrubbed with anger. Her hair had scorned the brush as her face had disdained the matin's lotion. Her mouth opened and shut and I tried not to listen and couldn't help myself thinking that maybe starting off trying not to look like an unkempt harridan might be a better way of persuading your husband not to have that affair which in any case he wasn't having. I mean, really surreal. Mega-surreal.

And then she started pursuing me about the house. And you have to decide that either she's sick or she isn't, and though she was behaving sick I couldn't convince myself that she was. Which meant that I was screaming back at her. And then I started to leave for work and she accused me of running away and going off to see my girlfriend, and we were just screaming at each other as I made it to the front door.

Then it went on. And on. She followed me out to the car, screeching like a crow. In the middle of the main street. Top of her voice, accusations of, as they say, a personal and professional nature, *mit* everyone looking. Screeching. Carrying Sal in her arms for some reason I couldn't fathom, and coming at me, just coming at me as I fiddled with the lock on the Peugeot. I was jumping, jumping, buzzing. And the fucking lock wouldn't open. And then she's right on top of me with her mad accusations. So I just hit her, hit her across the face with the keys in my hand and her face got cut, and I thought I was going to break and I looked at her as if to say, surely this isn't real, is it? Stop the film. Punch the rewind button, it's only a tape, isn't it? And she just carried on screaming with madness and hate in her face. I couldn't believe it. 'Shut up,' 'Shut up,' 'Shut up,' I shouted and when she didn't I hit her again. Then I jemmied the car door open, jumped in and drove off.

I looked in the mirror. She was still standing there, in the middle of the street, one hand holding the baby to her, the other hand pressing a handkerchief against the blood on her face. I drove. She was still there. I drove like a maniac, or as fast as a maniac can given that he's forgotten to change out of second gear. Then I two-wheeled the bend by the Cave Coopérative and the sight of her was gone.

Mme Rives *Sont fous, les Anglais.* That Canadian who took room 6 and only went out after dark: he was English. He told me twice he was Canadian but then he left his passport lying around when the girl and I went in to make up his room and he hadn't even told us his real name. He'd changed it. He was very silent, stayed in his room for a week, and when he left he shook my hand, smiled for the first time, and said he was happy.

And that young couple who bought old Bertin's house. They appeared to be sympathetic, she was very proud of her baby, he was very proud of that stupid old Peugeot which kept breaking down. I told him one day that he ought to get a little Renault 5 like everyone else. He told me he had renounced the modern world. He used to say stupid things like that, although in a perfectly charming way.

Then what happens? They've been here six months, people are beginning to like them, when they have a screaming quarrel in the middle of the street. Everyone stops to look.

Finally, he hits her twice across the face, jumps into his old car and drives off. She stands in the middle of the road for about five minutes, with blood on her face, then goes back into the house and doesn't come out again. That is the last we see of her. A week later they clear everything out and disappear. My husband said the English are a mad and violent race, and their sense of humour is very singular. The house is for sale: it's that one over there, you see? Let's hope we get someone sensible next time. If it has to be a foreigner, give us a Belgian.

Nothing much has happened in the village since. Lagisquet's dog got run down by a car. The dog was deaf and Lagisquet was an old fool. We told him he ought to tie the dog up. He said he didn't want to interfere with Poulidor's freedom and happiness. Well, he's interfered with its freedom and happiness now. He opened the front door, the dog shot out, and a car ran it over. Some people were sympathetic to Lagisquet. I wasn't. I said, 'You're an old fool. You've probably got English blood.'